An

Amish Kitchen

OTHER NOVELLA COLLECTIONS

OTHER BOOKS BY THESE AUTHORS

Visit AmishLiving.com for more information

An
Amish Kitchen

BETH WISEMAN

KELLY LONG

AMY CLIPSTON

THOMAS NELSON
Since 1798

NASHVILLE   DALLAS   MEXICO CITY   RIO DE JANEIRO

ISBN-13: 978-0-373-60234-6

An Amish Kitchen

The publisher acknowledges the copyright holders
of the individual works as follows:

A Recipe for Hope
Copyright © 2012 by Elizabeth Wiseman Mackey

A Taste of Faith
Copyright © 2012 by Kelly Long

A Spoonful of Love
Copyright © 2012 by Amy Clipston

Published in Nashville, Tennessee, by Thomas Nelson. Thomas
Nelson is a registered trademark of Thomas Nelson, Inc.

Thomas Nelson, Inc., titles may be purchased in bulk for educational,
business, fund-raising, or sales promotional use. For information,
please e-mail SpecialMarkets@ThomasNelson.com.

Scripture quotations taken from the King James Version.

Publisher's note: This novel is a work of fiction. Names, characters,
places, and incidents are either products of the author's imagination
or used fictitiously. All characters are fictional, and any similarity to
people living or dead is purely coincidental.

Cover Design: James W. Hall, JWH Graphic Arts

Original Package Design © 2012 Thomas Nelson, Inc.

Cover Photography: Steve Gardner, Almay.com, iStock.com

Printed in U.S.A.

CONTENTS

GLOSSARY

ab im kopp: off in the head, crazy

ach: oh

aenti: aunt

appeditlich: delicious

ausleger: undertaker

bauch: stomach

boppli: baby

bruder: brother

The Budget: a weekly newspaper serving Amish and
Mennonite communities everywhere

buss: kiss

buwe: boy

daadi: grandfather

daed: dad

danki: thank you

dat: dad

Derr Herr: God

dochder: daughter

dumm: dumb

dummkopp: dunce

Englisch: non-Amish person

fater: father

fraa: wife

freind: friend

freinden: friends

fremm: strange

froh: happy

gegisch: silly

Gern gschehne: You're welcome

Gott: God

grandkinner: grandchildren

grank: sick

guder mariye: good morning

gut: good

gut nacht: good night

hatt: hard

haus: house

hiya: hello

Ich liebe dich: I love you

kaffi: coffee

kapp: prayer covering or cap

kichlin: cookies

kind: child

kinner: children or grandchildren

kumme: come

lieb: love

maed: young women, girls

maedel: girl

mamm: mom

mammi: grandmother

mei: my

mudder: mother

narrisch: crazy

nee: no

Ordnung: the written and unwritten rules of the Amish; the understood behavior by which the Amish are expected to live, passed down from generation to generation. Most Amish know the rules by heart.

rumschpringe: running-around period when a teenager turns sixteen years old

schee: pretty

schtupp: family room

schweschder: sister

sei se gut: please

sohn: son

Was iss letz?: What's wrong?

wedder: weather

Wie bischt?: How are you?

Wie geht's: How do you do? or Good day!

willkumm: welcome

wunderbaar: wonderful

ya: yes

A RECIPE FOR HOPE

BETH WISEMAN

To Janet Murphy, with love and thanks

Chapter 1

It's going to be a long two months.

Eve Bender finished packing the necessities to take to her parents' home, trying to follow the same instructions she was giving to the children: "Pack light, take only what you must have."

Moving back in with her parents at age thirty-eight was bad enough, but she also had a husband and three teenage boys in their *rumschpringe* in tow.

Eve shook her head as she struggled to zip a large brown duffel bag. *Of all the things to happen.* Yesterday a storm had knocked a tree down onto their two-story farmhouse, and the damage was extensive. It was going to take members of the community two months to completely repair the structure, but Eve knew it was a miracle that none of them had gotten hurt. She'd been thanking God since it happened.

She placed the duffel bag next to an old red suitcase she'd bought at a mud sale in Penryn a few years before. She'd paid two dollars for the piece of luggage and only used it once when she and Benny traveled to Harrisburg to attend a cousin's wedding. She folded her arms across her chest and stared at the bags, hoping she'd remembered everything they'd need at her parents'.

Benny, along with several men in the district, had cleared the tree earlier this morning, using a chainsaw to break the large limbs into logs that could be carried to the woodpile. Her husband had also checked to make sure the boys could get safely to their rooms upstairs. The tree had fallen through Eve's sewing room upstairs and crushed the kitchen below it. They might have lived around the mess if it weren't the middle of January. Benny and the boys had done the best they could to hang thick tarps over areas exposed to the elements, but Eve wondered if the clear sheeting would hold against a strong wind. She pulled her long black coat snug around her and went down the hall to check on the boys.

She walked into Leroy's room. At eighteen, her oldest son was sitting on his bed with earbuds plugged into whatever his latest gadget was. He pulled one from his ear when she walked in.

"Are you packed?"

Leroy pointed to a dark-green duffel bag on the far side of the room. "*Ya.*" He put the plug back in his ear.

"Very *gut.*"

Shivering, Eve headed toward the twins' room. She knocked on the door, then entered slowly, not surprised to find Elias sleeping on his twin bed and Amos sitting on the other bed with his pet lizard lying on his stomach.

"I'm trying to keep him warm," Amos said when

Eve put her hands on her hips and scowled. She wasn't fond of the foot-long Chinese water dragon that Amos usually kept in a cage.

"*Mammi* is going to have a fit when you bring that lizard into her *haus*."

Amos's hazel eyes grew round as he sat up, cradling the reptile in his hands. "I—I can't l-leave him here. He-he'll freeze."

The younger of her sixteen-year-old twins—by nine minutes—Amos, stuttered when he was upset or nervous. "I know. I'm just saying *Mammi* isn't going to like it." She walked over to where Elias was sleeping and gently slapped him on the leg. "Elias, get up."

Elias rolled onto his back and rubbed his eyes. "It's Sunday. A day of rest."

"Not today. I told both you boys to pack whatever you need to go to *Mammi* and *Daadi's haus*."

Elias slowly sat up, his sandy brown hair tousled. "I don't know why we have to go over there. This half of the *haus* is fine." He rubbed his eyes again as he yawned.

"Don't be silly. It's going to be in the teens tonight and snowing. Even with the tarps and the fireplace, I can't even cook us a meal."

Eve's gas range was only a year old, and her propane refrigerator wasn't much older than that. Both would have to be replaced, along with the oak dining room set Benny had built when they were first married, with seating for eight. Losing the dining room furniture upset her more than the other losses. But she reminded herself that they were all safe and silently thanked God again.

"Now get moving," she said with a clap of her hands. "We need to be there before dark."

Back downstairs, she carefully stepped over debris and made her way to what was left of the kitchen. Benny was holding his black felt hat in one hand, stroking his gray-speckled brown beard with the other, and eyeing the mess.

"Is it really going to take two months before we can move back?" Eve shuddered. She and her mother didn't see eye-to-eye on most things, and *Mamm* wasn't used to having three teenage boys around either.

"Depends on the weather." Benny finished looking around before he walked to Eve and pulled her close. "It won't be so bad."

Eve's head rested against her husband's chest as he towered over her by a foot. "You don't know my mother the way I do." She sighed.

After making up the sleeper sofa in her sewing room, Rosemary put fresh sheets on the two beds upstairs where the twins would sleep, then made her way to Eve's old bedroom. Her daughter's room hadn't changed all that much since Eve had moved out to marry Benjamin over twenty years ago. She ran her hand along the finely stitched quilt on the bed with its mottled cream background, golden yellows, and soft blues bursting from a star in the center. Rosemary had given Eve the quilt on her sixteenth birthday, but Eve left it when she'd married, opting to take a brand-new double-ringed wedding quilt that Benjamin's mother and sisters had made for her.

As it should be.

Rosemary sighed.

She eased a finger across the top of the oak dresser and pulled back a layer of dust, then reached for a rag in her apron pocket. After wiping the piece of furniture from top to bottom, she inspected the rest of the small room, dabbing at a cobweb in the corner above where the rocking chair was. She could remember sitting in the rocker, Eve swaddled in her arms, rocking until late in the night. Her only child had suffered a bad case of colic. She turned toward the bedroom door when her husband walked in.

"Everything is *gut*, Rosie. You're fretting too much." Joseph pushed his thick, black glasses up on his nose. "You'd think the bishop was coming to stay. It's just Eve, Big Ben, and the *kinner*." Like most folks in the community, Joseph referred to Benjamin as Big Ben because he was a bear of a man, stout and tall, towering over almost everyone. Rosemary still called him Benjamin because that's what she'd called him since he was born.

"I'm not fretting." Rosemary raised her chin as she folded her trembling hands together in front of her. "I just want things to be nice for Eve and her family."

Joseph shook his head and stared at her. "You worry too much."

"I do not. I'm not worried about their stay. Why do you say that?" Rosemary looked away from her husband's soft brown eyes as she positioned the Bible and box of tissues on the nightstand.

"You know just what I'm sayin'." Joseph tipped back the rim of his black hat just enough so that Rosemary could see how much his gray bangs needed a trim. He tapped a finger against his thick beard of the same color and raised a bushy eyebrow. "You know that when Eve is here in our *haus* for two months, she will see…" He paused as Rosemary clenched her fingers tightly together. "She will see how things are."

"Joseph Chupp, you don't know what you're talking about." Rosemary moved toward the bedroom door and tried to ease past him, but Joseph blocked her, gently grasping her shoulders.

"Talk to Eve, Rosie. Tell her everything. Let her help you."

"There is nothing to tell." Rosemary shook loose of his hold. "And I don't need any help. I am quite capable of running *mei* own home, preparing meals for you, and tending to everything else around here. I'm not a feeble old woman." She scowled. "So stop acting like I've got one foot in the grave."

"I didn't say that, *lieb*. But I think——"

She maneuvered her way around him and shook her head. "Let me be. I have much to do."

Once she'd reached the bottom of the stairs, she crossed the den and went into the kitchen, going straight to a large pot of stew she had simmering on the stove. She fought the tears forming in the corners of her eyes as she picked up the spoon on the counter. With concentrated effort, she gripped the ladle full-fisted and shakily swirled it around the thick, meaty soup, praying that the Lord would keep her hand steady.

Eve's family lived almost nine miles outside of Paradise, just far enough to make it quite the haul by buggy, so most of Rosemary and Joseph's visiting with their daughter and her family was done after worship service every other Sunday. The thought of all of them under the same roof for two months was exciting. And terrifying.

Rosemary jumped when she heard a knock at the front door.

Chapter 2

Eve forced a smile when her mother opened the large wooden door, then pushed the screen wide. *"Wie bischt, Mamm?"*

"Gut, gut. Come in." Her mother smoothed the wrinkles from her black apron as she stepped aside so Eve could enter the living room, then waited while Benny and the three boys toted in the suitcases and duffel bags.

Eve breathed in the aroma of her childhood home. There was always a piney clean fragrance mingled with a hint of whatever *Mamm* might be cooking. Eve hung her black cape and bonnet on the rack by the door and glanced around the room. Her mother's oatmeal-and-honey hand lotion was on the end table next to her side of the couch. She'd been making and using the lotion for as long as Eve could remember. After devotion time in the evenings, her mother would smooth the silky balm on rough hands, worn from a hard day's work.

Eve hadn't been in her parents' home in a couple of months. She blamed it on the distance between their houses and the fact that she saw them every other Sunday at someone else's homestead for worship, but she knew it was more than that. Her mother didn't approve of the way Eve and Benny raised the children. "Too many freedoms," she'd always say. Eve had grown weary of her mother's lectures years ago.

It also upset Eve to see the way her parents lived. She'd tried for years to get her mother to upgrade to appliances and other household fixtures that would make their lives easier, things that Bishop Smucker approved of, like propane lighting. But *Mamm* insisted on using lanterns to light the entire house, which became more and more of a fire hazard the older her parents got. The same lantern was on the mantel from many years ago, and when Eve turned to her left, she saw another one on the coffee table—just the way it had always been. Both her parents had poor eyesight, especially her father, who was almost blind without his thick, black-rimmed glasses. Eve had told them repeatedly that propane lighting would brighten up the room and help them to see better, but *Mamm* said such technology wasn't necessary. She also used the same gas stove that she'd had since before Eve was born, one so ancient she had to light the pilot in the oven as well as the top burners.

Eve walked to the fireplace, pulled off her black gloves, and warmed her hands by the fire as Benny and the boys continued to haul in their necessities.

"I have you and Benjamin in your old room." *Mamm* joined Eve by the fire. "We'll put the twins in the extra bedroom and Leroy in my sewing room on the pullout couch."

"That sounds *gut*." Eve managed another brief smile, although she couldn't help but wonder if God was punishing her for something. Two months here with her mother would be a nightmare. That wouldn't be the case with her father. He mostly stayed in the background and let *Mamm* run things, which was exactly the opposite of how it should be. Everyone knew that the man should be the head of the household.

Her father came from his bedroom around the corner from the living room, waving to everyone as they entered. "Come in, come in...out of this *wedder*." He kissed Eve on the cheek the way he always did when he saw her, then shook hands with Benny and all three boys. Eve glanced at her mother, who had never been affectionate. Eve didn't have the energy to change things. Instead, she was overly affectionate with her own children and made sure they'd never feel unloved.

"Follow me, and we'll get you all set up while the womenfolk work on some supper." *Daed* motioned for Eve's clan to follow him upstairs, and Eve followed her mother into the kitchen. She could see snow starting to fall outside the window as night was almost completely upon them. They'd made it there just in time, and Eve was hoping her house wouldn't be damaged any further from bad weather.

"It smells *gut* in here." Eve walked to the old white gas range and fought the urge to say anything. She'd asked her mother only once why they didn't buy a newer model, one with an electronic ignition that would be easier—and safer—for them to use. *Mamm* had scowled and said it was too *Englischy*, a term that Eve had never heard anyone except her mother use. "What can I do to help?"

"You can set the table." *Mamm* pointed to a hutch on the far wall in the large kitchen. "And use the *gut* dishes."

Eve hesitated. Her mother only used the good dishes at Thanksgiving, Christmas, or other special occasions. But Eve didn't want to give her any reason to argue so soon after they'd arrived, so she went to the hutch and pulled out seven of the large white china plates. She was setting the last one in place around the large table in the middle of the room when her father, Benny, and the boys walked into the room. Eve had already instructed her sons about not using cell phones, earbuds, or other electronics around her parents—especially their *mammi*. After a small rebellion, they'd all agreed. And Eve had told Amos, "If possible, try not to let *Mammi* see that lizard."

Eve remembered when she'd turned sixteen, excited to participate in all the things that the *rumschpringe* offered. It should have been a time to explore the outside world, go to movies, ride in cars, wear *Englisch* clothes, listen to the radio, and own a cell phone—if portable phones had been common and affordable back then. But Eve's parents had been much too old-fashioned and overprotective for any of that. Eve had hidden the few things that she did do from her parents—the same way she was making her own *kinner* do now.

She wasn't thrilled that all of her boys were actively taking advantage of this time period, but that's the way things were done. Children should be allowed to experience the outside world, then make a decision whether or not to be baptized into the community. It was every parent's fear that one of their children would choose not to stay, but Eve knew that she and Benny had educated

the boys well about the *Ordnung*. All she could do was
pray that they'd all seek baptism. Leroy was scheduled
to be baptized in the spring, which made Eve think that
there would be a proposal in the works too. Her oldest
son had been courting Lena Byler for almost a year,
and Lena was going to be christened into the community at that time as well.

Eve's father sat in his spot at the head of the table,
Leroy and Elias took the two seats to his left, and Amos
and Benny sat across from them. When Eve's mother sat
down across from her father, Eve slipped into a chair beside Benny. They all bowed their heads in silent prayer,
and Elias was the first one to speak.

"It's so dark in here." He glanced at the lantern hanging above the middle of the table, then at two others on
the counter. All the *kinner* were used to the large propane lamps they had in their house.

"This is the way it has always been done, Amos."
Eve's mother raised her chin as she passed a bowl of
chow-chow to her right.

Eve cleared her throat. "*Mamm*, that's Elias."

Her mother shook her head. "*Ach*, I still can't tell
those boys apart."

Eve smiled. "Most people can't." She ladled herself some stew from the large pot in the center of the
table. Despite her anxiety about staying with her parents, she still thought her mother's cooking was the
best in the world.

Of course, if *Mamm* would wear her glasses more
often and invest in some propane lighting, she'd have
a better shot at identifying her own grandchildren. But
to be fair, everyone in the community confused Amos
and Elias. They were as identical as any twins could

be, and the only thing most people used to distinguish them was that Amos stuttered sometimes. As a parent, Eve could tell them apart instantly before they even came within ten feet of her. Elias's eyebrows were a tad bushier than Amos's, and Elias had a freckle to the left of his right eye. One of Amos's teeth on the bottom row was crooked a bit to the left, and his thumbnails were different from his brother's, rounder. And to Eve, the boys just had a different scent. Maybe that was something only a mother noticed.

"I'm the handsome one," Elias said with a mouthful of food.

Eve quickly corrected him. "Don't talk with your mouth full."

From there, the conversation turned to the work to be done on the house. The plan was that Eve's father, Benny, and the three boys would tackle outdoor chores here first thing in the morning—get the chickens and pigs fed, stalls cleaned, horses tended, and cows milked—then they would go to the house to work. Various members of the community would show up as they could to lend a hand. Eve knew they could raise a barn in a day, and at first she'd questioned Benny as to why they couldn't get her house put back together in a day too. Benny had started to explain the structural damage, but then he just shook his head and said, "We'll get it livable as soon as we can."

Eve glanced out the window, and the only propane light her parents allowed illuminated the yard, large flakes of snow falling in blankets. If bad weather continued, it was going to make repairs that much more difficult.

She thought about spending her days inside with no

one else but her mother, and she wondered how this part of God's plan for her life could be a good thing. It was only a matter of time before they began to disagree about everything from how Eve raised her children to updating this old house. As she finished the last of her stew, she determined that she was just going to keep quiet and let her mother run her own household and try not to cause any upset.

Elias put the lantern on the nightstand between him and Amos before he climbed under the covers fully dressed, leaving his shoes next to him on the floor. He flipped open his cell phone.

"You better not try to sneak out here. It ain't gonna be as easy as at home." Amos sat up on his bed, frowning in the dimly lit room.

"Mind your own business." Elias propped himself against his pillow and tapped Elizabeth's number. While it was ringing, he said to his brother, "Besides, I'm closer to Elizabeth's *haus* here. Just barely a run through the Lapps' pasture, and I can meet her at the barn behind her *haus*."

"I—I reckon if you'd got caught sneaking out at home, you would've been in a b-big enough heap of trouble. But if you get caught sneaking out of *Mammi* and *Daadi's haus*, you're r-really gonna get it."

Elias closed the phone when Elizabeth didn't answer, then glanced at the battery bars. Only one left. Tomorrow he'd need to find some power to recharge, which might be a challenge since he'd be with his father and other members of the community working on their house. His father had insisted both Elias and Amos take a leave from their part-time jobs at the market in

Bird-in-Hand to work full-time on the reconstruction. Leroy had also been told to put his job on hold at the construction company where he worked. Leroy's supervisor hadn't taken the news as well as the twins' boss at the market, but the older man had eventually agreed.

This new work schedule put a glitch in Elias's plans. First, it would be hard to charge his phone. Second, he wouldn't get to see Elizabeth. She'd been visiting him every day for two months during her lunch break from the bakery. Elias was sure their first kiss was coming soon.

"She's not answering anyway." Elias put the phone on the nightstand. He glanced out the window at the steady snowfall. It would have been a cold trek across the pasture, but seeing Elizabeth would have been worth it. "And ya know, Amos…you ain't ever gonna get a girlfriend if you don't give it more effort."

Amos grunted. "Give it more effort? N-Now you're talking like the *Englisch.* You probably want to—to be one of them."

"Don't be *dumm.* I'll never leave here. I'll marry Elizabeth, and we'll have lots of *kinner.*" In the darkness he pointed a finger at his brother. "You're the one always reading them *Englisch* magazines. You probably want to go live out there." He waved his hand toward the window.

"Ain't true. I mostly like the pictures anyway." Amos lay down.

"You're gonna be living with *Mamm* and *Daed* until you're old, like twenty or something." Elias folded his hands behind his head. His brother was so shy that he'd barely even talk to a girl; all he did was bury himself in books and magazines. Elias knew that it was partly because of his stuttering, but Amos was a good-looking guy. Elias grinned at the thought.

"Sh-shut up, Elias."

"You shut up, Amos." Elias shook his head, not in the mood to fight. He stood up and was just about to slip out of his trousers when the phone rang. He grabbed it and answered quickly as he sat back down on the bed.

Elizabeth's sweet voice was a whisper as she spoke. "Can you *kumme*?"

"*Ya*. Same plan. If I'm not there in thirty minutes, then I got caught leaving the *haus*." He paused. "But since I'm at *mei mammi* and *daadi's haus*, I'm closer, so maybe less than thirty minutes."

"*Gut*. I'll be in the barn. Be careful, Elias. It's snowing *hatt*. Sure you want to *kumme*?" Before he had time to answer, she said, "I really want to see you."

Elias smiled as his heart thumped in his chest. A blizzard wasn't going to keep him from Elizabeth. He swallowed hard. "I want to see you too. Putting on my shoes and leaving."

As soon as they hung up, Elias slung his feet over the side of the bed and reached for his flashlight on the nightstand. He looked at the clock. Nine forty-five. His parents were always in bed by eight thirty, since they started their day around four thirty, so he was pretty sure his grandparents would be asleep too. But their bedroom was downstairs, so he'd have to be extra quiet going out the front door. He reached for his shoes.

"I—I wouldn't wanta—wanta be you if you get caught." Amos sat up in bed, and Elias pointed the flashlight in his face.

"Don't worry about it. It's late. Everyone's asleep."

Amos chuckled. "I hope she's worth it."

"*Ach*, she is, *mei bruder*. And I'm going to kiss her tonight."

"I'm going to sleep." Amos lay back down. "When four thirty comes, you'll be sorry."

Elias didn't answer, but instead shoved his pillow beneath the quilt on the twin bed. His mother rarely checked on them, but just in case she poked her head in the room, he'd be covered. He bundled up in his coat, stuffed his hands in his gloves, and pulled a thick stocking cap over his head.

He cringed when the bedroom door squeaked, then two stairs creaked on his way down. Crossing the living room, he decided not to go out the front door, but instead use the door in the kitchen since it was farthest away from his grandparents' bedroom. He tiptoed into the kitchen, and a bright light hit him in the face.

"Going somewhere?"

Chapter 3

Elias's feet felt rooted to the wooden floor in the kitchen as he stared at his grandfather. "Uh..."

"Just going out for a late-night stroll?" *Daadi* pulled the flashlight from Elias's face and put it on the table so the light was shining at the ceiling. Elias didn't move. "Mighty cold for a walk, *ya*?"

"Uh, *ya*."

Daadi picked up a glass and took a swallow. "Nothing like warm milk to help a man sleep." He pointed to a plate on the table. "And a slice of your *mammi's* apple crumb pie. Have yourself one." His grandfather pushed his glasses up on his nose, then scooped up a bite with his fork.

Elias was sure his chance of seeing Elizabeth was gone. He pulled off his knit stocking hat—the black one his mother had made him two years ago—and rubbed his forehead. "I was just…" His heart ached at the thought of lying to his grandfather, and he wasn't sure what to say.

Daadi nodded as he swallowed. "*Ya, ya.* I know." He stood up from the table, pushed in his chair, and pointed a finger at Elias. "I reckon we don't need to speak of this."

Elias felt his face turning three shades of red, and he opened his mouth to respond, but his grandfather spoke first.

"Your *mammi* doesn't like when I get up to eat cookies or pie this late at night. Gives me heartburn, and she says it's not *gut* for me." He smiled, his coke-bottle glasses hanging off his nose again. He was dressed in a long white shirt atop black trousers and black socks. *Daadi* picked up the flashlight from the table, and Elias brought a hand to his face when his grandfather shined it in his direction. *Daadi* stroked his long gray beard. "Which one are you anyway?"

Elias considered his options for a moment, then told the truth. "Elias." He held his breath as he waited to see what *Daadi* would do next.

His grandfather lowered the light, shuffled past him, and patted him on the shoulder. "Well, Elias…have a nice stroll. *Gut nacht.*"

Elias stood still as his grandfather scooted in his socks across the living room. Elias heard the bedroom door gently close. Was this a trick?

He waited a full five minutes as he tried to decide what to do. Then he imagined how Elizabeth's lips would feel on his, and he tiptoed out of the kitchen and closed the door behind him.

* * *

Elizabeth's teeth chattered as she pulled the back door open, forcing it against packed snow. She pulled her flashlight from the pocket of her heavy black coat and turned it on, scanning for critters as she strode down the path to the barn. When she didn't see anything, she walked to a haystack in the corner of the barn and sat down. Luckily, their three horses, four pigs, and three goats didn't seem disturbed by her visit. She wrapped her arms around herself, knowing she shouldn't have tempted Elias to travel on foot in this weather, but her heart fluttered every time she thought about him. Seeing him only once a day at lunchtime had been hard enough, but now that he would be working on the family's home, she wasn't sure when they could get together. This seemed like the only way, and she was sure that he was going to kiss her soon.

She stood up and paced, thinking it had been longer than thirty minutes. She poked her head out the barn door to see that all the lights at her house were still off. It was a miracle she'd managed to get out of the house with three younger sisters in the same bedroom, two older brothers down the hall, and her parents around the corner. It would be worth it when Elias walked through the door.

Elizabeth had known both the Bender twins for as long as she could remember, and from the time she was six or seven she was sure that she would grow up to marry Elias. While the boys looked the same to most people, Elias was more outgoing and confident. He never got riled or upset, and he was always happy. Elizabeth loved that about him. Amos seemed like a fine fellow, but he was incredibly shy, kept his head down, and stuttered when he got nervous. Elizabeth had tried to talk to him lots of times after the worship service, but she doubted Amos would ever venture out into the night to visit her. The barn door eased open, causing her heart to skip a few beats. *Elias, or Mamm or Daed?*

Her heartbeat returned to normal as Elias crossed the threshold into the barn. She brought her hands to her chest and bounced up on her toes once. "You made it." She walked quickly toward him, stopping a couple of feet away. His face was drained of color, his breathing ragged. His black jacket and stocking cap were covered in white flakes, his teeth were chattering. She walked closer and began rubbing his arms. "You're freezing. I should never have asked you to do this."

But I'm so glad you're here.

Elias wrapped his arms around her and pulled her close. She wasn't sure if it was just to warm himself up; but whatever the reason, it felt good to be in his arms.

"*Ach*, Elias. You're trembling."

"I'm fine." He shook as he held her. "I just wanted to see you."

"I feel the same way." She nuzzled her head into his chest. "I can feel your heart beating."

He chuckled. Not what she was expecting. He eased away, grinning. "I almost got caught."

"*Nee*. What happened?" She'd thought it had taken longer than thirty minutes.

He peeled back the rim of his black stocking hat, which had almost fallen over his eyes. "*Mei daadi* was sitting at the kitchen table when I tried to sneak through the kitchen."

Elizabeth gasped. "What did you do?"

Elias shrugged, still grinning. "He was eating a piece

of pie and drinking milk. He asked if I was going for a stroll. I never really answered, and he went on to bed."

Elizabeth wrapped her arms around herself again. "That's *fremm*."

"I know." He pulled her back into his arms. "But I had to see you."

They stayed in the embrace for a few moments, both shivering, until Elias slowly pulled away. He gazed into her eyes, and Elizabeth was sure he could hear her heart beating.

"Elizabeth…" He leaned down until his lips were inches from hers. "I love you."

Before she could answer, his mouth was firmly on hers, and she went weak in the knees. The kiss went on forever. Twice he eased away, but kissed her again. When they finally parted, she said, "I love you too, Elias."

He pulled her into his arms. "I can't stay long. But I'll try to come tomorrow night."

Elizabeth pulled from his arms and gazed into his eyes. "*Nee*. Don't come." She cupped his cheeks with her gloved hands. "It's much too cold for you to travel by foot like this. And tomorrow is supposed to be even colder. It's enough knowing that you love me."

Elias smiled. "I'd walk through a blizzard to be with you, Elizabeth, even if it was only for a few minutes like tonight." He kissed the top of her gloved hand. "I'll be here."

"But—"

"Don't you want me to come?" Elias tipped his head to one side.

Elizabeth fell into his arms. "*Ach*, Elias. I always want to be with you, but it's just so cold."

"I'll be here."

And as Elias kissed her for the last time that night, Elizabeth was sure that she would one day be Mrs. Elias Bender.

On Monday morning the men and boys left to go work on the house, leaving Eve and her mother alone. Eve wasn't sure how much work the menfolk would be able to get done on the house with the weather predictions, but of more concern to her was how she and her mother were going to fare all day together. Eve noticed her mother's right hand trembling as she washed the breakfast dishes. They'd all known for over a year that *Mamm* had Parkinson's disease. Eve had tried several times to get her mother to see a doctor in Lancaster, but *Mamm* always said that Fern Zook's herbal recipes were working just fine.

Eve loved Fern and appreciated the work that she did, but she suspected that modern medications could help her mother's condition far better than an herbal remedy.

Mamm's right hand shook with might as her four fingers met with her thumb, then the familiar circular patterns began as her mother tried to steady the plate so she could run the dishrag across it.

"*Mamm*, I'll finish the dishes." She reached for the plate her mother was holding, only to have her mother shakily jerk it away.

"I'm not an invalid, Eve. I can wash the dishes. I take care of your father every day." She scrubbed at the white plate.

Eve's mouth hung open for a moment. "I didn't say you were an invalid. I just offered to help." She set her dish towel on the counter, walked to the table, and picked up the butter and jams, stowing them in the refrigerator. "What can I do to help around here today? I'll clean the bedrooms and bathroom upstairs, but what else?" She was hoping there was plenty to do to keep them both busy and out of each other's hair.

Her mother didn't look up. Her hands were still in the soapy water, and strands of gray hair had come loose from beneath her black *kapp*. "I was hoping you'd do a couple of things for me while you're here."

Eve stood still, dreading what might be coming. "What's that?"

Mamm slowly turned toward her. "I haven't updated the family Bible since you were born. I was wondering if you'd add the boys, their birthdates and such." She turned away and resumed washing another plate. "And there is a large section in the back for notes. Maybe you could write down certain dates that are special. Things like that."

That was an easy enough task. Eve pointed to the living room. "The Bible you keep on the end table?"

Mamm shook her head. "*Nee*, I have the big family Bible in *mei* bedroom. It goes back five generations." She turned around to face Eve again, wiped her hands on a dish towel, and smiled. "I always meant to update it after the boys were born, but I needed to verify the times and how much they weighed." She paused. "And especially note the differences in the twins, since most of us can barely tell them apart."

Eve smiled. "That's an easy task. I'll be glad to." *And that will take about five minutes.* "What else?"

Mamm picked up her recipe box from the kitchen counter and motioned for Eve to join her at the kitchen table. She pulled out a stack of blank index cards from the back of the box.

"Most of the meals you and I make we know in our minds, *ya*?" *Mamm* raised an eyebrow, and Eve nodded. "But someday the boys will marry, and we'll want to share the recipes. I thought you could spend some time while you're here writing them all down." Her mother flipped a finger along the top of the categorized cards. "Most of these are from friends, although a few of them are mine." She leaned over and touched Eve's hand. "But I've never taken the time to write down the ones I know by heart."

Eve glanced at her mother's hand on hers, a rare and welcome gesture, but then *Mamm* quickly pulled her hand away. Again Eve wondered why there'd always been such distance between them. Eve's grandparents had passed before she was born, and her aunts and uncles lived in Ohio, along with a few cousins Eve had never met. She'd often wondered what kind of relationship her mother and grandmother had.

Mamm handed her a pen. "Do you want to start now?"

Eve slowly took the pen. "There are probably hundreds. You've been showing me how to cook since I was a little girl."

"*Ya*. Exactly." Her mother tapped her hand to the table, then hastily got up. "You get started, and I'll bring you the Bible for updating. Don't worry about the upstairs, I'll get it."

Eve stared at the recipe box. She thumbed through the cookie section and randomly pulled out a card. It was a recipe for boiled cookies from Rachel King. Eve remembered when Rachel gave *Mamm* the recipe. Rachel's daughter, Hannah, couldn't have been more than a year old the first time Eve babysat her. She could still recall the scrumptious cookies that Rachel had left for her to snack on. Eve had made sure not to leave that day without Rachel's recipe. Her mouth watered as she thought about the chunky peanut butter cookies.

Eve placed the card back in its spot as she thought about Hannah, who was now a grown woman running the family's bed-and-breakfast. She pulled out another card from the box, a recipe for sour cream pancakes that had come from Esther Stoltzfus. Esther had died years ago, but her famous sour cream pancakes lived on. Eve recalled the first time her mother prepared them, when Eve was about ten. "But *Daed* doesn't like sour cream," she had protested.

"Then we just won't mention that there's sour cream in them," her mother had said, then giggled.

Eve stared at the recipe box, figuring that there was probably a story behind every card. The best times she'd ever shared with her mother were when they were cooking.

As memories filled Eve's mind, she positioned one of the blank recipe cards in front of her. Smiling, she started to work.

Chapter 4

Think, you old woman. Think. Rosemary thumped her palm to her forehead repeatedly.

"*Mamm*, are you okay?"

Rosemary spun around and grabbed her chest as she leaned against the kitchen counter. "What?" She scowled. "You scared me near to death, sneaking up on me like that."

Eve had taken up working on the recipes in Rosemary's recliner near the fireplace for almost a week. She wrote all day and kept the fire going while Rosemary cleaned, did the mending, and kept up with the rest of the normal household chores. Every day her daughter offered to help with the routine tasks, but Rosemary just needed her to write down those recipes. All of them.

She hadn't heard Eve get up and walk into the kitchen. Eve pulled her black sweater snug around her. "I didn't mean to sneak up on you. I was just wondering if it feels cold in here to you. I'm freezing."

"Add some logs to the fire." Rosemary waved a hand in the air as she tried to remember where she'd put her glasses. She'd looked everywhere: on the nightstand by the bed, on the coffee table and end table in the living room, in the bathroom, even in the refrigerator. Although she'd never admit it to a soul, she'd found her spectacles next to the butter on two separate occasions.

Eve took a couple of steps into the kitchen. "Those propane heaters in the bedrooms upstairs work great. Why don't we get a couple for down here?"

"What?"

"Heaters, *Mamm*." Eve walked closer to Rosemary. "*Heaters.*" She edged even closer and spoke louder. "Our Daily Bread has some nice propane heaters on sale. I can pick up a couple when I'm there tomorrow afternoon."

"That's fine." Rosemary grimaced as she scanned the countertop, continuing to look for her glasses. "And I'm not deaf."

"What are you looking for?" Eve moved closer, and Rosemary sidestepped to her left as she reached behind her and clutched the tiled countertop. She locked eyes with her daughter. For the life of her, Rosemary didn't know what Eve was talking about.

"What?" Rosemary's heart thudded in her chest. *This is what it's like to lose your mind.* It took a lot of effort to pretend it wasn't happening. "What?" she asked again in a calmer voice.

"You're looking around like you've lost something." *Yes, that's it. I've lost something. Now, what was it?* Eve moved closer, and it felt like every nerve in

Rosemary's body was twitching, then centered in her hand. She reached for her right hand with her left and squeezed, but the shaking was worse than usual. She could feel Eve's eyes on her, the same way people at church stared at her when the shaking started.

"*Mamm*, why don't you let me take you to Dr. Knepp? I'm sure he'll prescribe some medicine for your Parkinson's. Fern's herbal recipes are fine, but the *Englisch* doctor can give you some better medication, and—"

"My glasses!" Rosemary let out a huge sigh of relief. "I'm looking for my *glasses*." She smiled. "I've lost my glasses." She shook her head a couple of times. "Now, what were you saying?"

"Dr. Knepp, *Mamm*. Let's get you some better medication to help with the shaking. It's nothing to be embarrassed about."

"I'm not embarrassed. Fern's herbs are doing me fine. I just need to find my glasses."

"They're on the mantel. I saw them there earlier."

Rosemary lifted her chin and pressed her lips together. "Now why in the world would they be on the mantel?" *Maybe you put them there to confuse me.*

Eve shrugged. "I don't know. You were dusting the lanterns earlier. Maybe you set them down. I'll get them for you."

Rosemary sighed, then quietly whispered, "*Danki*."

Eve was working on the recipes in bed when Benny crawled underneath the covers beside her. "What are you writing on the back of the card, or is that just a very long recipe?" Her husband eased up against her, his beard tickling her face. She turned and gave him a quick kiss.

"I'm writing down things that I remember about me and *mei mamm*."

"Like what?" Benny nuzzled her with his beard again.

She gave him another kiss. "Now scoot over and let me work on this." She playfully pushed him away. "My fondest memories of me and *Mamm* are when we were cooking, so on the back of every card I'm writing what I remember related to the recipe." She shrugged. "I mean, I don't have something to write on every card, but if we had a *gut* time making this recipe, or if something *gut* happened… I'm writing it down."

"I think that's very nice." Benny smiled. "You're a *gut dochder*."

Guilt flooded over Eve. "*Nee*, I don't think so." She paused as she took a deep breath. "I haven't been seeing *mei mudder* enough, and she's gotten worse. She hides it well during worship, but being with her all the time, I really notice how much her hands shake. She still refuses to go see Dr. Knepp."

"I know it frustrates you to see her suffer, but you can't make her go."

Eve set the cards and pen on her nightstand, then rubbed her eyes. "She didn't even argue today when I asked her about buying some extra propane heaters for downstairs. She was too busy worrying about her glasses she'd lost." She rolled over on her side and faced Benny.

He eased onto his side and propped his head on his hand. Her sweet Benny. He always knew when to just listen.

"She's so cranky. Worse than ever."

"We're working on the *haus* as best we can, but the

storm is supposed to blow in tonight. If we get all the snow they say we're going to get, that will slow us down."

"I'm not worried about that." Eve blinked her eyes a few times as a knot formed in her throat. "I'm worried about her. About *Mamm*." She paused again, trying to find the words to explain her feelings. "It's not just the shaking. She's different. And I don't mean just crankier. Sometimes she looks at me in a *fremm* way." She took a deep breath, then heard a movement downstairs.

"Your *daed* eating a late-night snack again?" Benny grinned.

Eve looked at the clock. Nine thirty. She and Benny were up later than usual. "*Ya*." Eve pushed back the covers on her side and swung her feet over the side of the bed. "I'm going to go talk to him. About *Mamm*." She wrapped her hair in a tight bun, pinned it, then found her robe. After she picked up the lantern, she leaned down and kissed her husband. "Sleep, *mei lieb*. I'll be quiet when I come back in."

Benny nodded as he yawned, then his face faded from view as Eve moved with the lantern toward the bedroom door.

A minute later she entered the kitchen. Her father was sitting at the table with a flashlight illuminating a round circle on the ceiling. His eyes grew wide when Eve entered the room.

"*Ach*, you scared me," he said through a mouthful of cake. "I thought you were your *mudder*."

Eve smiled. *Mamm* had told her years ago that *Daed* got out of bed every night for a late-night snack. "He needs to feel he's getting away with something," her mother had said. "But it does give him an awful case of indigestion the next morning."

She pulled out a chair and sat down across from her father. He pushed a pan of sliced *kaffi* cake toward her. "Taste this." He frowned. "Something don't taste right about it."

Eve picked up a slice of the cake her mother had made yesterday. She took a bite. "It's not bad. It's just not really…good."

Her father frowned. "Your *mamm* is the best cook in the district." He put down his half-eaten piece of cake and shook his head.

"I wanted to talk to you about her. She's getting worse, isn't she? I mean, the shaking has increased, but she also seems so ill-tempered—"

"She's not ill-tempered."

Her father spoke with an authority that Eve wasn't used to hearing. Even when she was growing up, she'd rarely heard him raise his voice, and any disciplining had been left up to her mother. Although neither of her parents had ever laid a hand on her. *Mamm* would make her sit in her room when she'd misbehaved, but that was the extent of it.

Daed rubbed his forehead and sighed, then went on. "She's sick, Eve. I've been telling you that."

More guilt. Eve bit her bottom lip for a moment, blinked her eyes a few times. "I know that."

"*Nee*. I don't think you do. Until this past week, you've only seen her every other week for a brief time. You're just now getting an idea of how sick she is because you are with her every day."

"*Daed*, I have a family to take care of. It's not that I avoid you." *Especially not you.* "I've tried to get her to go see Dr. Knepp. *Englisch* medications could help with the shaking."

Her father sighed. "I know you to be right." He gazed at her across the table in the dimly lit room. "But she needs *you*. Modern medicine can only go so far."

A tear found its way down Eve's cheek, and she quickly swiped it away. She'd just lied to her father. She did avoid her mother as much as she could, and she'd been dreading this extended visit.

"*Mei* sweet *maedel*..." Her father reached over and put his hand on top of hers. "Use this time to get to know your *mudder*." He stood up, then leaned down and kissed her on the forehead. "You might be surprised by what you learn."

Eve heard her father's bedroom door close. She picked up the slice of cake and took another bite.

Sugar. That was it. There was no brown sugar, which Eve knew the recipe called for. She ate the rest of the cake anyway, not ready for sleep just yet. She folded her hands in front of her and bowed her head.

Elias chuckled. "It's been so easy, sneaking out this week." He pulled Elizabeth close and kissed her again. Afterward he pushed back a strand of loose hair that had fallen from beneath her *kapp*. "*Daadi* just sits at the table eating his snack and waves to me as I go out the door. He usually tells me to have a nice walk and to stay warm."

Elizabeth frowned. "He's on to you, Elias. He knows you're not just going for a walk every night at this hour."

Elias shrugged, grinning. "Maybe so, but I never lie to him, and he has never mentioned it in front of *mei mamm* or *daed*."

"I guess that's *gut*," Elizabeth said, shivering.

"I'm going to go. You're freezing." He pulled her into his arms, kissed her again, then sent her indoors. "Be careful," he said as she made her way to the barn exit. "We don't want you getting caught either."

Elizabeth nodded, and once she was safely inside, Elias fought the bitter cold across the Lapp pasture to his grandparents' house. He knew a storm was due to blow in, and he probably shouldn't have traveled to see Elizabeth tonight. He could see a faint light shining from the kitchen, and he was surprised that his grandfather was still up. Every other night, *Daadi* was in bed when Elias returned from seeing Elizabeth.

He trekked softly up the porch steps, pulled back the screen, and twisted the handle on the wood door. A light hit him in the face.

And this time it wasn't his grandfather.

Chapter 5

Elias cringed as his mother stood, yelling at him in a whisper from the other side of the kitchen table. "You are grounded, do you hear me?"

"*Ya*. Yes, *Mamm*." Elias was glad that the table was between them. He hadn't seen *Mamm* this mad since he dropped a frog down the back of Anna Mae Stoltzfus's dress after worship when he was nine. Usually she left the discipline to their father, but she'd been so furious about the frog incident she didn't even wait for *Daed*, opting to pull a switch from a nearby tree before they walked into the house. Elias wished he were young enough to take a spanking instead of being grounded.

"It is nearing zero degrees outside with a storm coming in. Do you have any idea how dangerous it is for you to be outside in this?" *Mamm* put her hands on her hips.

He could barely see her in the dim light of the lan-

.tern, but he was pretty sure her face was red as a beet, the way it usually got when she was really mad.

"How could you do this while we are staying at your grandparents' *haus*?"

Elias opened his mouth and almost said that *Daadi* knew about it, but there was no reason to get his grandfather in trouble too. "I'm sorry."

Mamm pointed toward the living room. "Go. We will talk of this in the morning. And you can be sure that I will tell Elizabeth's *mudder* about this."

Elias stopped breathing. "*Mamm*, you can't. Please. Don't tell her *mudder*. I'll never be able to see Elizabeth again. Her father will forbid it. *Mamm*…" He squared his shoulders, standing taller. "I'll die if I can't see her."

His mother rolled her eyes. "You will not *die*. And over time, I'm sure that you and Elizabeth will be able to see each other again."

Just the thought of not seeing Elizabeth every day caused Elias's stomach to ache. "What about the singing on Sunday?"

"That's in two days. I promise you'll still be punished."

Elias put a hand on his hip and looked at the floor. "Some *rumschpringe* this is."

His mother came around the table and held the lantern up. As he'd suspected, her face was beet red.

"You watch yourself, mister. We've allowed all of you boys plenty of privileges, but sneaking out when a storm is coming is dangerous, and you should know better." *Mamm* frowned, her eyes locked with his. "I don't want your grandparents to know about this. Now up to bed you go."

Elias stomped across the living room to the stairs.

He wasn't a child and shouldn't be treated like one. He would find a way to see Elizabeth. No matter what his mother said.

Four o'clock came early on Saturday morning. Eve had trouble going to sleep after catching Elias sneaking back into the house. She knew she'd reacted out of fear more than anything. As predicted, the storm had come during the night and dropped almost twelve inches of snow. Despite the weather, her father, Benny, and her three sons left to go work on the house. She'd told Benny about catching Elias, and they agreed that two weeks' punishment would be sufficient. Benny had talked her out of telling Elizabeth's parents.

Her father's words weighed heavily on her heart. *"Use this time to get to know your* mudder," he'd said.

What is there to get to know? Eve and her mother were nothing alike. Her mother had shown little to no affection toward Eve when she was growing up. Eve had made it a point to shower her children with affection. Rosemary Chupp was also stubborn, refusing to change with the times or make use of modern medicine to help herself. Eve took advantage of certain luxuries that the bishop allowed—things that still kept them separated from the outside world, but that also improved quality of life or saved time—propane lights, certain canned goods, battery-operated mixers for baking, a modern gas range for cooking, and a sewing machine that was run by a small generator...just to name a few.

Eve gathered up the recipe box, blank cards, and her pen. After she stoked the fire, she curled up in the recliner and tried to focus on the happy times she and her mother had shared. Even now, as they prepared meals

together in her childhood home, there was a peaceful-
ness between them that was absent the rest of the time.
Just like when she was young.

"How are the recipes coming?" *Mamm* walked into
the room toting a yellow feather duster. Eve didn't think
the house could get any cleaner, but she didn't comment.

"Fine. I can't believe how many recipes I have in my
head. It was a *gut* idea to get them all written down."

"*Danki* for doing that." *Mamm* smiled, and again
Eve's father's words flowed through her mind.

"You're welcome. I'm enjoying it." Eve paused. "We
cooked a lot of things together over the years."

"*Ya*. We did." *Mamm* exhaled, sounding content, and
Eve wondered if her mother wished they were closer
too.

They were quiet for a few moments, then Eve decided to share her project. "I—I hope you don't mind,
but on the back of each card I've written memories I
have of us preparing the recipe." She bit her bottom
lip for a moment, keeping her head down. "Or maybe
where we took the food, or what we were doing when
we first made it." She shrugged. "Just little things like
that." She looked up after a moment and was shocked to
see tears gathering in the corners of her mother's eyes.
"Mamm?" Eve waited, not sure what to do. She wasn't
sure she'd ever seen her mother cry.

"I think that is *gut*. Very, very *gut*." *Mamm* raised
her chin, blinked her eyes several times, then began
dusting around the lanterns on the mantel.

They were quiet while Eve wrote and her mother
cleaned the living room. Eve had already gone upstairs
to make sure that Amos's lizard and cage were still
safely hidden in the closet behind a bunch of boxes. So

far they'd been lucky that Eve's mother hadn't stumbled upon the reptile while tidying up the boys' room.

Eve finished her card for Chicken in a Cloud. It was a favorite of both hers and her mother's, although Eve had long ago given up making the sauce from scratch, opting for cream of chicken soup instead. It wasn't as tasty, but it was much easier. However, it was her mother's recipe, so Eve wrote it out the way her mother had originally taught her—to save some chicken broth, then mix it with flour and butter to make the creamy sauce. But the best part of Chicken in a Cloud was the story that went with it. She turned the card over and wrote.

I remember the day we had chicken and potatoes, and you suggested we do something other than just bake the chicken and make mashed potatoes as a side dish. I was standing on the little red stool as usual, so I was tall enough to help. You always stood to my left.

Eve paused, looking up. She could see the red stool through the doorway into the kitchen, tucked into a nook on the other side of the refrigerator; same place it had always been. She smiled.

You added milk and cream cheese, the way you always did when making mashed potatoes, but I asked you why you didn't add any butter. You told me to wash my hands, and we both did. Then you thrust your bare hands into the mashed potatoes and pulled out two handfuls and laughed. I wasn't sure what to do, but you nodded for me to do the same. Then we tossed the mashed potatoes into a casserole dish you had laid out, both of us laughing the whole time.

I was eight or nine, I think, and I couldn't believe we were playing in the food! We formed a crust with the potatoes, then talked about the chicken filling. I felt so much a part of the process, and when we were done, you told me to name our creation. And Chicken in a Cloud was born.

Eve leaned her head back against the recliner, noticing that her mother had left the room. *Mamm's* bedroom door was closed. She'd been known to sneak in a nap this time of day, so Eve closed her eyes and let the Chicken in a Cloud memory linger in her mind. There'd been so many good days for them; she wondered why she allowed herself to focus on the negative in their relationship. Maybe they were just two different women with varying ways of doing things.

She opened her eyes and looked into the recipe box. She'd written close to a hundred, she figured, and probably had at least a hundred more to go. There wasn't a story to go with every card, but each time she recalled a fond memory, she felt one step closer to her mother, even if it was only one-sided. Glancing at the clock, she knew she was going to miss the two o'clock prayer gathering at Our Daily Bread, but Benny had asked her not to travel in this weather. She knew he was right, but she would miss the fellowship of the local women in the community. Her mother hadn't been to the prayer gathering since the tremors in her hands had started. Sometimes Eve was surprised *Mamm* still went to church.

Shaking her head, she once again forced out the negative thoughts.

* * *

Rosemary sat on her bed staring at the plain white wall as shadows of her past danced in front of her. She'd gone for years without the haunting images surfacing. *Why now, Lord? Why are these demons in my head?*

She thanked the Lord every day that her relationship with Eve wasn't like the one she'd had with her own mother. Rosemary had never laid a hand on Eve. She'd made it a point to stay distant from her only daughter, just in case that type of thing ran in the family genes—like mother, like daughter. Now she wanted to be closer to Eve, but they'd been this way for so long that Rosemary wasn't sure how to change. She saw the outpouring of affection that Eve gave to her own children, even if she wasn't raising them the way Rosemary would have liked. The boys had brought all their electric gadgets along, and she reckoned everyone thought they were hiding them. But there were small boxes with wires in the twins' room, a radio in Leroy's, and Eve had lotions from Walmart. Rosemary cringed.

If there was one thing she'd learned from her mother, it was that change wasn't good. That belief had been beaten into her and her siblings. She'd tried to make sure Eve didn't evolve with the times, but she and Joseph had rarely disciplined their daughter. Maybe it was their fault that Eve didn't feel the same way about change. As another generation was nearing adulthood, Rosemary could see that things were only getting worse. Soon there'd be generations of Amish folk who wouldn't rely on the Lord's will, but instead on all those gadgets and what-nots.

Rosemary heard a ringing in her ears—so loud she brought her hands to her head. But she could still hear

Minerva screaming. *Mamm* must have the horse whip after her again. Rosemary didn't understand why Minnie couldn't just mind her manners with their mother. Most of Rosemary's beatings had come from defending her sister. She hauled herself up off the bed and burst out the door.

Minerva was curled up in a ball in the recliner. Rosemary ran to her and dropped to her knees. "Minnie, hush your cries. Stop it now." She pulled the girl into a hug to try and muffle her sobs before *Mamm* came back again. Minnie pulled away and said something, but Rosemary could barely hear her for all the buzzing in her ears.

She blinked a few times, then her heart started pounding in her chest when she realized the mistake she'd made. "Eve, is that you?"

Chapter 6

"It was terrible, Benny." Eve leaned her head back against her pillow Saturday evening. "She thought I was her sister, Minnie, and then when I tried to talk to her about it, she walked away. Did you see how quiet she was during supper?"

Benny didn't say anything as he got underneath the covers.

"I think she must be going crazy." Eve thought again about what her father said. This must be what he wanted her to know, that her mother was losing her mind. "Because she is surely *ab im kopp*."

"Remember, Dr. Knepp said that Parkinson's disease can cause some mind problems. Didn't he say that?" Benny propped himself up against his pillow, then stroked his beard. "It wonders me how often this happens."

"I don't know. I wish *Daed* would have told me about

this, but I guess he wanted me to find out on my own."
Eve shook her head, frowning. "He said she wasn't ill-tempered, and that's true. It's even worse; she's losing her mind."

"Maybe that's why she wanted you to write all the family recipes down."

"You're right. I didn't even think of that." Eve thought about the *kaffi* cake with no sugar in it. She rolled onto her side, her long brown hair cascading past her shoulders. "Do you think *Daed* is punishing me somehow—that he's mad at me for not coming around enough, so he wants me to see how bad things are with *Mamm*?"

"That doesn't sound like your father. Plus, only our heavenly Father judges us." Benny leaned over and kissed her on the cheek. "Pray about it. And I will too."

Eve closed her eyes and said her prayers.

But sleep didn't come for a while.

Rosemary was glad that worship and the meal afterward had occupied a large part of the day, but she knew that come tomorrow she'd be left alone with Eve again, and her daughter was bound to say something about Rosemary's bout of insanity.

It had seemed so clear in Rosemary's mind... Minnie screaming and Rosemary comforting her.

She pulled her heavy coat tighter around her, thankful for the windshield on the buggy, but freezing nonetheless. Joseph's teeth were chattering when she glanced his way, and he kept pushing his glasses back up on his nose. Twisting her neck, she turned to see Eve, Benjamin, and the twins behind them in their own buggy. The Bylers had hosted worship on this frigid Sunday, so Leroy had stayed to be with Lena.

"I want to talk to you about something, Rosie." She recognized the slow steadiness of Joseph's voice. He was about to say something important.

She looked his way.

"I want you to let Eve carry you to see Dr. Knepp."

Rosemary hadn't mentioned the Minnie episode to Joseph, so Eve must have told him. "What did Eve say?" She faced forward, raising her chin as her own teeth clicked together.

"About what?"

Rosemary turned toward him again. "About me. Did you and Eve have a conversation about me? I don't want you talking behind *mei* back like—" She sighed, unable to pick the right word for her rant...*like I'm a crazy person.*

"No one's talking behind your back, *mei lieb*, but I want you to get some better medication for your sickness."

Rosemary thought about the day before and briefly considered it. "*Nee.*"

"Don't you want to feel better?" Her husband pushed his glasses up on his nose again.

"I don't feel bad." Rosemary gripped her hands together in her lap, hoping Joseph wouldn't notice the shaking. She'd been praying that she wouldn't lose her senses anymore, and she'd keep praying about it. As awful as life had been with her own mother, Rosemary still remembered the day her father took her mother to see the *Englisch* doctors in Lancaster. *Mamm* never came home.

Joseph slowed the horse to a slow trot. "Rosie..." He turned toward her and sighed, then looked back through the plastic shield in front of them. "I know that you think we need to avoid the modern things of the world. And we mostly do. But I want you to think about seeing the *Englisch* doctor."

Tears gathered in the corners of her eyes for the second time this week. She couldn't remember the last time she'd cried, and yet it had almost happened in front of Eve, and now Joseph. She looked down at her hands. The shaking had been getting worse, but more fearful was a trip to see Dr. Knepp.

Elias tossed and turned beneath his covers. He'd spent as much time as he could with Elizabeth after worship service, but now as the moon shone brightly through his window, his mind filled with visions of her. They'd sneaked behind the Bylers' house twice to kiss, and Elias was sure he wanted to spend the rest of his life with her.

He glanced at Amos on the other side of the room and wished his brother would quit snoring. Usually it didn't bother him, but tonight he was just jittery in general. *This must be part of being in love.* He was glad no one could see the thoughts floating through his mind. Turning on his side, he thumped his pillow with his fist until it flattened. He was a frustrated man; he couldn't sleep, he missed Elizabeth, and work would come early in the morning. He'd be glad when he was back at his job at the market, able to see her every day for lunch.

He folded his hands behind his head and scowled. Every day this past week *Daed* had sent Amos to the hardware store for something they'd needed for the house. Once it was for more nails, and then yesterday they'd run out of wood putty. It didn't seem fair that Amos always got to make the run to the store. Elias

could have used the opportunity to see Elizabeth, which
was probably why his father didn't assign him the task.
Amos was sure taking advantage of his break away
from the job site, taking an extra long time every day.
He was probably stopping in some bookstore or library
to bury his head in a book.

Elias rolled over again. Elizabeth had insisted that
Elias not sneak out during the two weeks while he was
grounded. She was worried about his health out in the
cold, and that he would get caught again and be in even
more trouble. He was thankful his parents had not told
Elizabeth's parents that they'd been meeting.

*I love her so much. I hope she loves me half as much
as I love her.*

He flipped onto his other side. And wished Amos
would quit snoring.

Rosemary couldn't sleep. She had been awake when
Joseph slipped out of bed to go have a snack, and she
was still sleepless as he tried to sneak back under the
covers without her knowing. She smiled for a brief moment, but worry filled her heart. She was afraid to go
to sleep. What if her mind wasn't intact when she woke
up? She'd been praying about it all night, but maybe this
was God's plan for her.

She watched the clock for almost an hour, and it was
nearly eleven when she climbed out of bed to go to the
bathroom. As she felt her way through the darkness, a
glow outside the window caught her eye. She walked
toward the window and leaned her face toward the pane
to peer outside, then she walked to the bed and nudged
her husband.

"Joseph, wake up."

He grunted.

Rosemary gave him another gentle push on the shoulder. "Wake up. One of the boys is outside in this weather."

"Is he coming or going?"

Rosemary went back to the window and peered out. "He's coming up the walk toward the porch."

"*Gut*. Then all is well."

She turned around and faced her husband. His voice didn't express one bit of concern. "How can you say that? No *kinner* should be out this time of night in this *wedder*."

"It's Elias. He goes to see the Lapp girl."

Rosemary watched out the window as Elias came up the porch steps. "Elizabeth?"

"*Ya*. That's her name. Now come back to bed."

Rosemary waited until she saw Elias safely up the porch steps and heard the gentle *click* of the door in the living room closing behind him before she went to the bathroom. A few minutes later she shuffled back to bed in her socks, pulled the covers back, and got into bed. She nudged Joseph. "That's disrespectful, sneaking out." She shook her head before she slid down onto her pillow. "What next?"

"He's in *lieb*. I used to sneak out to meet you too. Now go to sleep."

Rosemary remembered meeting Joseph at the nearby shanty when she was seventeen. She cringed, recalling the risks she'd taken. But she knew Eve wouldn't react the way her own mother would have if Rosemary had been caught. "Eve will hear of this in the morning."

"Let it go, Rosemary. I'll talk to Elias tomorrow."

Her eyes rounded in the darkness. "Let it go? I can't keep this from Eve."

"I will talk to the boy in the morning."

"You make him understand that this type of behavior is unacceptable. And in our *haus*." She rolled onto her side. "Eve would have never done anything like that."

"Really?" Joseph chuckled. "I doubt we know half of what Eve did during her *rumschpringe*. We didn't give her many freedoms, but *kinner* that age are going to break the rules, explore."

"Eve would have never sneaked out of the *haus*."

"Ask her, then."

"I will."

"Go to sleep."

Rosemary let out a heavy sigh and closed her eyes.

Elias grunted as he pulled the covers up over his head. "What do you want, Amos? It can't be time to get up yet." His brother poked him in the arm for the second time, and Elias eased his head out of the covers. Amos was holding a lantern, and Elias glanced at the clock. "I could have slept thirty more minutes."

"George is missing."

Elias bolted up. "What?"

"I must not have closed the latch on his cage good." Amos held up the lantern and shined it toward the closet, the door wide open. "He ain't there."

Elias rubbed his eyes as he stretched the length of the bed.

"Help me look for him."

"He's your stupid lizard. And I can smell breakfast cooking." Elias rolled out of the bed.

"*Danki*, Elias. I'll—I'll remember when you need

mei help for something." Amos dropped to his knees, shined the lantern under each bed, then actually called George by name as if he were calling for a dog.

Elias shook his head but then lit the other lantern. He pulled out the dresser and held the light close, shone the light behind the rocking chair, then held it at arm's length around the room while Amos did the same thing using the other lantern. "I don't see him."

"That's not *gut*." His brother scratched his head as he continued to move the lantern around the room.

Elias pulled on his black work pants and a dark-blue long-sleeved shirt. "Let's eat breakfast. I'll help you find him when we get home from work tonight."

Amos leaned down and stuck his hand inside each of his shoes that were by the bed, then went to his empty duffel bag in the corner and pulled it wide at the zipper. "*Nee*. Not in here." He dressed quickly. "Shut the door *gut* behind us," Amos said as he left the bedroom in front of Elias. "That way he won't get out of this room while we're at work."

Elias did as Amos asked, but sighed as he glanced behind him at the space between the bottom of the door and the wood floor.

Plenty of room for George to squeeze his way out.

Chapter 7

The next morning Rosemary wanted to tell Eve about Elias. It seemed the right thing to do despite Joseph's insistence that he would speak to the boy. Eve should know that her son had been sneaking out. But she looked so peaceful curled up in the recliner writing on the recipe cards. Rosemary stared at her for a few moments, still unable to believe that she'd actually mistaken her own daughter for Minnie. She shook her head, struggling to clear the images.

As she ran a broom across the wooden floor in the living room, she fought the tremble in her right hand and the ache in her back. She paused, straightening for a moment as she put a hand across the small of her back.

"Mamm..."

Rosemary turned to Eve. *"Ya?"*

"Why don't you take advantage of my being here

and let me help with the housework?" Eve laid her pen across the card in her lap.

Rosemary shook her head. She was already taking advantage of Eve being here by having her write down the recipes. Eve didn't know that Rosemary had referred to them several times already, sneaking a peek when no one was around.

"No..." She smiled as she waved a hand in Eve's direction. "It's important for you to write the recipes down, and..." She paused. "And *mei* hand trembles too much to do that." It was easier to admit that than tell her daughter that she couldn't remember how to make things she'd been cooking for over forty years. She wondered if Eve was going to mention yesterday's episode. Surely she already suspected that her mother was losing her mind.

Eve twisted her mouth back and forth. "Well, you should at least let me get you something better than that old broom. They make nonelectric sweepers, *Mamm*, that are very light and easy to use."

"No need." Rosemary began pushing the broom across the floor again. "This is the way I've always done it."

"*Ya*, I know." Eve's tongue was thick with sarcasm, and Rosemary's eyes darted to the right just in time to see Eve rolling hers.

Rosemary held the broom out to her side like a pitchfork and put her other hand on her hip. "Did *mei* own *dochder* just roll her eyes at me?"

Eve put the recipe box, cards, and her pen on the end table next to her and leaned forward. "*Mamm*, I'm sorry. I don't mean to be disrespectful, but I can't understand your unwillingness to change. Bishop Smucker allows us certain items that make our lives easier, like better appliances and a new sweeper. It just doesn't make sense to me." Eve lifted her hands and shrugged. "So maybe explain it to me."

Rosemary's blood was about to boil, but she reminded herself that Eve was of a new generation. Rosemary would have never spoken to her mother in such a way. And for good reason.

"Why is it that you feel the need to change everything about our ways?" Rosemary lifted the broom a few inches off the ground. "I've had this broom for years, and it's cleaned every room in this house just fine without buying an *Englisch* sweeper. Besides, hard work is *gut* for the soul."

"*Mamm*, God doesn't distinguish your place in His kingdom based on whether or not you use a broom or a sweeper—which, by the way, isn't an *Englisch* sweeper."

"Well, the good Lord doesn't want us veering from our simple ways either." Rosemary put the broom down, turned, and ran it across the floor again. "And I reckon He doesn't want us giving our *kinner* all the freedoms that they seem to have nowadays."

Eve's eyebrows drew into a frown. "All three of *mei* boys are in their *rumschpringe*, *Mamm*. You know there are certain freedoms that go along with that." Then Eve mumbled under her breath, "Even though I didn't have any."

Rosemary thought about what Joseph had said, and she faced Eve, brushing back a piece of gray hair that had fallen forward. "Did you ever sneak out of our *haus* in the middle of the night?"

The color drained from Eve's face. "Why do you ask?"

Well, there; Rosemary had her answer. But if Eve sneaked out because Rosemary and Joseph had not allowed her enough freedom, then why was Elias sneaking out? Those *kinner* surely had more than enough privileges. Her thoughts were quickly resolved—it was just never enough these days. There was never going to be a return to the times when a hard day's work and simple pleasures were enough to keep a person satisfied. With each generation the birds wandered farther from the nest, which only set them up to be swallowed by the world around them.

She finally answered Eve. "I was just wondering. Your *daed* suggested that maybe we didn't give you enough freedom during your *rumschpringe*, but if we didn't, it was only to keep you close, to make sure that you chose correctly—to be baptized into the community."

Eve smiled, not showing any teeth. "I chose correctly."

"I hope that your boys will all make the right choices." Rosemary slowly stooped to push the little bit of dirt she'd gathered into a dustpan.

"They are all *gut* boys, but they deserve to explore the world so that they know this is what they want. You're lucky I didn't..."

Rosemary looked up. "What? We're lucky you didn't what? End up in the *Englisch* world? It was surely our biggest fear when you were growing up."

"I worry about that too, but you can't criticize the way we raise our *sohns*." Eve stood up. "At least they know they are loved." She turned to go up the stairs. "I'm going to straighten their rooms."

Know they are loved? Her daughter didn't know she was loved? Rosemary's head started buzzing again, and she started to call out, but instead she squeezed her eyes closed.

She put her face in her hands. *Dear Lord, please don't let me have another episode.*

Deciding that maybe a nap would help the dizziness she was feeling, she opened her bedroom door, then grabbed her heart. *It's happening again.* Another hallucination.

She didn't move as she eyed the small alligator perched atop her bed. Slowly she backed up two steps and opened her mouth to call for Eve, but stopped herself.

This isn't real.

She eyed the imaginary reptile for several moments. Then she shrugged and crawled into bed beside it.

Eve knew she shouldn't have spoken to her mother that way, but it was getting harder and harder to take the constant criticism about the way she and Benny raised their children and how she continued to move away from the simpler ways she'd been brought up with.

She walked into her mother's sewing room, which was exactly as Eve remembered. The treadle sewing machine was against the left wall, and the shelves next to it were filled with quilting scraps, bolts of material, and other sewing supplies. On the opposite wall was the yellow-and-blue plaid couch that *Mamm* had picked up at a mud sale in Bird-in-Hand. She'd said the couch was much too fancy for the living room, but she'd bought it anyway since it folded out into a bed and had only cost her ten dollars.

Eve pulled up the green and white quilt that Leroy had tossed back this morning, then fluffed his pillows and positioned them against the back of the couch. She glanced around the room. Leroy's dirty clothes were in a hamper Eve's mother had put in the room, and his other clothes and personal items were neatly folded and displayed atop *Mamm's* sewing table in the corner. Eve smiled. If Leroy did choose to marry Lena Byler, the girl would be glad that Eve had trained up her son to be neat and tidy.

She closed the door behind her and went down the hall to the extra bedroom where the twins were staying. As she eyed the mess before her—mostly on Elias's side of the room—Eve knew that the twins' future *fraas* would have their work cut out for them. She picked up two dirty shirts off the floor. As she made Elias's bed, she thought about the way he'd slipped out to meet Elizabeth. It wasn't the worst thing in the world, but it had certainly been worthy of punishment. She'd avoided letting her parents know about the incident, but maybe she should have told them. Maybe she should have made a point for her mother to see that she was quite capable of disciplining her children when they needed it.

She smoothed the wrinkles from the quilt on his bed before she went to the other bed, which was covered in a matching quilt. Once both the beds were made, she sniffed a few times, recognizing the smell of dirty socks. She bent to her knees, and sure enough...two dark black socks were underneath Elias's bed. Picking them up with thumb and first finger, she held them at arm's length as she looked around for any other dirty clothes. When she didn't find any, she walked to the small hamper and tossed in the socks.

Unlike some of the rooms in the old farmhouse, this room had a closet. Eve had inspected the contents when she and the twins were deciding if it would be a good place to keep George. There were boxes stacked along the left side, and Eve knew that her old faceless dolls were in one of the crates, cards and letters that her mother had saved in another, and various keepsakes. Eve didn't open the closet, hoping Amos was remembering to feed the reptile.

The boys had managed to sneak the lizard in with a blanket draped over the cage while Eve distracted her parents. She felt a little guilty for deceiving her folks about a Chinese water dragon, but it would have been just one more thing for her mother to fret about.

Eve hadn't been happy when Amos came home with this unusual pet. Her son had saved his money and begged his parents for what he called a lizard, but the frightful-looking beast had grown much larger than any lizard Eve had ever seen. If it gave Eve the shivers, what would her mother think…

Elias bit down on his ham sandwich, his teeth chattering from the frigid temperatures. As he sat on the couch in his family's living room, wind blew around the plastic sheeting and swirled throughout the damaged structure. *Daadi* was sitting next to Elias, eating his own lunch. His father and Leroy had eaten earlier and were outside toting lumber from the wagon to a designated pile on the north side of the house. Amos— as usual—had been sent to town for supplies, and was probably thumbing through magazines or books some-where.

"Elias…" His grandfather sighed as he locked eyes with Elias, shaking his head. "I reckon when a fellow is grounded, he should respect his parents enough to follow the rules." *Daadi* pushed his glasses up on his nose, frowning.

"Uh, *ya*. You're right." Elias wondered what his grandfather was getting at.

Daadi ran a shaky hand through his beard. "Your *mammi* caught you coming into the *haus* last night. She wanted to go straight to your *mudder* and tell your busi-ness, but I told her that I'd give you a friendly talkin'-to, and that I was sure you wouldn't disobey your parents again." He stuffed his lunch trash in his black lunch box and stood up from the couch.

Elias's jaw dropped. "But I didn't…" He scratched his head for a moment before he went on. "Are you sure it was last night?"

"*Ya*. It was last night." *Daadi* pulled on his heavy gloves, then pushed his black felt hat firmly onto his head. "I won't be able to help you next time."

"But I…" Elias wondered if his grandfather was con-fused. Or more likely, his grandmother was. He stood up and watched the older man walk out the door to help his father and Leroy. Moments later Amos walked in.

"I'm starving!" His brother's whole face spread into a goofy smile, and Elias walked closer to Amos, squint-ing.

"Where've you been?"

Amos's teeth were chattering, but the grin wasn't going away. "You know where I was. Running errands."

Elias moved even closer to Amos and thumped him

lightly on the arm. "That the only place? And what about last night, *mei bruder*?"

Amos's mouth pulled into a sour grin. "Wha-wha-whatcha talkin' about?"

"I just took the blame for you sneaking out of the *haus* last night. So you best start talking."

Chapter 8

Elias turned up the propane heater in the bedroom, set the lantern on the end table between his and Amos's beds, then crawled under the covers and waited for his brother to come in after taking a bath.

Amos's hair was wet and sticking straight up when he walked in towel-drying it, barefoot, wearing blue pajama bottoms and a white T-shirt. "*Ach*, it's cold in here."

Elias rolled his eyes. "Put some shoes on, you *dummkopp*." He looked at his cell phone. One bar left, but no word from Elizabeth yet. He scratched his chin. He'd been trying to reach her for an hour and no answer.

Amos got into bed shivering and tucked himself beneath the covers.

Elias turned on his side to face his brother. "So where'd you go last night?" It seemed unlikely that

Amos would have a girlfriend, but Elias couldn't think of any other reason for a man to trek into this weather.

"N-None of your business." Amos reached over the side of the bed and between the mattresses, pulling out a magazine with bent edges and a shiny red car on the front.

Elias glared at his brother. "It ain't, huh?" He sat taller. "I'm the one who took the blame for you. *Mammi* saw you last night, and she and *Daadi* think it was me who snuck out."

"Sorry a-about that." Amos flipped through the pages of the magazine.

"You don't seem too sorry." Elias glared at his brother, then grinned. "Find that lizard of yours?"

Amos's jaw dropped and he sat taller, tossing the magazine to the side. "*Ach!* I forgot!" He jumped out of the bed, grabbed the lantern, and began searching the room. "Help me look for George."

Elias yawned as he snuggled into his covers. "I think one *gut* deed for the day is enough for me."

Amos grumbled under his breath, and he was still shuffling around the room when Elias drifted off to sleep.

Eve carried the lantern down the stairs, tiptoeing, knowing she was early for breakfast. She could smell sausage and biscuits already going, but she didn't realize her father was up also until she heard her name.

"Eve and Benjamin give those *kinner* too much freedom. I could hardly sleep last night, worrying one of them young'uns would be wandering around out in this *wedder*." Eve's mother paused. "And all over a *maedel*."

Eve slowed her step, gently turning the lantern down

as she listened to her mother go on. "I hope you told Elias that we don't allow such doings in our home."

"*Ya, ya.*"

Eve came to a complete stop, still listening.

"Eve and Benjamin will be lucky if those twins don't end up in trouble or living out in the *Englisch* world." Another pause. "I don't think they had those types of troubles with Leroy. Or maybe they did, and we just didn't know about it."

Eve heard her father's chair scoot from the table, and Eve picked up the pace, not wanting to get caught eavesdropping. She came face-to-face with her father in the middle of the den.

"*Guder mariye, Daed.*" She scooted around him as he smiled and nodded.

"I'm gonna go milk the cows. Send those boys when they get up."

"It's still early. I'm sure they'll be down shortly." Eve edged into the kitchen, kept her head high, and poured herself a cup of coffee.

"*Guder mariye*, Eve."

Eve returned the sentiment but couldn't look at her mother. Her thoughts assailed her, but she bit her tongue. For a moment. Then she swirled around, leaned up against the kitchen counter, and glared at her mother as *Mamm* pulled biscuits from the oven.

"We live in different times, *Mamm*. We don't allow our *kinner* to do anything that other parents in the district don't let theirs do." She bit her bottom lip, wondering why she had never been good enough in her mother's eyes.

"Were you eavesdropping?" *Mamm* set down the oven mitt and raised an eyebrow in Eve's direction.

Eve folded her arms across her chest. "*Nee.* I just happened to hear the end of your conversation with *Daed.*"

Her mother sighed as she walked to the refrigerator and pulled out two jars of jam. "I just don't think you know what's going on with your own *kinner,* that's all." She shrugged, putting the jars on the table.

Eve took a deep breath, remembering to respect her parents no matter what. "At least I *love* my children. And they know that." She glared at her mother and trudged across the kitchen. "I'm going to go help *Daed* in the barn."

"Eve, wait." Rosemary watched her daughter stomp out to the barn, pouting as if she were a small child. Rosemary knew she shouldn't have said anything about Eve's child-rearing, even if it had been the truth. Eve and Benjamin were going to lose control of those twins if they didn't do something. If Rosemary had those boys under her roof for a while, she could teach them a thing or two about the old ways. They'd get rid of all that modern technology—and no one would be sneaking out of the house. And twice now, Eve had mentioned how her boys knew she loved them.

But did Eve just insinuate that Rosemary didn't love her?

Rosemary shuffled across the kitchen, grasping her right hand as it began to shake. She'd hoped that she and Eve would get closer while Eve was here, but instead, she was just pushing Eve further away.

With a heavy heart Rosemary finished cooking breakfast, hoping Eve would come in before everyone else so that maybe she could make amends with her daughter. When that didn't happen, she turned to the Lord. She'd been praying that God would show her the way to get closer to Eve, but she also wondered if God was talking and she just wasn't hearing Him.

Ten minutes later everyone was seated at the kitchen table. After they'd prayed, Benjamin spoke up.

"Eve and I have something to ask you both." He reached for a biscuit, glancing back and forth between Rosemary and Joseph.

Rosemary briefly looked at Eve, but her daughter was picking at her scrambled eggs and didn't look up as Benjamin went on.

"Cousin Mary Mae has fallen seriously ill, and Eve and I feel it would be *gut* to pay her a visit." Benjamin sighed. "The timing is bad with the *haus* and all, but it would be a *gut* chance to also pick up some supplies. I'm having trouble finding some of the hardware we need for the old door in our kitchen and a few other small things we could cart back in the van with us."

Joseph pushed up his glasses. "How long would you be away?"

"We'd like to stay for a week." Benjamin took a bite of his biscuit and swallowed. "The boys could still help you on the *haus* while we are away." He glanced at Eve. "Mary Mae and Eve write letters and are close. Eve feels we should make the trip, and I do too."

"She's got the cancer, huh?" Leroy scooped up the last of his eggs and quickly reached for the bowl in the middle of the table.

"*Ya*." Eve kept her head hung low, and Rosemary wondered how much of her sadness was due to Mary Mae...or how much of if it was from this morning's scuffle.

"It's no problem." Joseph sat taller as he spoke directly to Benjamin. "You go, take the time you need to be with Mary Mae. We will keep working on your *haus*, and all will be well."

As the others chatted, Rosemary grew quiet, thinking. She and Joseph would have these three teenagers to tend to on their own. Could she maybe show them some of the old ways? Tell the boys stories about how things used to be, before all this modern technology invaded their world? And would they listen, maybe even get rid of some of their gadgets?

Rosemary glanced around the table. Leroy was a good boy. He kept busy and seemed to stay on task. He seemed mostly interested in spending his free time with Lena.

She looked at the twins. Elias was making a move for the last piece of bacon when Amos reached for it too, beating his brother to it. Rosemary was pretty sure that the slight bump under the table was one of the boys kicking the other. She'd seen the twins picking at each other continuously, more so than normal. She'd never raised any boys, and these two seemed a bit of a handful.

Well, she had hoped for this. A chance to have some say in her grandchildren's lives.

She took a deep breath as Benjamin sat up taller and firmly told the twins to mind their manners.

Careful what you wish for.

Chapter 9

The next day Eve shivered all the way out to the van that was waiting in the driveway, large flakes of snow dotting her heavy black coat and bonnet. Benny had already loaded their luggage, and Eve had talked to the twins about behaving themselves while she and Benny were gone.

She felt bad about spouting off to her mother yesterday, although neither had said anything about their unkind exchange.

Maybe a week away from each other would be good for both of them. Her heart hurt for Mary Mae, and Eve was anxious to spend time with her cousin, but she was also apprehensive about leaving the twins with her parents. She'd instructed Leroy to keep a close eye on things. She was almost to the car when Amos called out to her.

"What is it, *sohn*?" She turned around, putting a hand to her forehead as she tried to block the snow.

Amos lifted his feet high in the snow as he crossed through part of the yard that hadn't been shoveled. He was breathless when he reached Eve.

"We—we—we..." Amos blinked a few times, and Eve knew he must really be upset about something to be having such a hard time saying the words.

"What is it? What's wrong?" She brushed snow from her cheeks with the back of her glove.

"We can't find George." Amos's teeth chattered as he spoke.

"What?" Eve swallowed hard. "Did he get out of his cage? He is a big lizard, Amos. Where is he?"

Amos raised his shoulders and held them up before slowly dropping them. "I—I guess I left the cage open a few days ago."

Eve thought she might fall over. "A few *days*? How can George be missing for that long? Have you looked everywhere?"

"*Ya, Mamm*. I've looked all over the *haus*, everywhere except *Daadi* and *Mammi's* bedroom." He tipped his felt hat down with his hand, shielding himself from the snow. "Their bedroom door is always closed."

"I'm sure George isn't in their bedroom." Eve shivered, shaking her head. "We would have already heard about it." She tried to picture the expression on her mother's face if she stumbled upon a large lizard running around in her bedroom. Eve suspected that George had either died or gotten outside if he'd been missing this long. Maybe he'd gotten into some poison her father kept in the basement for mice, or slipped outdoors somehow.

Amos hung his head, sighing heavily. He was sixteen in years, but in some ways he seemed much younger, especially now as she watched him fighting tears. She touched him on the arm.

"Keep looking. Maybe he's hiding somewhere." She gazed up at him and grinned. "Just find him before your *mammi* does." Eve gave him a hug before she made her way to the car, then turned around and pointed a gloved finger at him. "You boys behave yourselves while we're gone."

Amos nodded as he trekked back to the house up the cleared walkway. Everyone had delayed going to work this morning until they saw Eve and Benny off.

As the van pulled away with Eve and Benny in the backseat, Eve said a quick prayer—another one—that all would be well while they were gone.

And she prayed that Amos would find George.

The house was quiet, the way it had been before Eve and her family had come to stay. Once Eve and Benjamin had gotten on their way, Joseph, Leroy, and the twins had hitched up the buggies and gone to work on the house.

Rosemary stared out the window at the snow and knew that this weather was slowing down progress. After a few moments she shuffled about the house, wondering if she'd stumble upon her glasses. She'd already checked the refrigerator but had quickly closed it. The jars and jellies had looked like they were dancing on the shelf, which Rosemary knew was not the case. But she'd had the vision just the same, and her anxiety level was rising. What else would happen? Would she lose more things? Would all objects start looking like they were dancing? Would she remember how to cook Joseph his supper tonight?

She picked up the recipe box on the counter and brought it to her chest, thankful that Eve was writing everything down. *Now if I could only find my glasses, I could read the cards.*

Sighing, she put the container back down and made her way to the cookie jar. She'd been keeping the jar filled for the boys—and to facilitate Joseph's late-night sweet tooth. She took a peek inside but decided some dried cranberries would better suit her. Grabbing the plastic bag of fruit from the cabinet, she headed to her bedroom to read the family Bible. She'd enjoyed looking at Eve's latest entries about the boys, but today she wanted to just sit quietly and read from the Good Book.

She sat down on her bed, crossed her legs, and eased the Bible from her nightstand before she remembered that she hadn't found her glasses. She set the bag of fruit down beside her on the bed. In some ways she was no better than Joseph, eating late at night. Her secret indulgence was to eat a snack in the middle of the day while sitting on her bed reading. Joseph said the bed was no place for eating, so in her own way Rosemary felt like she was getting away with something too. She kept the Bible in her lap as she enjoyed a handful of the cranberries, trying to remember where she'd put her glasses.

It was about ten minutes later when she heard movement from underneath her dresser. She'd learned not to get alarmed anymore. Her hallucination had shown up twice before. She'd almost told Joseph about it night before last, but he surely would have dragged her to see Dr. Knepp at that very moment. She watched the lizard crawl out from underneath her dresser.

Her imaginary friend was looking a little parched today.

Rosemary left the room, went to the kitchen, and dribbled some water on a small plate. When she returned, the creature was up on her bed where she'd first spotted him. She wasn't sure how he slithered his way up there, but for all she knew, her hallucination was capable of flying or a number of other things she didn't care to think about. She set the plate carefully on the floor, a few droplets splashing onto the wood surface. Then she watched the reptile eyeing her cranberries. She eased past where he was on the bed, reached into the bag, and placed a few in front of his long snout. Or was it a *her*?

And, dear Lord in heaven...does it matter?

Rosemary shook her head, watching as the lizard nibbled at the dried fruit. When he was done, he slid down her bedspread, stopped at the water for a quick drink, then went back under her dresser.

She eased herself back on the bed, picked up the bag of cranberries, and leaned back against the headboard. She grasped her hand as it began to shake so fiercely that the motion of it slapping against her leg was painful.

Rosemary knew she could handle the pain.

It was all these hallucinations that she feared the most. Losing her mind.

She wondered if maybe Eve and Joseph were right. Maybe *Englisch* medications could do more for her than Fern's herbal remedies. She closed her eyes, and after a minute or so the trembling began to subside. She opened her eyes and crossed one foot over the other.

If she began to turn to modern ways for medication,

where would it stop? First it would be *Englisch* pills, and next thing she knew they'd be installing propane lamps and using mobile telephones. *Too much.*

God was in control. Not Rosemary. What good could come from giving up their simple ways? If the Lord wanted to ease her ailments, He could do so, without her having to engage in worldly ways.

Elias tried not to fidget during devotions, but something was gnawing at his gut. He kept his head buried in the Bible as his grandfather recited from the book of Matthew, but he wasn't hearing much. He'd have to pray on his own later to make up for being so unfocused.

He hadn't heard from Elizabeth in several days, and he hadn't been able to reach her by phone. Earlier today he'd begged Leroy to let him use the buggy to go see her after work, but his older brother refused his plea, citing his punishment. Didn't Leroy understand that without Elizabeth's love he could hardly function? And with no phone conversations, Elias had no way to schedule a late-night meeting with the woman he planned to marry someday. Even grounded, he was ready to take the risk to see Elizabeth.

"Let us pray..." *Daadi* said the words loudly, as if he knew that Elias wasn't following along.

Once devotions were over, his grandmother began to tell stories about the old times, how there were no electronic gadgets or many of the modern things that their people used today. She'd never made a secret of her thoughts on the matter, and Elias had heard his mother complain about *Mammi* not accepting the new ways that the bishop allowed.

Elias tried to show as much respect for his grandmother as he could—despite the knot in his stomach—by responding to her questions, nodding when he should, and so on. But something was wrong. He could feel it.

He glanced at Amos. His brother carried on with their grandmother as if he were really enjoying her lectures and reflections on the old ways. Elias scowled, wishing he'd never taken the fall for Amos. His twin wasn't perfect—he'd sneaked out the same way Elias had—yet Elias was the one still grounded, and the one who was going to miss a party at Elizabeth's house on Saturday. Her sister Rebecca was turning fifteen, and the family was having a get-together. Elias had been to parties at Elizabeth's house before, and he knew there would be lots of food, the Ping-Pong table set up in the basement, and mostly there would be enough people there for him and Elizabeth to go lose themselves somewhere. Elias couldn't wait to kiss her again, but every time he thought about the feel of her soft lips, he thought about how she hadn't called him and how he couldn't reach her.

There had to be a way for him to attend the party on Saturday.

"Elias, are you hearing me?" His grandmother's sharp tone caused him to sit up straighter on the couch.

"*Ya, Mammi.* I'm listening."

It was a small lie, and Elias regretted it, but an idea had danced into his mind.

He knew exactly how he was going to be at Elizabeth's house on Saturday.

Chapter 10

"Y-You're *ab im kopp*." Amos shook his head. "You kn-know what *gut* parties the Lapps throw, and I—I ain't missing one, no matter what you try to promise me."

Elias stood over his brother, who once again had his head buried in one of his dumb magazines. He snatched the magazine away from his brother.

"Hey!" Amos jumped up and grabbed the book back from Elias. "I—I said I ain't d-doin' it, so just leave me alone." He cut his eyes at Elias before he settled back down on his bed.

Elias eased onto his own bed and sighed. "All right, then. I'll give you fifty dollars instead of twenty-five if you'll let me go in your place. You know *Mammi* and *Daadi* can't tell us apart."

Amos chuckled. "You don't even have fifty dollars."

"*Ya*, I do. I've been saving. Unlike you, *mei bruder*, I don't spend my money on expensive *Englisch* magazines." He paused, shaking his head. "You're not ever gonna own a car, so why do you like looking at them so much, anyway?" Before Amos could answer, Elias said, "Come on. Just think of all the books and magazines you can buy with fifty dollars."

There was silence for a few moments before Amos said anything. Then his brother lifted his eyes over the top of the magazine. "Maybe—maybe Elizabeth doesn't want to see you or talk to you."

Elias had thought of that plenty of times, and he was sure the notion was what kept his stomach tied in knots. "What makes you say that?"

"You ain't talked to her. There's been no sneaking out to see her, and you can't even reach her by phone." Amos shrugged. "Sounds to me like she's trying to end it."

Elias clenched his hands into fists and took a deep breath. "You don't know what you're talking about. I'm going to ask Elizabeth to marry me. I wouldn't do that if I wasn't sure about the two of us."

Amos chuckled. "Well, you won't be asking her at the Lapps' party, will ya?"

Elias glared at his brother and decided to ask him something that had been rooting around in his mind. "Who'd you sneak out to go see?"

"I told you. N-None of your b-business." Amos didn't look up as he flipped another page.

Elias shook his head, then got his nightclothes out of the dresser. He was moving out of the room when he turned around, feeling the need to jab at his brother. "Ever find that stupid lizard of yours?"

"No." Amos sighed, not looking up again.

Elias regretted poking fun about the lizard. He knew how much his brother cared for George.

He wished Amos knew how much he cared for Elizabeth. If he did, he would swap places with Elias so that Elias could see her.

Shuffling down the hall to the bathroom, Elias's mind was still whirling. There had to be a way to get to that party.

Rosemary sat on the side of the bed brushing out her thinning gray hair while Joseph was all tucked in on his side reading a book.

"Did you see how a little bit of influence from us made a difference tonight?" She smiled, recalling all the stories she'd told the boys about the old days, before modern ways invaded their lives. "I bet it won't be long before those boys give up some of those unnecessary gadgets."

Joseph grunted. "*Ach*, I'm sure they'll be tossing those cell phones and radio plugs right into the trash first thing in the morning."

Rosemary twisted to face him. "Why do you speak to me like that, Joseph? You're poking fun about a serious situation. If we don't do our part to straighten those boys out, they are going to end up fleeing to the outside world, and that will break everyone's heart, especially Eve's and Benjamin's."

Joseph closed his book and pushed his glasses up on his nose. "*Mei lieb*, those boys are fine. Eve and Big Ben have done a *gut* enough job raising them up. They'll make the right choices."

"I hope you're right, but I have a couple more days

to try to talk some sense into them through the Scriptures." Rosemary stowed her brush in the top drawer of the nightstand, then crawled in beside Joseph. "Tomorrow, during devotions, I want us to spend some time on respecting your parents and elders." She poked him on the arm. "And you speak up and say something about not betraying our parents. Maybe they'll take heed and not keep up that sneaking out."

"Yes, dear."

Rosemary huffed. "You are patronizing me, Joseph. When instead you should be thinking about how we can make a difference in those boys' lives." She grasped her hand when it started to shake and quickly stuffed it beneath the quilt as she leaned back against the headboard. Her head started to spin a bit, so she closed her eyes.

"Yes, dear." Joseph eased himself down into the covers, popping his pillow with his fist a few times. He snuffed out the lantern on his side of the bed. "Go to sleep."

"I'll go to sleep after I finish tending to Minnie. Momma gave her another lashing. I'll be right back." Rosemary sat straight up, ready to go tend to her sister. She picked up the lantern on her nightstand, but Joseph quickly caught her by the arm.

"Rosie, Minnie ain't here. You know that. She's playing with the good Lord in heaven. You're thinking in the past again." Joseph held tight to her arm, and Rosemary struggled to organize the thoughts in her head. She stared at the gray streaks running through her husband's beard. *If Joseph is old, Minnie can't still be here.*

"But…but I heard her cries." Rosemary grasped her shaking hand and eased the lantern back down.

She turned to Joseph, tears in her eyes. "I'm losing my mind."

He pulled her into his arms, running a hand through her damp hair. "You need to go see Dr. Knepp, *lieb.*"

She melted into the comfort of his arms and buried her face in his chest. "I'm too afraid. He'll tell me that I'm goin' crazy, and they'll lock me up somewhere."

"That's not what they do, Rosie. They'll give you some medicine to help you, that's all."

Rosemary squeezed her eyes closed and fought the visions of Minnie crying, along with the moaning she could hear in her head.

This isn't real.

But sleep didn't come for a while.

Elias was glad that they stopped work on the house early Saturday afternoon. The party at the Lapps' started at four o'clock, and he had to figure out a way to be there. He'd been trying to call Elizabeth, but still no answer. And no calls from her.

He'd caught Amos sneaking back into the house last night, and once again his brother refused to tell Elias what he was up to. It must be a girl after all. He resented the fact that Amos hadn't gotten caught, that Elias himself had taken the blame for him once, and mostly he resented Amos's smug attitude.

I'm going to that party.

Elias was having a cup of hot cocoa with his grandfather when Amos came marching into the kitchen wearing his Sunday clothes and a smile as wide as it was irritating.

"Off to the birthday party?" *Daadi* took a sip of his cocoa, and Amos nodded. Elias resisted the urge to tackle Amos to the ground. His nostrils flared as Amos grinned on his way out the door.

"I know you're fretting about not being able to go," *Daadi* said to Elias after Amos was gone. "But the Lord always has a plan, and…" His grandfather shrugged. "It's just not in the plan for you to go today."

Elias nodded and fought the urge to tell his grandfather that Amos had been sneaking out. It wouldn't make a difference right now, though, and Elias wasn't a tattler.

As he sipped on his cocoa, he thought about Elizabeth. Her parents must have taken her phone away for some reason. That had to be it.

Daadi stood up, gulped the rest of his cocoa, then put his glass on the table. He pulled his hat and jacket from the rack near the kitchen door. "Tell your *mammi* that I'm going to town for a few supplies for the *haus*. I'll be back in a couple of hours."

"Yes, sir."

Elias tapped his fingers on the table, thinking. It wasn't long before an idea came to mind. He jumped from the table and ran upstairs.

Chapter 11

Elizabeth opened the door and smiled at her handsome man. "I'm so glad to see you."

"Me too. I've missed you."

As she stepped to the side so he could come in, she knew they needed to talk, but her father was standing only a few feet away stoking the fire.

"Everyone is in the basement. There's lots of food, and there's already a Ping-Pong game going on. Go get something to eat, and I'll be down shortly." She resisted the urge to whisper in his ear that she couldn't wait to sneak off with him somewhere.

As he walked past her, he nudged her hand. She glanced down and saw a piece of paper, which she quickly took and stuffed into the pocket of her apron.

The front door was still open, and she saw Abram Fisher pulling up to drop off his younger brother Matthew. Two more buggies were coming up the driveway. She'd been given the job of greeting all of Rebecca's guests, and she was anxious to be done with the task so she could head downstairs.

She fumbled at the piece of paper in her pocket, anxious to read it.

It was twenty minutes later when the buggies finally stopped pulling up, and Elizabeth hurried to the bathroom. After locking the door, she pulled the note from her pocket and read.

Dear Elizabeth,
A new love is so tender, the heart fluttering and wanting to render.

It is with you that I feel renewed and alive, like a swim in the pond after taking a dive; crisp and refreshing, but much more than that—it's the sound of my heart as it goes pitter-pat.

My feelings for you are as pure as a new baby's soul, and once lost, I now have a goal—to be the best person I can be, to spend my life loving you eternally.

She brushed a tear from her cheek as she pressed the poem to her chest. It was the third one she'd received, and with each one she knew she loved him that much more. She couldn't wait for him to kiss her later today. Somehow they'd find a place where they could go to be alone. Stuffing the note back in her pocket, she slipped out of the bathroom and made her way back to the living room.

Her father was standing at the window, and she could hear her mother puttering about in the kitchen, but oth-

erwise all their guests had moved downstairs. Elizabeth headed toward the basement stairs, but her father
spoke up.

"Hold yourself, *maedel*. Someone is walking up to
the porch."

Elizabeth sighed as she turned and walked back
across the living room. "*Danki, Daed*."

She walked onto the front porch, closed the door
behind her, and pulled her sweater snug as her teeth
chattered. Straining to see who the last guest was, she
gasped when he came into view.

Her jaw dropped, and her heart began to pound in
her chest. "What are you doing here? I thought you
were grounded."

Elias looked around, grinned, then kissed her on the
mouth. "Where have you been? I've been trying to call.
I've missed you so much."

Elizabeth eased away and swallowed hard.

Oh, this is a mess.

Rosemary found an old magnifying glass so she
could read one of Eve's recipe cards. Tomato pie
sounded good, and one would be enough to feed her,
Joseph, and Elias. Amos wouldn't be home from the
Lapps' house until later in the evening, and Leroy had
gone to supper at Lena's.

As she sliced the tomatoes, she thought about Elias
having to miss the party, but rules were rules. Before
Eve and Benjamin left, Eve had told her that Elias was
grounded, but she didn't tell her what for. It had to be
for sneaking out; she'd seen him with her own eyes as
he sneaked back in. She supposed she should be glad
that Eve had punished him in such a manner, but as a

grandmother, she assumed it was all right to feel a little sorry for him.

"Smells mighty *gut* in here." Joseph walked in from feeding the animals.

"That's just freshly baked bread you smell. I haven't even cooked the tomato pie yet." She leaned down with the magnifying glass to see how much milk the recipe called for.

"Still haven't found your reading glasses?" Joseph pulled out a chair at the table, sat down, and began thumbing through the most recent copy of *The Budget*.

Rosemary shook her head. "No. And I've looked everywhere."

"They'll show up."

"I hope."

She was quiet as she finished putting the pie together, seeing that Joseph had his head buried in the paper.

After a few moments he looked up. "Is that one pie going to be enough for you, me, and Elias?"

Rosemary nodded. "I made a fruit salad to go with it, and I have a shoofly pie for dessert." She pulled the oven door open and put the pie in. "When Amos left around four, I told him there would be some cake for him when he got home, although I'm sure there is a mountain of food at the Lapps' house."

"Four? I saw him leave a little before three."

Rosemary turned around, wiping flour from her black apron. "Well, I chatted with him for a minute or two before he left, and I know it was around four o'clock."

Joseph twisted his mouth from one side to the other. "Okay, dear."

She walked closer, hands on her hips. "I dislike when

you do that. You patronize me like a child. That boy left around four o'clock. I haven't completely lost my mind, and I can still read a clock."

"Well, that's good and fine, Rosie. But one of the boys left a little before three. That's all I'm saying."

Rosemary shifted her weight, pressing her lips together for a moment. "It was Amos that left, right?"

Joseph shrugged. "I reckon. He's the one who isn't grounded."

"Well, then who left at four o'clock while you were still in town?"

Joseph closed the newspaper. "Sure you don't mean Leroy?"

"Joseph Chupp, I know the difference between Leroy and the twins. It wasn't Leroy who came through here at four. He left much earlier. It was Amos."

"Well, then I guess we both saw Amos leave, or those boys have pulled a fast one on us."

Rosemary chuckled. "I don't think so. Not on my watch."

Joseph stroked his beard, grinning. "Then you better hope that there is a twin upstairs. 'Cause I suspect there ain't."

"Well, why in the world would Elias sneak out, pretending to be Amos, when he knows he'd get caught at supper time?"

"Probably didn't care, if it's all about a girl." Joseph stood up, kissed Rosemary on the cheek, then smiled. "I think one got away on your watch."

Rosemary marched directly to the stairs and up she went. When she returned a few minutes later, Joseph was casually sitting in his rocker sipping a cup of coffee.

"Well, we are missing one," she said as she folded her arms across her chest and tapped her foot on the floor.

"*Ya*. I figured as much."

"Well, when young Elias gets home, you will extend his punishment. He's under our roof, and I reckon it's our job to—"

"Someone's coming." Joseph stood up and walked to the window. "I hear a buggy turning."

Rosemary joined him at the window, and they both waited. A few moments later Rosemary gasped, then covered her mouth with her hands.

"*Ach*, Joseph. Oh no."

She hurried to the door and out onto the porch, her heart pounding.

Chapter 12

Rosemary almost stumbled down the snowy porch steps, Joseph on her heels. She met Samuel Lapp in the yard; Amos and Elias were on either side of him. Although she wasn't sure who was who.

She went to the boy on Samuel's left, since blood was running down his chin from a split lip and he had a bulging black eye. After a quick inspection she moved to the other one, who'd taken quite a beating himself based on his swollen cheek and shiner.

"Who did this to you?" Rosemary's eyes watered as she glanced back and forth between the twins. They both lowered their heads as Samuel spoke.

"They did this to each other." Samuel shook his head, frowning. "I heard a commotion down in the basement, and the *maeds* starting screaming." He pointed to Amos, then to Elias. "These two were down on the floor pounding on each other."

Rosemary was speechless. Joseph stepped forward.

"*Danki* for bringing them home, Samuel. And we're sorry for the trouble."

"Well, it wonders me what would cause two *bruders* to do this to each other when it surely isn't our way." Samuel shook his head again. "Not *gut*. And Rebecca's pretty cake her *mamm* made her ended up in a pile on the basement floor."

Rosemary opened her mouth to apologize, but nothing came out. She couldn't believe the boys could do something like this.

"Please send our apologies to your *fraa*, to Rebecca, and to the others there." Joseph waved a hand toward Amos and Elias. "You boys head into the *haus* and start cleaning yourselves up. We'll be in shortly."

"I'll tend to them," Rosemary finally said, tucking her head as she pulled her sweater around her and hurried into the house and away from Samuel's accusing eyes. She wasn't out of earshot, though, when Samuel spoke.

"I'm sure you'll be hearing from the bishop about this matter."

Rosemary moved faster, shivering. From the cold. And the thought of the bishop coming out to see them. She couldn't recall a time that Bishop Smucker had come calling about a "matter."

When she walked into the living room, Amos and Elias were glaring at each other as if they weren't done with whatever was ailing them.

"We need to get some ice on your eyes, both of you." She glanced back and forth between the two of them. "Who's who?"

"That's Amos!" Elias yelled. "Someone who is supposed to be *mei bruder*, but who tried to trick Elizabeth into loving him by pretending he was me."

Rosemary put a hand on her chest, hoping to calm her rapid heartbeat and wishing Eve and Benjamin were here. This was way too much for her and Joseph to handle.

"And—and she d-does love me!" Amos stepped toward Elias, his bottom lip trembling, his eyes beginning to tear.

Elias stood taller. "How'd you stop your stupid stuttering while you were with her?" He leaned forward as his hands curled into fists at his side.

Oh, dear Lord. No more. Rosemary took in a deep breath and held it, not sure what to say. Or do.

"Fern t-taught me some breathing exercises t-to help." Amos's voice cracked as he spoke.

"You're a bad person, Amos." Elias ran up the stairs.

Amos swiped at his eyes.

Rosemary swallowed back a knot in her throat, hurting for all involved. She stepped closer to Amos, putting a hand on his shoulder. "We need to get some ice on that eye before it swells shut."

"*Mammi*, I have to go." He pulled away from her and dashed out the door.

Rosemary stood in the middle of the room, hoping Joseph would intercept him. But a few moments later Leroy walked in.

"I just saw Amos running down the road. Where's he going?"

"I don't know." Rosemary looked out the window. "It's dark outside. Did you see your *daadi* out there?"

Leroy pulled off his boots and left them by the front

door where the twins usually left theirs. "He must be in the barn. I saw a light flickering out there."

"Leroy, there's been a problem with your *bruders*. You might want to go talk to Elias. I'm going out to the barn and talk to your *daadi*, see what we need to do." She pulled her black bonnet and heavy coat from the rack by the door. "I don't want Amos running around at night like this, especially when he's so upset."

"I already know what happened." Leroy pulled off his heavy coat. "Lena's younger sister was at Rebecca's party, and she told us when she got home." He pulled his hat off and hung it and his coat on the rack. "Can't believe Amos done what he done."

"Well, he's hurting now, and we need him at home so we can all work this out." Rosemary opened the front door but turned to face Leroy first. "Go talk to Elias. He has to forgive Amos. He's his *bruder*." Then she hurried to the barn.

Elias was shaking, he was so mad. Mad at Amos, and angry at himself for losing control. He sat down on his bed, propped his elbows on his knees, and held his head in his hands. His lantern was almost out of fuel, but he didn't care if the room went dark, just as his world had.

"*Mamm* and *Daed* are going to ground you both for the rest of your lives." Leroy walked across the threshold and sat down on Amos's bed. "How'd this happen?"

Elias didn't look up at his older brother. "Amos betrayed me. He's been giving Elizabeth love letters and pretending he was me. All this time I've been wondering why she hasn't been calling to meet somewhere. She's been meeting with Amos." He looked up, blinked a few times, and shook his head. "What kind of person does this?"

Leroy shook his head. "But Amos is your *bruder*. You will have to forgive him."

Drops of blood dribbled from Elias's lip as he reached for a tissue on the nightstand. "I ain't forgiving him for nothing."

They were quiet for a few moments, then Leroy spoke again.

"He must have secretly loved Elizabeth for a long time to go and do something like this. And I reckon he's hurting too."

Elias flinched as he dabbed at his lip. "Don't defend him. What he did is unforgivable."

"Nothing is unforgivable."

"Fine. Then you don't mind if I secretly start courting Lena behind your back?"

Leroy shifted his weight on the bed, then crossed one ankle over his knee. "Look…she wasn't the right girl, Elias. If she could so easily be swayed by Amos, then you don't want her anyway."

"She thought he was me."

"But it wasn't you, and she still must have felt something."

"She felt confused. That's what she felt. And now she's mad."

Leroy leaned forward. "That's what I'm saying. If it was the kind of love that is meant to be, all this wouldn't have happened. This is God's plan. You have to accept that. And you have to forgive Amos."

"Get out, Leroy. Please. Just go." Elias thought he might cry, and he didn't want his older brother seeing that, nor did he want to keep listening to Leroy's lecture.

Leroy stood up. "I'm going to go check on things. *Mammi* is worried 'cause Amos took off."

"*Gut.* I hope he never comes back."

Leroy walked toward the door but turned around to face Elias. "You don't mean that. And you need to go get some ice on that eye."

Elias didn't say anything. His head was throbbing, his lip burning, and his heart hurting. "Close the door on your way out."

A few moments later he heard Leroy's footsteps down the hallway. Elias leaned back on his pillow, and a tear trickled down his cheek.

Joseph tinkered about in the barn, organizing tools on his workbench and acting as if the world hadn't just come crashing down around them. Rosemary knew better, and by the light of the lantern she searched Joseph's face for some hint of concern.

"Joseph, are you listening to me? What do we do? Should we go after Amos? Do we need to call the emergency number that Eve left for us at Mary Mae's shanty?" Rosemary edged closer to where her husband was standing.

"*Nee,* don't call Eve and Big Ben." Joseph picked up four loose nails and put them in a tin box on his bench. "Amos will be back, and Elias needs some time to cool off."

Rosemary bit her bottom lip, swallowing back an urge to say that these things happen when *kinner* are given too much freedom. However, her thoughts ran amok as she struggled to understand how something like this could happen while the children were in her and Joseph's care.

"There's nothing we could have done to prevent this from happening," she said after a minute, hoping to convince herself.

"*Nee.* I don't think so." Joseph picked up the lantern and held it up, nodding for Rosemary to walk with him.

"*Ach,* the bishop will probably come calling, like Samuel said." Rosemary pulled the rim of her black bonnet down in an effort to block the wind as she and Joseph left the barn. She wondered if Amos had grabbed his coat. She couldn't remember.

Shivering, she walked faster, and so did Joseph. "We can't be held accountable for what the boys did," she said.

Joseph stopped abruptly and turned to face her. "Why not? You hold Eve accountable for every single thing that happens with the boys."

"Joseph…" She put a hand to her chest. "They are her children, and…" Rosemary stopped talking as Joseph held the lantern high, showing the scowl on his face.

"Rosie, everything happens according to the Lord's plan. You know this. But I don't think I've ever seen two women who judge each other more than you and Eve." He started walking again, shaking his head. "And it's a shame too."

Rosemary didn't say anything as they trudged to the house, the cold wind stinging her face.

Lord, is that what I do…judge?

It only took a few seconds to know the answer.

Three hours later Rosemary paced her bedroom as Joseph silently read the Bible.

"Where can Amos be? We need to go find him."

Joseph pushed his glasses up and scratched his nose.

"If the boy is not home in another hour, I will go search for him."

Rosemary folded her arms atop her white nightgown. "I'm not sure I like that idea, you being out in this cold."

Joseph put a hand to one ear. "Listen. Is that the front door?"

Rosemary walked to their bedroom door and eased it open, relieved to see Amos walking in. "It's him."

She pulled on her robe, walked back to her nightstand, and grabbed the lantern, then hurried to the living room. "Amos?"

He was almost to the stairs when he turned around, but he didn't say anything.

"Are you all right?"

The boy's left eye was swollen shut. "*Ya*. I'm sorry, *Mammi*. I just had to go b-be by my-myself for a while."

Rosemary wondered if there was going to be more trouble when Amos went upstairs and confronted his brother. "Do you want to sleep down here on the couch? I can fetch you some blankets, and you'll be warm with the fire still going."

Amos turned around. "Would that be okay?"

"*Ya*." She held the lantern up. "Wait here."

A few minutes later Rosemary returned with two sheets and a large quilt from the closet under the stairs. Once she'd fixed the couch, Amos lay down right away. "You call for me if you need anything."

He nodded, but Rosemary sensed that he wasn't in the mood to talk, so she slipped back into her room and closed the door behind her. After she set the lantern on the nightstand, she climbed into bed.

"I'm so glad he's home." She turned to Joseph. Her husband was slowly closing the Bible, and his eyes were

round as saucers behind his thick lenses. Rosemary
brought a hand to her chest. "What is it, Joseph? Why
do you have that look on your face?"

Joseph didn't say a word; he just pointed to the floor
near the dresser.

Rosemary gasped. Her hallucination's beady little
eyes glowed in the dim light. She quickly waved a hand
in front of Joseph's face.

He pushed it aside, frowning. "What are you doing?"

"Seeing if your eyes move back and forth. Do you
know who I am?"

He narrowed his eyebrows. "Good grief. Of course
I know who you are. I'm just wondering who that is
down on the floor…that long green lizard."

Rosemary put her hands to her chest. "Oh, Joseph!
You see him *too*. I've been seeing him for days."

Joseph gave his head a quick shake as he blinked his
eyes a few times. "What?"

Rosemary patted his arm. "It's all right, dear. He's
not real." She smiled, feeling a bit smug that she wasn't
the only one losing her mind.

Joseph held up the lantern as he stepped out of the
bed and moved toward the creature, who quickly van-
ished under the dresser. Her husband struggled down to
his hands and knees, groaning as he did so. After taking a peek under the dresser, he looked up at Rosemary.
"He's as *real* as the dust balls underneath that dresser."

Rosemary frowned, then joined him on the floor
with her own lantern. They both peered underneath
the dresser. "I thought I was just imagining things, like
the jars in the refrigerator dancing, or thinking Eve is
Minnie."

Joseph held the light up in her face. "The jars in the refrigerator dance?"

"Never you mind." Rosemary lifted herself up until she was sitting on the bed. "Where do you think this thing came from?"

"I suspect I know." Joseph lifted himself up and carted the lantern out into the living room.

"Don't wake the boy," Rosemary whispered when she heard Amos snoring, glad he was sleeping soundly.

"*Ach*, that thing has to belong to the boys. They must have it as a pet." Joseph headed back to the bedroom and held the lantern up as he stared down at the dresser. "I'm not sleeping in my bedroom with that critter in here."

Rosemary thought about all the times she'd shared bed space with the reptile, even given him water and dried fruit. She chuckled softly. "Oh, Joseph. Get into bed. I've slept next to him plenty of times."

Joseph was still standing, a blank look on his face, when Rosemary climbed beneath the covers.

"Good night, dear." She winked at him, but then had to bury her head in the pillow to keep from laughing at his silly expression.

Chapter 13

Eve had the strangest feeling as they neared home. Her stomach was churning, her head splitting, and she could feel her heart beating in her chest. As she and Benny sat in the backseat of the van, the radio was playing Christian music. Eve usually enjoyed such a treat since their people didn't listen to music, but her thoughts were elsewhere.

She leaned closer to Benny and whispered, "Do you think everything is all right at home?"

"*Ya*, of course it is." He reached for her hand and gave it a quick squeeze, but kept his eyes straight ahead, looking past the driver's shoulder at the flurry of snow that had started a few minutes ago. "I don't remember the last time I've seen this much snow in Lancaster County."

Eve took a deep breath and tried to relax. Mother's intuition was a peculiar thing, often sneaking up on a woman and taking hold. She recalled the time Elias tried to convince Amos that he could fly off the roof. Eve had dropped her broom and run outside before Amos ever hit the ground. And when Leroy was five, she'd taken him to a neighbor's house while she went to a doctor's appointment. Throughout the appointment, she'd had the same feelings she was having now, and when she returned to pick up Leroy, he'd fallen and bumped his head so hard he had to have stitches.

Something is wrong at the house.

Elias knew that he and Amos were going to be in big trouble when their parents got home. He had stayed away from his brother as best he could, but they'd been forced to work together on the house the past couple of days, which they'd done without speaking. It seemed to Elias that their grandfather had intentionally assigned them projects that forced them into the same work space.

Amos had spent the past few nights sleeping on the couch downstairs, which was fine by Elias. Then his brother would go upstairs to get dressed in the morning after Elias came downstairs. Elias knew it couldn't go on like this forever, and he'd prayed a lot about what happened. In his mind he'd forgiven Amos, but his heart was having trouble catching up. He wanted to ask Amos how he could do such a thing. But even more, he wondered how Elizabeth could have mistaken Amos for him, unless she was longing for more than Elias had given her. He wasn't one to write mushy poems like his brother. Didn't she know that about him? And he wasn't as soft-spoken or shy as Amos. Didn't Elizabeth recognize that difference?

He sighed. *The kisses.* Couldn't Elizabeth tell that she was kissing someone else? He leaned down to tie his shoelace. *Daadi* had said that there would be no work on the house today because of the weather.

Amos walked into the room as Elias walked out. Once again they avoided eye contact or speaking.

Elizabeth had searched her heart and tried to sort out her feelings for Elias and Amos, trying to forgive herself for her role in all of this. But after a few days alone with her thoughts, she was sure that Amos was the one for her. Not Elias.

It was terrible, what Amos had done, but Elizabeth knew she wasn't innocent either. Amos did what he did out of love for her, and she'd responded in kind. Amos had wanted her so badly that he'd taken risks, penned her beautiful poems, and even betrayed his own brother. She didn't feel good about that last part, but deep within she was flattered that he would go to such extremes.

Now she just had to tell Elias that she wanted to be with Amos. It was a horrible situation, but both of them needed to know how she felt. If she'd been meant to be with Elias, she could have never fallen into another man's arms. In a dark place in the back of her mind, she felt smug that she had her choice of the two men.

She leaned up against the headboard, glad to have some quiet time to think. She pictured herself and Amos lying next to each other in bed after they were married. Amos would read her a poem he'd written just for her, then he'd ease over next to her, holding her gently in his arms.

Opening her eyes, she couldn't help but think about Elias. His ways were more abrasive, even his kisses weren't as soft and gentle as Amos's, yet his outgoing nature, strength, and confidence were qualities that had drawn her to him in the first place.

She tapped a finger to her chin. Too bad she couldn't roll them both into one and make the perfect man; a nice mix of gentleness and manliness, making her laugh when she needed to, or writing her sweet poems that spoke to her heart.

But that wasn't the way it worked, so she'd chosen Amos.

It obviously wasn't a matter of looks. Most folks couldn't tell Elias and Amos apart. Elizabeth grinned, knowing she wasn't one of those people. No, it was Amos's poems that sealed the deal and showed her what she really wanted and needed in a partner.

Tomorrow she would go talk to them both. Hopefully both Elias and Amos would have calmed down by then.

Eve didn't wait while Benny paid the driver, nor did she stick around to help him unload the supplies they'd brought home or their luggage. She hurried up the sidewalk, knowing her stomach wouldn't calm down until she saw that everyone was okay.

It was almost the supper hour, and the scent of something simmering on the stove hit her as she opened the door. Breathing in the aroma of her mother's good meat loaf, she almost choked when she saw Elias walk across the room in front of her.

"What happened?" She rushed to him and reached up to cup his cheek as the churning in her stomach intensified. His eye was black and blue, and a scab was forming on his lip.

"Amos looks worse." Elias's voice sounded almost proud as he spoke, and Eve was still confused when her mother walked into the room.

"*Ach*, I didn't hear you come in." *Mamm* locked her hands in front of her, bit her bottom lip, and narrowed her eyebrows. Then she looked at Elias and spoke in a firm tone. "Best to go help your *daed* with the luggage."

Elias pulled his coat from the rack and went outside. Eve waited until the door closed behind him before she said anything.

"What's going on? And what did Elias mean about Amos looking worse?" Eve just stood there, a hand to her chest, her coat still buttoned. "What happened?"

Her mother waved a hand. "Come to the kitchen before I burn supper." She shook her head. "It's been a mighty mess around here since you've been gone."

For the next few minutes Eve listened to her mother describing what happened between the twins. All the while *Mamm's* right hand shook viciously as she struggled to stir a pot of beans on the stove. Eve was surprised her mother hadn't yet dropped the spoon.

After *Mamm* was finished, Eve rubbed her eyes as she tried to sort it all out. She had always thought that Amos was the more sensitive of the two boys, and she felt guilty for being surprised that it happened this way when she could have more easily seen Elias doing something like this. She looked up when she heard the front door open and close. Peeking around the corner, she saw Elias and Benny carrying luggage toward the stairs.

"And…" *Mamm* spun around to face Eve. "If all that isn't enough, there was a big giant lizard living under my dresser, which I have since learned is named George and lives in a cage upstairs in the closet."

Eve clamped her mouth tight and avoided her mother's eyes. "Oops. Guess we should have told you about George."

"Well, someone should have. Especially when he escaped." *Mamm* sighed. "I thought I was hallucinating…" Her mother didn't finish, but instead lifted her chin and turned back to the beans.

Eve knew that her mother was thinking of the time when *Mamm* had called her Minnie, something they still hadn't talked about. "I'm sorry that happened." Eve was sorry about both instances, but she didn't specify which she meant. "I guess we shouldn't have left you with the boys."

Eve's father walked into the kitchen then, shaking his head and grumbling.

"*Daed*, what is it?"

"Elizabeth is pulling up the driveway. One of the boys is out there—Amos, I think." *Daed* pulled out his chair at the kitchen table. "I'm too old and hungry to monitor that situation right now, but someone probably needs to make sure both boys aren't together around that girl, since they go all *ab im kopp*."

Eve walked to the window in the kitchen. A full moon lit the yard. Their people had their superstitions about the power of the full moon, as well as lots of other things, but Eve had never believed in such things. Although, today…she couldn't help but wonder if the moon didn't have something to do with the troubles her boys were having.

"Sit. We will pray and eat." Her father spoke with authority, but Eve didn't move. She wasn't hungry. Holding her spot at the window, she watched Elizabeth walk across the yard toward Amos.

She knew she'd never hear the end of this from *Mamm*. She would have to listen to what a bad mother she was, how the boys had too many freedoms, and on and on. She waited until her father raised his head from prayer, then asked, "How much longer on the *haus*?" It had only been three weeks, and one of those weeks she and Benny had been away.

"Big Ben will be surprised when he sees how much we got done while you were traveling." Her father reached for a slice of butter bread. "I think probably in a couple of weeks you can go back. Everything might not be perfect, but it will be livable."

Eve nodded as she forced a smile, then joined her father and mother at the table.

Elizabeth stepped out of her buggy, and Amos was quickly by her side.

"It's t-too cold for you t-to be out, Elizabeth."

"I had to see you." She glanced around him to make sure no one was on the porch, especially Elias, then she touched his arm. "Does it still hurt?"

He reached up and touched his face, flinching. "A—A little. It's okay, though."

She glanced around him toward the porch. "Where is Elias?"

"He was helping *mei daed* carry luggage upstairs. D-Do you w-want me to get him?"

"*Nee*." She reached up and touched Amos on the cheek and smiled. He must have thought she was here to make amends with Elias. "I'm so sorry that this happened, but..." She took a deep breath. "I know that it's you I want, Amos. Your sweet words have won my heart." She smiled. "And your gentle ways."

Amos hung his head for a moment, then looked back at her as his eyes darkened with emotion. "I don't think I showed my gentle ways by fighting with *mei bruder*."

"You were fighting for the girl you love," she said softly, gazing into his one opened eye. *And you won.*

"You're shivering, Elizabeth. You shouldn't have come this late." Amos's teeth chattered as he spoke. "But since you're here, I have something very important to tell you."

Elizabeth brought a hand to her chest as she felt herself blush, knowing he was surely going to tell her that he loved her. "Oh, Amos…"

Chapter 14

Somehow they'd all gotten through the rest of the week and worship on Sunday, even though Elias had said he was sick and asked to skip church. Eve had agreed, knowing it might be a bad situation with both boys and Elizabeth at church. Eve still didn't know much about what was going on, only that her younger sons were not speaking to each other. If Elizabeth had made a choice between her boys, no one had mentioned it to Eve. But she did notice that Amos and Elizabeth seemed to be keeping their distance from each other during worship service and afterward. *Maybe Elizabeth chose Elias?*

With no snow in the forecast, Benny, her father, and the boys had all left early this Monday morning. Eve was ready for a lecture from her mother about her *sohns'* behavior, but she would avoid it as long as she could. She curled up in the chair with the recipe box, but she could hear her mother upstairs. And she was talking. To herself.

Eve sighed, put the box on the table by the chair, and walked up the stairs. Her mother's voice grew louder the closer Eve got.

"You're not such a bad fellow," Eve heard her *mamm* say.

"You and George are friends now?" Eve grinned from the threshold as she folded her hands in front of her. *Mamm* was leaning down in the closet talking to George through the cage.

But when her mother stood up and faced her, Eve gasped. Both of her mother's arms were jerking and shaking. "*Mamm*, we need to go see Dr. Knepp."

"No." Her mother stood taller, but the shaking only grew worse.

"Why not? Don't you want to feel better? Don't you want medicines that will help with the shaking?" Eve didn't give her a chance to reply. "Things are changing, *Mamm*. And change can be *gut*. Going to see an *Englisch* doctor isn't forbidden by the bishop. Neither is having more modern kitchen appliances or using a sweeper in the kitchen." She could hear her voice rising, but seeing her mother like this frightened her. "It just doesn't make any sense. These things do not take away from our relationship with God."

Her mother gripped her hands together in front of her, but her shoulders still bounced forward as she edged closer to the bed and sat down.

Eve couldn't stand to see her suffering like this. "*Mamm*, please. Let's go get you something that can help you."

"I'm fine, Minnie. Just let me be, and I'll be better soon."

Eve's eyes filled with tears. "It's me, *Mamm*. Eve." She eased closer, squatted down in front of her mother, and put one hand on her leg. "It's me."

"I know that."

Eve could feel her mother's leg tense from her touch, so she pulled back her hand, but she wanted nothing more than to wrap her arms around her and comfort her. "You called me Minnie."

"I must have been thinking about Minnie." *Mamm* shrugged her shoulders as spasms still shook her.

Eve stayed where she was. *Please, Lord, help me to say the right things. Help me to help her.* She blinked back tears, longing for a different kind of relationship with her mother, yet fearful to open herself up to more hurt. But the words sprang from her mouth. "I love you, *Mamm*."

Her mother locked eyes with Eve. "I've been a bad mother, haven't I?"

"No. You haven't." *Just tell me you love me.*

"I know you think all of this change among our people is *gut*. But I don't agree, Eve. And I don't think I ever will. The more we stray from our ways, the more it scares me."

Eve bit her bottom lip, struggling not to cry. *Just wrap your arms around me and say you love me.*

"They'll lock me up. The *Englisch* doctor will." Her mother's gaze drifted over Eve's shoulder, her expression blank.

Eve's jaw dropped. "What? They won't lock you up, *Mamm*. They might ask you to have some tests, but they won't lock you up. You just need some medicine to help you with the symptoms you're having."

"They locked up *mei mudder*." Mamm paused, still staring over Eve's shoulder. "Because she was crazy. And not so *gut* of a mother, I might add."

Eve didn't know much about her grandparents; they had both died before Eve was born, and her *mamm* never really talked about them. "What do you mean, they locked her up?"

"She had the crazies. I guess like I do." Her mother's gaze didn't leave the faraway place over Eve's shoulder, but her eyes filled with tears. "Your father wouldn't do *gut* without me, though."

"You're not crazy, *Mamm*. These hallucinations are from the Parkinson's disease. I read about it, and problems with your mind can be a symptom." Again the urge to pull her mother close was overwhelming, but she didn't move.

Finally *Mamm* shifted her gaze and locked eyes with Eve. "I was so careful with you growing up. I never wanted to hurt you."

Eve narrowed her eyebrows. "What are you talking about?"

Mamm was quiet for a few moments.

Eve's knees were cracking, so she eased herself up and onto the bed next to her mother and waited for her to continue.

"If I've been critical of the way you raised your *kinner*, it's only because I feared that the freedoms they have will pull them from our district."

"I don't want them to leave, but they deserve a chance to experience *Englisch* freedoms during their *rumschpringe*. And it's always been done that way."

Eve paused, sighing. "Except in our *haus* when I was growing up."

Her mother hung her head. "I know you don't think I'm a *gut mudder*, Eve, but I did the best I could."

"I have never said you were a bad mother. I just want to feel…" Eve shook her head. "Never mind." She shouldn't even have to say it. It should be obvious.

Her mother stood up from the bed and turned to face Eve. "*Danki* for doing the recipes. It will be a big help to me."

Eve jumped up off the bed. "Don't you do that!" She couldn't recall ever yelling at her mother before, but as tears threatened to choke her words, she went on. "Every time we start to have a meaningful conversation—about anything—you change the subject. Why can't you tell me you love me, *Mamm*? You've never said it! I don't even remember you hugging me. Was I so awful a child that you couldn't even hug me?" She pointed a finger at her mother. "*Mei kinner* will never feel that way. I tell them I love them all the time." She sniffled. "And I hug them."

"Is that what you think, Eve, that I don't love you?" *Mamm* was shaking so bad that her voice trembled as she spoke. She clasped her hands in front of her, but it did little to help. Her eyes filled with tears. "I've loved you since the day God graced me with the gift of you. Every breath I've taken has been for you."

Eve knew her parents had wanted more children but were never able to have any. So many times Eve had longed for a brother or sister.

"Really?" Eve rolled her eyes, then brushed tears from her cheeks. "Because except when we were cooking together, I never felt it."

Mamm briefly smiled. "The times we cooked together were my favorites too." Then she frowned, pulling her eyes from Eve's. "I never wanted to be like my mother. She was so…strict…with Minnie and me. Sometimes she'd just beat Minnie like you beat the dust out of a rug. I thought if I stayed distant from you, then I'd never be tempted to be like mother, like daughter."

"You never touched me." Eve swiped at her eyes.

"I know. I guess in my mind it was safer that way. I'm sorry, Eve. And I'm sorry for judging you for the way you've raised your *kinner*. It's not my place to judge. Only the Lord can do that." She locked eyes with Eve. "And I know we've disagreed about so many things, but all this change going on among our people frightens me."

"It doesn't have to, *Mamm*. Change can be a *gut* thing."

Her mother hung her head. "*Nee*, I don't think so." She tried to steady the shaking in her hands, arms, and shoulders. She looked at Eve as a tear rolled down her cheek. "Look how much *I'm* changing."

"We can get help with that." Eve closed her eyes for a moment, then reached for her mother's hand, grabbing it so firmly that there was no chance her mother could pull away. "I'll make a bargain with you."

Her mother's eyebrows shot up.

"If you'll let me take you to the doctor, then I won't say another word about upgrading the kitchen with more modern appliances, a sweeper for the kitchen, or anything else."

"You're sure they won't lock me up the way they did *mei mudder*? She was an awful woman most of the time, but I loved her and missed her just the same when she didn't come home."

"I will never let anyone lock you up. I will always take care of you."

Her mother pulled her hand away, then buried her face in her trembling hands and sobbed. "I'm afraid, Eve."

Eve wrapped her arms around her and pulled her close, until her mother finally relaxed in her arms and cried. "I know you are."

Elias climbed into bed following another day of not speaking to Amos. *Daed* had told Amos that he couldn't sleep on the couch downstairs anymore, so Elias waited for Amos to come in from the bathroom down the hall. His brother hadn't said a word about his conversation with Elizabeth, and prior to tonight Elias hadn't cared to hear about it. He had gotten his answer the night she'd come over. When Elias walked outside and saw her talking to Amos, Elizabeth had run to her buggy. She'd clearly made her choice.

The betrayal by both his brother and his former girl-friend was gnawing away at him, despite the prayers he'd been saying daily for strength to forgive them both.

"You and Elizabeth planning your wedding?" Elias crossed his ankles and put his hands behind his head when Amos entered the room.

"*Nee*." Amos pushed back his covers and got into bed. He snuffed out his lantern and fluffed his pillow.

Elias reached for his lantern on the nightstand and turned it up. "You ain't going to sleep, Amos. We're going to talk about this." He swung his feet over the side of the bed and held the lantern high.

Amos sighed, but he sat up on his bed and faced Elias. "Fine."

"How could you do this to me, Amos? I'm your *bruder*." Elias dabbed at his swollen lip, not that his physical injuries were as important as the hurt in his heart.

"I-I'm sorry. I…really am." Amos hung his head, sighing again.

"*Ya*, well, that's all *gut* and fine, but I love Elizabeth. And you stole her from me." Elias put the lantern on the nightstand, struggling with the feelings of rage and love comingling in his heart.

"If she was really yours, then I reckon I couldn't have stolen her from you."

Elias grunted, locking his one good eye with his brother's. "What's that supposed to mean?"

Amos shrugged. "I-I'm just saying that if sh-she was so in love with you, she wouldn't have had anything to do with me."

"She thought you *were* me!" Elias spoke in an angry whisper.

"*Nee*. She d-didn't. Fern's herbs helped a l-little, but I still stuttered. She knew the first time that I saw her for lunch that I wasn't you."

"I don't believe you."

"It's true. And—and I know I hurt you real bad, Elias, and I'm sorry f-for that. But I love her too."

Elias let out an exasperated huff. "She wasn't yours to love."

"She flirted with me. A-All the time. I think she liked some things 'bout me, and she liked other things about you. But she couldn't have us b-both."

"When? When did she flirt with you?" Elias swallowed hard as he tried to keep his emotions under control.

"Anytime she could. A-After church sometimes when you—you weren't around. Other times too."

"Well, now you've got her, *bruder*. Congratulations."

Amos lowered his gaze. "She's not the right girl for me." He paused. "I—I figure she'd probably flirt w-with you behind my back." He looked up. "I ain't proud of the way I acted, but I've never had a girl really like me. I'm a-ashamed." He sat taller, chin lifted. "But no *maedel* should come between us."

Elias grunted. "She already did."

Amos shook his head. "*Nee*. I told her I ain't gonna date her, much less marry her."

Elias rubbed his chin, cocking his head to one side. "Are you saying you could have had Elizabeth, and you turned her down?"

As Amos nodded, Elias wondered if he would have done the same thing if the situation were reversed. If Amos was right, and Elizabeth did like some things about each of them, then things were as they should be. He extended his hand to Amos. "I'm sorry I threw the first punch."

"I'm s-sorry too."

For the first time in days, Elias felt like he might get a decent night's sleep. He snuffed out his lantern and crawled underneath the covers. His heart still hurt over Elizabeth, but Amos's heart was hurting too. A huge knot formed in his throat, knowing what his brother had so unselfishly given up.

"Amos?"

"*Ya?*"

Elias dabbed at his eyes in the darkness. "*Bruders* forever."

"*Ya. Bruders* forever."

Chapter 15

"Two weeks have passed, and it still feels *gut* to wake up in *mei* own bed." Eve rolled over and gently touched Benny on the cheek.

"It feels *gut* to sleep in on a Saturday morning too."

Eve snuggled closer to her husband. "*Ya*, it does. We don't do it often, but when we do, it's nice."

"Are you going to Our Daily Bread today?"

"*Ya*." She poked Benny playfully on the arm. "And guess what? *Mei mamm* is going with me."

She was looking forward to going to the prayer gathering. She hadn't been in weeks. Today would be extra special since her mother had agreed to go, and Eve and her mother had something to share with the group.

"I'm glad Dr. Knepp's medications are helping her," Benny said. "You were right to keep pushing her to go to the *Englisch* doctor."

It had been two weeks since Eve had hired a driver and they'd gone to see Dr. Knepp. There'd been good news and bad news. *Mamm's* Parkinson's disease was progressing, but the doctor had said that with medication she could better control her shaking, and he'd also prescribed something to help with her mind. Eve's father had said just yesterday that *Mamm* was still putting her glasses in odd places, and sometimes she forgot things, but overall he could see an improvement.

Mamm had purchased a floor sweeper too, and Eve knew that was a big step—a statement, really, of not wanting to be so judgmental. It had taken a lifetime for them to see inside each other's heart, but Eve was hopeful that she and her mother had begun a journey toward a better relationship.

Eve glanced at the clock by the bed. "I bet the boys are starving. You know they won't get started on chores until they have some breakfast. It's almost six thirty."

Rosemary put on a freshly ironed *kapp* and one of her best Sunday dresses. For months she'd avoided going to the prayer gatherings at Our Daily Bread because she was self-conscious about all her shaking and twitching. Many times she would have stayed home from worship service for the same reason, but every time she was tempted, she reminded herself how much Jesus had suffered. Her aches and pains were of no comparison.

Today, however, was a good day. Very little trembling.

"You look pretty," Joseph said when Rosemary walked into the living room.

"*Danki.*" She smoothed the wrinkles from her black

apron as she looked around the room. "It still seems so quiet in here with all the *kinner* back in their own *haus*."

Joseph pushed his glasses up on his nose and closed the book he was reading. "Been real nice having Eve over here so much, even after they moved back home. Good to see the two of you cooking together."

Rosemary smiled. "That's when Eve and I were always at our best. I guess it still is." She walked to the door and put on her black sweater and bonnet, glad the pre-spring temperatures had arrived. Peeking out the window, she saw Eve's buggy coming up the driveway. "See you soon." She kissed Joseph on the cheek.

Eve followed her mother into the white cinder-block building where the local women had been gathering since well before Eve was born. As they walked down the aisle with the fabrics, Eve was reminded that she needed material for some new shirts for Benny and the boys.

She followed her mother up the stairs to the upper room of the store. Familiar faces lit up when they entered. Eve swallowed back a lump in her throat as she watched her mother hugging some of the women. *What a blessing today is.* She silently thanked God for her mother's improved symptoms and that she and her mother were finally able to work on being closer.

After chatting in small groups for about fifteen minutes, the women settled into chairs and prayed for each other and their families. Then Ann Lapp offered prayers for all those who couldn't be with them today. Eve knew that she had been on that list the past few weeks, and her mother even longer. Eve was thankful for so many things today. A restored home, her family, and a newfound relationship with her mother. When Ann was done, Eve bowed her head and spoke aloud. "I would like to thank the Lord for our newly repaired home." She glanced around the room at the women.

"And please thank your husbands and *sohns* who took time when they could to help Benny, my boys, and *mei daed* work on the *haus*."

Ann clapped her hands together. "I think it would be nice if we all said what we're thankful for today." She waved her hand toward the window, bright sunshine streaming into the room and onto the wooden floors. "It's such a beautiful day in so many ways." She paused. "I'm thankful that Hiram is almost completely recovered from the flu he's been suffering from this winter."

All of the women nodded, and then each one thanked God for something they were thankful for on this glorious day. Eve was relieved that Elizabeth wasn't in attendance today. She would always wish Elizabeth well, but after what happened with the twins, she wasn't ready to face the girl yet. The feeling was probably mutual.

"I'm thankful for my first taste of love," Fern Zook said, her green eyes glowing. She reminded Eve of herself when she'd first fallen in love with Benny all those years ago.

Hannah King was the next one to speak up. "I'm thankful that God led Stephen to Paradise and our bed-and-breakfast." Her wide smile was indicative of more new love in the air, and Eve was extra thankful—if that was possible—that she and her mother were here today.

Eve's mother was the only one in the group who hadn't spoken up yet, and she raised a trembling hand to her chest, then reached for Eve's hand with her other one. "I'm thankful that *mei dochder* convinced me to go see Dr. Knepp for medication that helps with my shaking." She glanced at Fern. "Not that Fern's herbs weren't *gut*…" She smiled. "I just needed something a bit stronger." She squeezed Eve's hand. "Most of all, I'm thankful for the time I spent with my family while their house was being rebuilt."

Eve squeezed her mom's hand back, blinking her eyes. After a deep breath, she eased her hand away and reached into her apron pocket. She unfolded the piece of paper, recalling fondly the time she and her mother had spent together in preparation for this moment.

"*Mamm* and I have been cooking a lot," Eve began, smiling. "And we've been writing down all of our recipes so that future generations will always have them. On the back of some of the recipe cards, we wrote down fond memories we have of times we cooked together. And last week we created a recipe together that we would like to share with you." Eve glanced at her mother, who dabbed at her eyes. "It's a recipe for hope, and I'd like to read it to you." She read aloud:

A Recipe for Hope

Ingredients:
A taste of faith
A spoonful of love
3 cups of prayer
1 cup of trust
4 ounces of kindness
2 cups of forgiveness
1 bucketful of laughter

Mix all of the above together—but be careful not to let judgment, bad attitude, pride, or bitterness mingle with ingredients. Adjust measurements as needed to fit your daily needs, and always have ingredients on hand.

Serve abundantly every day, sharing with as many people as you can.

Some of the women laughed, others smiled. Eve looked at her mother and felt God's hand on them, revealing a love that had always been there, just hidden beneath the very human qualities that were a part of them all.

* * * * *

ACKNOWLEDGMENTS

Much thanks to my friends and family for your encouragement and support, and especially to my husband, Patrick, who puts up with my tight deadlines and related mood swings. Love you, dear. :)

To Janet Murphy, the best assistant on the planet—it's an honor to dedicate my novella to you. Thank you for all your help getting folks to test the recipes. You are a gem. Irreplaceable.

Thanks to my agent, Mary Sue Seymour. I hope another trip to New York City is in our future. What great memories!

To my editor, Natalie Hanemann—the journey continues, and I'm so incredibly blessed to have you in my life.

Barbie Beiler, thank you for making our "girls' weekend" in Lancaster County so much fun. You are the best. Miss you!

And to Kelly Long and Amy Clipston—it was so great working with both of you.

And last, but certainly not least—thanks be to God for all He is in my life.

ABOUT THE AUTHOR

Beth Wiseman is hailed as a top voice in Amish fiction. She is a Carol Award winner and author of numerous bestsellers, including the Daughters of the Promise and the Land of Canaan series. She and her family live in Texas. Visit Beth on the web at bethwiseman.com, look for her on Facebook or follow her on Twitter: @bethwiseman.

A Taste of Faith

Kelly Long

For my Gram

June 25
To: Henry Fisher
Paradise, Pa.

Dear *Bruder* Henry,
It seems that *Fater* has taken a turn lately, and the doctors at the hospital say they are worried about his breathing and heart condition. He's home now, using some oxygen. He asks after all of you often, even when he's poorly, and I thought you might like the chance to visit with him. You know that I love the *kinner*, but we've had a hard time even keeping the twins quiet so *Fater* can rest. I wondered if you and Martha might come for a visit alone, and perhaps Abram can tend to the young ones and the farm. I long to hear from you and would be glad to see you both. Matthias says "Hello" and "*Kumme* on with you."

Your loving sister,
Elizabeth

Chapter 1

July 3
Paradise, Pennsylvania

The light of the waning summer day filtered through the unadorned glass and played amid the profusion of plants in coffee cans that lined the windowsills. Twenty-year-old Fern Zook liked the way her silhouette blended and appeared to lengthen with the multitude of shadowy leaves and stems as she stretched to make sure each container took a few drops from the watering pot.

She reached a tender fingertip to the face of a pansy and murmured to the plants, as was her custom. "If only a man could be grown among you all. It would be much easier than trying to find one in Paradise. But then, God made man in a garden, so maybe…" She closed her eyes and indulged in her favorite fantasy…that of a tall, dark, handsome man, someone with a frame large enough to find her generous curves…interesting, instead of unappealing. Someone who—

"Hiya! Anyone in there?"

Fern spun from the plants to see the materialization of her reverie standing outside the kitchen screen door. She blinked when he hollered again.

"Can't you hear? I've got a sick little girl here!"

Fern sighed. It was Abram Fisher, the twenty-three-year-old eldest son of her grandmother's next-door neighbors. Tall and handsome, *ya*. He was broad-shouldered and lean-hipped, and his tousled chestnut-brown hair brushed overly long at the collar of his dark-blue shirt, which matched the color of his eyes. Darkly brooding and big, for certain. She'd passed Abram solemn and sure at church and seen him working in the fields, his strong forearms straining at some task or another, his large hands easily managing a team of four horses behind the plow. And apparently those same hands could cradle a little girl with abject tenderness as he was doing now with his sister, Mary. But Fern doubted he even knew she was alive; he certainly had never paid attention to her growing up. And now he was a dyed-in-the-wool bachelor, married to the land, who'd never given her a passing word until this moment.

"Hey!"

"I'm coming," she said in a calm voice and went to open the door. As he brushed past her, carrying Mary, his elbow grazed her dress, setting her heart to miss a curious beat.

Forcing her mind to the matter at hand, Fern assessed the red face of the fretful child. Sunburn…but not sunstroke, not by the way the child was moving about and fussing. Fern breathed a sound of relief when she laid her hand against the little red forehead and felt for a moment, sliding her hand gently to the sides and back of the child's neck. She could tell there was no fever, just the external heat from the sun exposure.

"Let's take off her *kapp*. A lot of heat escapes through the head, and she needs to cool down." *And so do you, Abram Fisher...*

The man was positively radiating tension from his big body. She was used to dealing with anxious parents, but not upset older brothers who looked like they could be models in an *Englisch* magazine.

She searched out the pins holding the prayer *kapp* on the tightly braided mass of brown hair and then threaded her fingers through the braids.

"That feels *gut*." Mary half-smiled.

"I'm glad." Fern peered down into the child's face, then looked back up to catch Abram's eyes. "Didn't she have her sunbonnet on?"

His blue eyes, which she fancied could make a girl forget herself if she wasn't careful, were as cold as the sea and met hers with a suppressed fury. *"Nee,"* he snapped. "I thought that it wouldn't hurt to let her play in the creek with the boys a bit. She had her dress off and just her underclothes on. I was wrong, all right?"

"*Ya*, you were," Fern murmured. The man certainly had an easily aroused temper. She turned from the table. "Well, it's not sunstroke. She's moving around fine, and I can feel no fever. I'll brew some tea."

He blew out a breath of what could only be disgust. *"Nee*, thanks. I have no time for tea."

Fern flushed. "Not to drink," she said patiently. "The tannin is a soother to the skin; it will help the burn cool and heal it faster."

"*Ach*," he grunted. "All right then."

She turned away and went to gather tea leaves to brew; it would take a few minutes and then have to cool. She had no idea what they'd talk about while they waited. She fussed at the stove awhile, then went back to lean over Mary, deciding that ignoring Abram might be the best course of action. She wasn't adept at talking to men unless it concerned her work and their immediate ailments.

"Would you like a peppermint stick?" she asked the little girl.

Mary's smile brightened her red face. "*Ya*."

"Me too!" An excited boy's face appeared at the screen door, and Fern had to laugh.

"I think you have company," she remarked, going to open the door. A mass of boys tumbled in, and she didn't miss Abram's faint groan.

"Matthew, I told you to keep the *kinner* at the house."

Fern waved an airy hand in Abram's direction. "*Ach*, it's fine. They were probably interested in their baby sister, right?" Her grin took in the group with ease. Children, she could deal with.

"We was worried about Mary," the smallest boy announced.

"Of course you were," she said, handing candy from a glass jar to eager hands. "Let's see, we've got John, Luke, Mark, and Matthew, right?"

The boys nodded tousled and damp heads, and Fern turned with a diffident stance to Abram. "Would you like a sweet?" She held the jar out to him and was surprised when he accepted with a brief nod, reaching long, tanned fingers into the glass to take out the candy. She couldn't help but notice when his white teeth took a decisive snap of the stick, and the sugar that was meant to be leisurely enjoyed was gone in two bites.

"Some things are better when they're savored," she said, watching him.

He grinned at her in what she considered to be a sarcastic fashion. "So they are—but not candy...or anything else that flits across a woman's mind."

Fern frowned. She didn't like his dismissive attitude about a woman's thoughts. Her lips framed a retort when Matthew spoke up, a solemn expression in the brown eyes behind his glasses.

"A woman's mind is just as *gut* as a man's, Abram. I believe that Fern wanted to tell you to slow down and taste things in life, right?"

Abram wanted to roll his eyes at Matthew, but the boy was thirteen, sensitive, and overly *gut* at studying; he needed a gentle hand. And, of course, he was absolutely right about what Fern had wanted. *Fern...what a ridiculous nickname...*

He recalled that her true name was Deborah, not that he'd ever thought about it, though they'd grown up beside each other. He eyed her covertly now as she put a gentle hand on Matthew's shoulder and bent to praise him for his insight. The gentle curves of her body were appealing to the eye, he decided, but she was probably as pushy as a mule about what she wanted and when she wanted it. He felt a simmer of emotions cross his mind and had to haul himself back to attention.

"Abram!" Mark shrilled his name.

"What?" he snapped, looking everywhere but at Fern Zook.

"We're going out on the porch like Fern said... three times now!" His younger brother poked him in the *bauch* to emphasize his words, and Abram slid his hands to his hips.

"Well, go on with the lot of you, then. I'm coming."

"*Neeeee*...you are staying here to help put the tea towels on Mary." Mark got one last poke in, then scurried behind Luke and hit the door. The boys piled out, and Abram had to look at Fern then.

She was laughing, a bright smile on her rosy lips. "You must have your hands full with your parents gone for the month."

He frowned. "*Ya*, they're a bunch." He found himself wondering if the soft curves of her shoulders would fill the palms of his hands. What was wrong with him? He must be addled in the head from the heat himself. He kept his voice level, then turned to the couch to bend over Mary, who held up her arms for him. He buried his face in the baby-soft curve of her neck, then kissed her hot cheek.

He straightened and avoided Fern's observant green eyes. "All right, what do we do?"

Mary spoke up. "Why do they call you Fern?"

Fern smiled. "It was what my mother called me, because as a baby I loved the outdoors so much. I guess I tried to chew on a fern one day, and somehow it became my name."

Mary giggled, and Abram had to admit that Fern was a good healer, capable as she was of distracting a patient in pain…in spite of her silly name.

Chapter 2

"Who was here?"

Fern looked up from gathering damp tea towels when her aged *mammi* came into the room, leaning heavily on her cane.

"*Ach*, the Fisher *kinner*. Little Mary has a sunburn."

"Did Abram bring her?"

Fern suppressed a sigh. If there was one thing her grandmother wanted more than to see her trained in the arts of herbal healing, it was to get her married. She'd remarked on Abram Fisher as a possible candidate on more than one occasion.

"*Ya*, he was here."

"Fine figure of a man."

Fern didn't reply; she did not want to contradict, nor could she in truth. She loved her grandmother. Esther Zook had taken her and raised her when both her parents had died from influenza when Fern was five. The old woman had been a balm to Fern's heart and flagging spirits when she longed for the gentle laughter and love she remembered from her *mamm* and *daed*. And through the years, as her *mammi's* arthritis had worsened, Fern had learned the ways of plants and general first aid, following in her grandmother's footsteps as a healer to her people. Of course the more serious cases always were sent to Dr. Knepp, an *Englisch* physician who was widely embraced by the community, but the Zook women were kept quite busy nonetheless.

Fern put the jar of peppermint sticks back on the counter, a flash of Abram Fisher's handsome grin coming to her mind. She turned determinedly to her grandmother.

"What would you like for supper?"

"Ach, anything you want that's cool from the garden. I'm not a bit hungry, to tell the truth."

Fern moved to cover the soft-veined hand of the older woman and frowned in concern. "Are you all right? Is there anything I can do?"

Her grandmother sank into a rocker. "To cure old age? *Nee. Derr Herr* has His own cure for that. But to aid my heart, you might take a basket of those cherry tomatoes from the kitchen garden over to the Fisher *kinner*. Boys always love them, and we've been blessed with more than a few this year."

Fern bit back her frustration. "I'm sure the Fishers have plenty of tomatoes."

Her grandmother held up a wrinkled hand. "I spoke with Martha before she left for Ohio; she said her cherry tomatoes had caught the blight."

Fern closed her eyes against the image of knocking

on Abram Fisher's door. She had no problem running something next door if she knew he was in the fields, but to go now, right after he'd been here, would look like she was chasing him. Still, she could say she also wanted to double-check on Mary...

"*Ach*, all right. I'll take the tomatoes over."

Her grandmother smiled, all gentle wrinkles and kind blue eyes. She reached out to pat Fern's hand. *"Gut* girl."

Abram watched Mary dash across the family's kitchen, a fistful of blueberries in hand and a smile on her rosy cheeks. He leaned back in a chair and felt like he'd suddenly aged in one afternoon; his baby sister had scared him half to death. And then it had not been the old woman who had answered his call for help, but the quick-mouthed Deborah, *nee*, Fern. He decided his momentary musings on the girl were because she was helping Mary. Besides, he didn't like her way of fixing things—she was too practical and straightforward for a woman. Not that he'd really been noticing in that much detail. He said a brief silent prayer of thanks for Mary's health and added the hope that he'd not have to be seeing Fern Zook again anytime soon for her services.

"She's nice...and has a quick mind," Matthew said, lifting his head from his book where he sat at the kitchen table.

"Hmm? Who?" Abram asked.

"Fern Zook."

"Ya," Mark chimed in, his pug nose in Abram's face for a second. "Mebbe you should maaarry her."

Abram made a feint swat at him, and the boy laughed.

Mary stopped running about for a moment. "What's maaarry mean?" she asked.

"Death," Mark quipped.

Mary's lip began to quiver. "Like my puppy died?"

"Close your mouth," Abram said to his younger *bruder* and held out his arms to Mary. "*Kumme* here, sweetheart."

She came readily and nestled herself on his lap. "What is it really, Abram? I don't want my kitty to die."

"*Nee*...of course not. Married is—like *Mamm* and *Daed*. Two people love each other, and then there's a wedding and they start a life together. That's all."

"That's a lot," Matthew said.

"*Ya,* well..." Abram brushed a strand of hair from his sister's forehead.

"Are you gonna do that with Fern Zook, Abram?" Mary asked, peering intently into his eyes.

He laughed. "*Nee*...married is not for your old *bruder.* I'll wait around someday till you marry, okay? But not until you're at least thirty-five."

"Thirty-five?" Luke laughed from where he sat eating the last of *Mamm's* molasses cookies. "That's too old. You gotta marry after *rumschpringe, ya*?"

"I don't want no *rumschpringe*. Girls are yucky— 'cept *Mamm* and Mary," John muttered, then he looked anxiously to his big brother. "Is that okay, Abram?"

Abram nodded at the eight-year-old boy. John was nervous at times, unsure of himself, but anxious to please. "You can have it or not...any way you want," Abram assured him, setting Mary back down to run around.

But his brother's question got Abram thinking back to his own *rumschpringe*. Women had been for then—

when he was seventeen, eighteen…playing at kissing and never meaning any of it beyond the passing pleasure of the moment. *Nee*…he'd seen the difficulties that friends had faced upon marrying, the tight-lipped responses to his teasing comments about married life, and he wanted none of it. His best friend, Joe, had married right out of the chute and now looked about twice his age, with two *kinner* born and another on the way… It was enough responsibility to break a man. *Nee.* The land was Abram's wife, his soul. He understood the soil and the seasons each in turn; there was struggle but never strife, and adding a woman to his life would without a doubt bring more than trouble.

He blinked, then jumped from his chair as Mary tripped over her own feet and fell across the floor, slamming her head against the stove in her descent. Just then someone knocked on the door.

"Rest and ice…and a visit to Dr. Knepp if she should start to throw up or lose consciousness in the next few hours or even days."

Fern watched Abram nod as he pressed the ice wrapped in a towel on Mary's forehead while the little girl squirmed in his lap. Fern glanced around the messy kitchen and then at the boys devouring the cherry tomatoes and wondered if Abram Fisher was actually capable of caring for five children for a month's time. She knew probably a dozen women in the community who'd give their right eye for the privilege of helping him, but she sensed that asking for help was not one of his normal activities.

She said a silent prayer that he might receive her words well, then cleared her throat. "Uh… Abram, it seems like you might benefit from a bit of help here and there. I would be glad to—"

"We're fine," he interrupted.

"I want *Mamm,*" Mary wailed.

"Shhh," he soothed in his deep voice, bouncing Mary on his knee. He turned to Fern. "What can I do for you to pay for this?"

Fern had to stop and think. Although he'd pressed a few dollars in her hand for the sunburn treatment, the community at large knew that the Zooks, being women alone, preferred work in exchange for their services. She glanced into his blue eyes and wondered what he'd do if she asked for a kiss in return payment. She smiled at the absurd thought and caught his quick frown.

"What are you thinking?"

What was wrong with her? It was probably being so close to him that set her pulse racing. Later, when she was back home, she'd feel more like herself. Fern shook her head and grasped at the first thought that came to mind. "A ladder."

"What?"

"We need a new ladder. So I can clean the upper windows outside that I didn't get to this spring."

"I'll do the windows," Abram said with a look of surprise on his handsome face.

"Why?" Fern asked, then flushed. Perhaps he thought that she was too big and clumsy to accomplish such a task.

"I don't want you—I—it's dangerous, that's all."

Abram couldn't help but notice how green her eyes were as they widened at his words or the way her pretty mouth formed a soft expression of surprise. She probably thought he was *narrisch* about the ladder. He was confused himself at his concern. She'd probably done the windows a dozen times over and then some.

"Abram, can me and Luke go outside and play?" Mark hollered above his sister's cries, an innocent expression on his face.

Abram kept jogging Mary on his knee and eyed his brother dispassionately. "*Ya*, but no creek, no bees, snakes, or spiders—no trouble, all right?"

"*Ya, ya!*" Mark yelled. He brushed past Fern with Luke in tow and hit the screen door running.

Abram waited as Mary wore herself out crying and settled for sniffling against his shirt. He took a brief glance around his *mamm's* normally neat kitchen and realized he hadn't even thought about supper or getting the cucumbers that were running riot in the kitchen garden…and then there was the washing. Still, his pride won out. He'd assured his parents that he could take care of things, and he would. He didn't want Fern Zook and her soft mouth telling him what or how to do things.

"I'll be over tomorrow with a new ladder and get at those windows," he said in a tone of dismissal.

"*Danki.* What are you reading, Matthew?"

She advanced into the kitchen, stepping over John's cookie crumbs, and he watched his brother smile and push his glasses up on his thin nose as he showed her the book. Abram found himself studying the soft, white curve of her neck as she bent in profile over the table. A stray golden-brown strand of hair had escaped the back of her *kapp* and hung long and tempting against her shoulder. Her hair seemed like it was shot through with sunlight, and he wondered idly how it would look unbound…

Abram stood up, feeling irritable and restless, and set Mary down.

"Your hair's down," he said.

He felt the weight of the children's gazes as Fern straightened.

"What?"

He frowned and gestured toward the single sunshiny strand. "I said your hair's down."

He watched her lift a self-conscious hand to her neck and catch the hair between her capable fingers. "*Ach,* I didn't know." Her face reddened in embarrassment.

Abram felt his petty irritability drain. He wanted to kick himself for making her feel bad. *It was one silly strand of hair...*

But Fern was already headed for the door. She stumbled over the small pile of wooden blocks that John had left on the floor and cried out as she started to fall. But Abram moved fast and caught her close with ease.

Chapter 3

Fern had the strange sensory experience that she was weightless as she felt herself held against him, his arms solid as oak and the press of his long legs against the back of her skirt like mountain rock. Yet there was restraint present as well. She felt his quick intake of breath, and she herself breathed as if she'd just run across two plowed fields. Her heart hammered loudly in her ears.

"Are you all right?" His voice was low in her ear.

She remembered his comment about her hair and stiffened in his arms. "Of course. You may let me go... I wouldn't want to offend you any further with my hair being down."

Instead of removing his arms, Abram bent closer so that she could feel the brush of his own hair against her cheek. He laughed. "Hair like yours could never offend. I was being irritable, and I apologize."

She sniffed, breathing in the strange male scent of him—like spices with a deeper musky undertone that did little to help her focus on the matter at hand.

"May I?" he asked, and she scrambled desperately for the response to a question she couldn't recall.

"Are you going to kiss her?" Matthew asked eagerly.

Abram turned her in his arms as if she were light as thistledown, until they both faced the interested face of the boy at the table.

"*Nee*," Abram breathed, then abruptly let her go.

Fern straightened her spine. "*Nee*, he most certainly is not. I must be leaving. A *gut* day to you." She carefully marched over the pile of blocks on the floor and hit the screen door handle with force, feeling it give with a satisfying squeak that echoed behind her in the drifting silence of the Fisher kitchen.

Had he been about to kiss her? The thought teased around his brain like the water touching his wrists as he stuffed an extra shirt into the generator-powered clothes washer. The daylight was fading fast. His *mamm* would never have been caught doing wash at this hour, but Abram figured that the order of chores didn't matter much with housework. He'd busied Matthew in setting the table for a supper of warmed-up stew that their mother had left in the freezer. Mark and Luke were nowhere to be found, as he might have expected, and John was struggling with some wooden clothespins in an attempt to hang up a sheet on the line Abram had lowered nearby.

He glanced sideways at Mary as she knelt in the shadowed grass, making a "house" for a toad he'd caught for her. He remembered his little sister's expres-

sion of mingled delight and surprise when he'd caught
Fern Zook close in the kitchen that afternoon. Mary's
little mouth had formed a gentle O, and he couldn't
help but think that Fern's mouth had probably been in
the same shape...

He shook his head and slammed the lid of the washer
down. Mary looked up.

"Are you mad about somethin', Abram?"

"Nee." He wasn't mad, but he sure was acting crazy.
He told himself sternly that it was simply a passing
phase or the result of not being in the surety of the
fields for a few days.

He looked up as the rustling of cornstalks alerted
him that someone was coming, cutting across his family's field. His friend Joe Mast stepped lightly from
between the waist-high stalks, a smile on his usually
sober face.

"Hiya, Joe!" Mary cried, then laughed as Joe swung
her and the toad up into his gangly arms. He balanced
her easily against one hip, called a greeting to John,
then looked at Abram.

Abram felt it no light mistake on the Lord's part that
Joe should come round for a visit just when he was having addled thoughts about a woman. Joe was Abram's
unspoken cornerstone against marriage...and kissing,
which for women had a funny way of leading to the
idea of wedded bliss.

"How's Emma?" Abram asked the question with purpose, wanting to see the familiar droop to his friend's
shoulders and the tightness around his mouth. Instead,
Joe's expression brightened considerably, and he jiggled
Mary against his side.

"Emma's right as rain, and the babe's due any day now."

"Uh-huh," Abram grunted, knowing he was not being the best of friends, but unable to help himself. "Any day now—that'll make three *kinner.*"

"Yep." Joe grinned. "And I know you're getting some practice with kids yourself since your folks are away. I came over to see if I could give you a hand."

Abram stared at him. Joe worked two jobs—one as a hand on an *Englisch* dairy farm and then trying to keep his own cows going. He and Emma lived in a small house of little means and neither had parents to help out. Yet here Joe was, offering to help and looking as cheerful as fresh pie.

"Are you all right, Joe?" he asked before he could stop himself.

Joe jostled Mary and smiled wider at her giggles. "Who, me? Doin' *gut* for once… Had a long talk with Emma one afternoon while her *aenti* watched the little ones. Realized we hadn't made any time for just us, me and Em, in a long while. I figured out that I gotta have that with her, and then everything feels real calm and settled…like when we were first running around together." He gave a sheepish shrug.

"*Ach,*" Abram mumbled, his friend's words of intimacy piercing him to the quick. He'd based a lot of years of thinking on Joe's silent communications that marriage was not such a great state of affairs. Now the man he'd thought terminally unhappy because he'd wed was giving him lessons in sustaining love. What could it mean?

Nothing, he told himself. It meant nothing. He was overworked, out of his mind with the kids, and generally

not himself; that was all. Fern Zook and her loose honeyed hair was nothing more than a mirage…a distrac-
tion when what he really needed was to work out some
sort of schedule and get things running well on the farm
and with the kids. But he couldn't accept Joe's offer
to help, not when his friend was so sincere in having
found happiness despite his own workload. He smiled.

"Joe, we've known each other since we were kids.
You know if I get into something that I can't handle I'll
ask for help. Things are fine here—"

A high-pitched scream cut off his speech. Both men
turned in alarm to the cornfield where the sound had
echoed with eerie intensity. John ran over from the
clothesline and took Mary's hand as Joe eased her to
the ground. The scream came again, then Abram saw
smoke rising from the tops of the cornstalks, followed
by a colored combustion of red and blue. Fireworks. He
might have known…the Fourth of July had just passed,
and the boys had probably gotten hold of some of the
things from the *Englisch* boy they played with at times.

"Stay with Mary and John, will you, Joe? I'll be right
back." He began to move through the field.

"Luke Fisher? Mark Samuel Fisher? When I get my
hands on you, I'm going to tan both your—" He broke
off as he came to a sudden clearing where the cornstalks had been trampled down. Mark was fooling with
a sparkler and matches while Luke held his fingers to
his mouth, jumping up and down.

Luke took one look at Abram, pulled his fingers out,
and started to bawl.

"*Ach*, it's just a little burn, Luke. Come on!" Mark
said.

"Let me see your fingers," Abram demanded.

Luke snuffled and held out his left hand. Abram frowned at the heavy blisters on the boy's fingers. Great. Just great. Back to Fern Zook…

Three times in one day, he considered grimly as he hauled the boys along through the field… The girl would think he was either off in the head or plotting ways to see her. Either idea was enough to make him feel sick himself. He tightened his grip on his *bruders'* collars as he marched them home through the cornstalks in the twilight.

Chapter 4

Fern tried to compose herself on the walk back to her grandmother's house; there was no way she was going to let the keen old eyes see how flustered she had been by being held by Abram Fisher. *Had* he been going to kiss her?

It certainly had felt like it. But maybe it was just wishful thinking.

She entered the coolness of her kitchen and saw her *mammi* at the table, carefully taking rose petals off several of the big fragrant roses that they grew in the kitchen garden.

"I had a taste for some rose tea," *Mammi* said with a smile.

For the second time that day, Fern looked at her *mammi* with concern. "I thought rose tea was only for special occasions."

"It is."

"Well, what's so special about today, or is your *bauch* ailing you? You know, maybe we should pay a visit to Dr. Knepp. You haven't been in a while, and I know that—"

"Fern, you're warbling on like a pretty songbird on the first of spring. Everything is fine. More than fine, really."

Fern blew at her forehead where a loose strand of hair had escaped her *kapp*, then flushed as she remembered Abram's comment about her hair being down. She sat down at the table and plucked at a rose, accidentally tearing one of the petals.

Her grandmother eyed her with a faint smile. "Did the Fisher boys like the fruit?"

"Ya, danki."

"And how is Abram faring?"

Fern looked at her squarely in a game effort to throw her off the scent. "He's fine. Doesn't need any help at all." She didn't quite succeed in keeping the dryness out of her tone, and her grandmother laughed.

"Gets to you, he does," the old woman said, her brow wrinkled in satisfaction.

"Nee." Fern told herself to remain calm. "He is going to give us a new ladder, though. Mary had a bit of a spill when I took the tomatoes over." *And I nearly did too*, she reminded herself.

"Well, I guess you can get at those windows, then."

Fern hesitated. "Uh… Abram said he'd bring the ladder round tomorrow and do the windows himself."

"Ach…"

Fern rose abruptly. She felt flustered and distracted and needed to do something to unwind. "I think I'll have a bath and wash my hair after supper."

Her grandmother looked up. "Didn't you do that yesterday?"

"Ya…but…what's the special occasion?" Fern said, remembering the roses.

"Hmm?"

"You never said, *Mammi*…the special occasion for the rose tea?"

"Never mind, child. Simply something that makes an old woman have faith. You wouldn't understand quite yet."

And with that, Fern knew she had to be content. Her *mammi* would talk when she was ready.

By the time Abram had waved Joe off, spent a few pointed moments with Mark, and got the kids seated to supper under Matthew's watchful eye, the gloaming had faded to darkness. He needed a lantern to light the way to the Zooks'.

He'd wrapped Luke's burned fingers in a cool cloth, settling his tears somewhat, but the boy still let out a faint sob now and then as he hopped to keep up. Abram slowed his steps and looked down at his little *bruder* in the circle of light from the lamp.

"Hurt bad, does it?" He softened his voice, suddenly remembering pinching his own fingers as a child in between floorboards in the hayloft and then lying manfully to his *fater* that he'd felt no pain.

"Ya…a little now."

"Well…she'll make you feel better."

She'll…she… As though Fern Zook had become definitive of all that was healing and feminine, like he'd corralled an idea of her goodness and tenderness in a corner of his mind, a soft reference point on a lost map.

What had other girls been to him? Too skinny for one thing, too eager with their kisses, too many elbows and angles and hasty touching in the crunched confines of the buggy…and *Englisch* girls at that, not ones who'd know how to tend a little girl or soothe a boy's pride… not like Fern Zook.

"Can we, Abram? Can we?" Luke was jumping up and down, and Abram realized he'd come to a full stop on the dark path while his mind wound with slow satisfaction toward the idea of a woman he'd seen all of his adult life and never given more than a passing glance before today. It was like he was under a spell.

"What do you want?" he moaned, more to himself than to Luke. But the boy's face grew cheery in the ring of light.

"I said, for the thirteenth million time, can we catch lightning bugs on our way back? Can we?"

"Sure…ya. If the Zooks will loan us a jar."

"*Ach*, she will," Luke said with a confident grin that belied the pain of his burns.

She will. Abram felt the words pulse with curious promise down the back of his neck with each step he took toward Fern Zook's home.

Her grandmother had retired to her bedroom on the first floor when Fern slid the metal tub and screen into place in the middle of the kitchen floor. Many Amish had modern showers, but that was an unnecessary convenience as far as her *mammi* was concerned. She said an herbal bath brought as much cleanliness, plus a sense of peace that no newfangled showerhead could ever provide.

Fern didn't usually take such an early bath, as people sometimes came to the door seeking help after dark. But this evening she felt grubby and decided to take the chance. When she'd filled the tub with warmed water, she turned to consider various herbs in their neat rows of jars. Then she spied a bowl of citrus fruit on the end of the counter. The juice from a lemon and an orange, in addition to a few floating circles of fruit, soon gave off a zesty, pleasant scent that had her senses tingling.

She peeked behind the screen once to make sure she'd latched the door, then hastily stripped off her clothes and let down her hair. She wiggled her toes in the water, flicking at an orange slice, before slowly sliding in with a murmur of satisfaction. She had just finished pulling on a clean dress and stockings when she heard a knock at the door. She listened carefully, hoping she'd misheard, but the sound came again. Yet why should she be surprised—it was why she changed into clothes and not a nightgown after a bath. Perhaps she should call for her grandmother. But then, the old woman had not quite seemed herself today, and Fern hated to disturb her. She quickly bent over and bound her long hair up in the towel, turban style, and decided that it would have to be *gut* enough for whoever had come calling, needing treatment at this hour.

She padded over the hardwood floor and flung the door open in frustration, then felt the color drain from her face when she saw Abram Fisher, his blue eyes gleaming in the light of a lantern.

"What do you think you're doing, answering the door like that?" Abram heard the angry words but somehow couldn't connect them with his own voice.

"I beg your pardon...I was having a bath," Fern Zook snapped. "My hair might be down, but it's well covered."

"Well, obviously you were having a bath. Do you realize that anyone could come along here, any stranger, and you fling open the door, carefree as a bluebird, when you look like—" He broke off in midbluster, unsure how to describe how she looked without giving away how much of an effect it was having on him. He felt his face flush with warm blood when he took in the way that the towel turban she wore only revealed more of the soft contours of her face, widening the twin pools of her green eyes and forcing her light brows into a higher arc. And she smelled like Christmas, all citrus and spice, enough to make a man forget everything but the pleasure of the moment. He wondered briefly what it would be like to come home late from the fields and find her waiting, like this, for him...

"My fingers are burnt bad!" Luke's interjectory wail shook Abram from his treacherous thoughts.

He glared at Fern. Clearly, she could not provide treatment without her hair up properly...and safely. They'd have to come back tomorrow.

"Well, why didn't you say so?" Fern asked, widening the door so that her small feet became evident.

Abram swallowed hard. "It's only a bit of a burn; it can wait until tomorrow."

But Luke jerked from his hand to run and cling to Fern's waist, leaving Abram to wish he might exercise the same privilege.

"Of course you're not leaving," she sniffed. "Come in and I'll help."

Oh no, you won't... , he thought grimly. Not with

what apparently ailed him. He swallowed his thoughts with determination, trying to get the idea of touching Fern Zook's delicate ankles out of his foolish brain.

"Are you coming?" she asked, then let go of the screen door so that he had to catch it quickly with his elbow. He entered the kitchen and saw the puddled floor, the screen, and the silhouette of the tub. He rubbed the back of his neck and tried to look everywhere but at her while he listened to her soft voice soothing Luke as she examined his fingers.

"This should have been attended to sooner," she murmured. "Why did you wait?"

Abram felt irritation mingle with attraction in a strange dance down the center of his chest. "Look, at least I knew enough not to smear it with butter."

"I'm simply pointing out that it might have spared Luke some pain to have had it looked at sooner."

"I had the kids to feed, and I—"

"Never mind." She waved him off and turned to the windowsill, half in shadow, and broke the pointed stems off a healthy aloe plant. She returned to Luke and squeezed the juice of the plant out onto his fingers.

He gave a small gasp of relief, and Abram couldn't resist the half smile that tugged at his lips. So simple. Aloe vera. His *mamm* probably had some growing in a pot at home.

"I should have thought of that," he said.

"It's not always easy to think of the right thing to do in a stressful situation."

"*Ya,*" he agreed, his irritation forgotten as he considered her words.

Ya, stressful...like right now, when my bruder's a half foot from your hip and the lantern light's illuminating you like a candle, and I feel that if I touched you, you would disappear into a fevered dream.

Abram swung on his heel away from her abruptly. "Luke, let's move. Who knows what the kids will have gotten into by now."

"But I thought we wuz gonna ask for a jar to catch lightning bugs," the boy protested.

"I've got plenty of jars," Fern offered.

Abram felt the light brush of her dress against his back as she swept past him.

"Never mind," he said hoarsely. "Come on, Luke. I mean it." He spoke over his shoulder to Fern. "I'll do the downstairs windows tomorrow too, to pay for tonight."

"Forget it—the aloe was nothing."

"I said the downstairs too… *Gut* night." He shepherded a glum-faced Luke out the door and escaped the citrus-smelling, feminine torture chamber.

Fern doused the lights and went to lie down in her simple bed upstairs. She snuggled deeper under the nine-patch quilt her grandmother had given her long ago and tried to sleep, but she was met with visions of Abram Fisher's not-too-happy face at every toss and turn. She should have known that a man who'd be bothered by a loose strand of hair would have no tolerance for a woman answering the door with a towel on her head.

"Besides, he probably thinks I'm plump," she muttered aloud to herself. Most likely Abram Fisher favored someone as slim as a wand—and someone who definitely would not come to the door with her hair wrapped in a wet towel. She found a comfortable position and started to pray, but long before her petitions and praises were finished, she fell fast asleep.

Chapter 5

"Say you've got a woman who gets a bit blue or cranky before her monthly time."

"Are you asking about me in particular?" Fern joked, but her grandmother frowned. Their Friday weekly herbal review sessions were not to be taken lightly, and Fern knew it. She straightened up in her seat at the kitchen table and answered properly.

"Evening primrose oil."

"Properties of garlic?"

"Anti-inflammatory in nature, increases anticlotting potential…though the FDA may debate the last."

Her *mammi* grunted. The two often disagreed about what the Food and Drug Administration did and did not know, with Fern favoring the testing and potential regulation of herbs as healing agents.

"Migraine…which you're giving me right now, impertinent child."

"Feverfew." Fern leaned across the table and peered into the beloved face of the older woman. "Do you really have a headache, *Mammi?*"

"*Nee*, now sit back. Upset *bauch?*"

"Green tea."

"Abram Fisher?"

Fern opened her mouth, then closed it again.

Her *mammi* gave her a mischievous smile. "That was for your FDA remark."

Fern had to laugh out loud. "Very nice. But tell me, what would you prescribe for one Abram Fisher?"

"Hmm…as an ailment or cure? Or both, as the case may be."

Fern rose and came around the table to give her grandmother a hug. "You are impossible, but dear. So what do you want us to take to Our Daily Bread tomorrow?"

Our Daily Bread was a local Amish store that housed a women's prayer group on the second floor every Saturday afternoon. Both of the Zook women were faithful attendees and often brought refreshments for afterward.

"Gingerbread."

Fern raised a brow. Gingerbread was too quick and simple for her grandmother, who liked the challenge of outbaking Leah Mast, prayer meeting or not. *Nee…* the gingerbread was for the Fisher boys, Fern had no doubt. But she dutifully went to get the chipped yellow mixing bowl down from its shelf.

She'd just assembled ingredients when a brisk knock sounded on the screen door. Ignoring the sudden catch in her heart, she tried not to be too hasty in turning round as her grandmother called, *"Kumme* in."

"Danki." The voice was that of Abram Fisher.

Fern was making what she considered to be a graceful turn when the bowl somehow slipped and she practically had to drop to her knees to catch it from meeting a crashing end on the floor.

She got back up, feeling a blush mount in her cheeks.

"Are you all right?" he asked politely, and she had to look at him then.

He looked even more handsome today, in his burgundy shirt and black suspenders and softly curling hair. Then she remembered his hasty departure the night before and resolved not to make herself look silly in front of him.

"I'm fine. You've come to do the windows? Where are the children?"

"I turned them loose to weed in your kitchen garden. Even little Mary can tell a *gut* plant from a bad."

"Well, don't let us keep you, then." There. She sounded composed and dismissive.

"Fern Zook." Her grandmother spoke sternly. "At least offer the man a cup of coffee before he begins."

Abram held up a large hand. "*Nee, danki.* I'll get to work." He flashed them a smile, then headed back outside.

Her grandmother nodded. "A fine figure of a man, as I said before. He'd produce *gut*-looking *kinner.*"

"*Mammi!*" Fern was shocked, but her grandmother merely gave her a conspiratorial smile.

"*Ya*, indeed…*gut*-looking *kinner.*"

Abram had a good view of the Zooks' kitchen garden from where he perched on the ladder outside the second-floor window. He was pleased to see the kids working quietly, but he still felt wound up inside. Seeing Fern's rosy complexion in the light of day was more than charming, and he forced himself to scrub hurriedly with his rag.

He was surprised to note that the windows in the older house, casements and all, were in such good shape. As he thumbed the wet edge of a well-set pane, he noticed movement from the room inside. He bent his head to look closer and saw Fern pick up an apron off the bed, then leave the room. It must be her bedroom. He sloshed the rag in the bucket and let the soapsuds run their race down the glass before peering more intently inside. A simple room, but pretty, with a mason jar of roses on a bureau amid a tangle of *kapp* strings and feminine clutter...

"Having a *gut* time?"

He jumped and nearly lost his balance as he stared down to the ground where Fern stood, one hand shielding her eyes from the sun.

"Don't sneak up on a man like that."

"Even one who's peeking in my window?"

He shook his head. "I was but admiring the fine windows and—"

"Never mind the windows; they're not fine. I came outside to ask if you and the children would like some gingerbread."

Something in her voice made him shift his weight on the ladder, and he slowly came down to stand next to her. "Why aren't they fine?"

"What?" she asked, her pretty brow wrinkling.

He nodded upward with his chin. "The windows... Tell me why they're not fine."

He was alarmed to see her beautiful green eyes

suddenly well with tears before she whirled away. He caught her arm. "Wait, *was iss letz*? What did I say?"

"Nothing. It is an old hurt, best forgotten. Do you want the gingerbread?"

"Sure." *Sure...but you've got me curious, Fern Zook. And I don't like the feeling one bit...*

He loosed her arm and saw the damp imprint of his hand on her sleeve. "I've got you wet," he said roughly.

"It's no matter. Please...come inside. I'll get the *kinner.*"

He watched her go, then glanced back up at the shining window frames. He shook his head... *Definitely too curious.*

Chapter 6

"They ate it all," Grandmother Zook said, satisfaction lacing her tone.

"I should say so." Fern smiled from where she wiped plates at the sink. "I'll have to make a new batch for the prayer group tomorrow."

"Ya...and the windows look nice. I took a walk round while you and Abram were talking. He seemed real interested in those window frames."

Fern stifled a frown. It was true that Abram had not been content with her answer to his question about the windows earlier. She had put him off by concentrating on the children. And she was surprised that the subject of the silly windows had still pained her to embarrassed tears.

"Mammi...you know that we never talk about those foolish pieces of glass and that time in my life."

"Did you tell Abram?" the old woman asked, a gentle persistence playing about her lips.

"*Nee*...there's nothing to tell."

"Tell him sometime."

"*Mammi*...please."

"Suit yourself. I'm going to have a bit of a lie-down. Mind that you take that tincture of stinging nettles over to Tabitha Yoder if you're out walking today. She told me Sunday that her sinuses were really acting up."

Fern didn't care at the moment about the Widow Yoder's sinuses. "You're going to rest? Why? I know you're not feeling well, and I think we should see Dr. Knepp. I'll bring the buggy round."

Her grandmother smiled and held up a protesting hand. "Deborah Zook...you're forgetting one of the first lessons I taught you. Can you name it?"

Fern frowned. "Listen to the patient," she mumbled.

"Correct. I'm saying that I am fine, so what do you do?"

"Hound the patient until she admits her problem?" Fern put her arms around her grandmother, and they laughed together.

"Not quite what I've taught you, but I'll settle for that nap."

"Fine, but when I get back, if you're not feeling well... *Ach*, all right. Have a nice rest."

Fern watched the beloved bent figure as she left the room and then turned back to her baking with a heavy heart.

"Now I want you kids to be *gut* for Emma, you hear?" Abram called over his shoulder to the crowded wagon behind him. The dutiful chorus of *ya's* did little to soothe his mind or his conscience.

Although Joe had insisted that the *kinner* come over and help Emma with some cleaning to give Abram a breather, he still didn't feel quite right about ditching the kids so that he could go off in search of advice about women from his other *gut* friend, the Widow Tabitha Yoder. Yet he had to find some way to get his addled head straight again, especially after watching Fern laughingly take bites of the moist gingerbread, licking her lips with the small pink tip of her tongue and…

"Abram!" Matthew called. "We're here."

He hauled on the reins as he realized that he'd nearly passed Joe and Emma's small but neat home. Emma came outside on the front porch, and he forced a smile to his lips as he hopped down, trying not to look at the ponderous protrusion of her abdomen. Maybe having the kids help her wasn't such a *gut* idea after all, but she smiled in greeting, looking capable and happy as Mary scrambled from the wagon to run to her side.

"Got your hands full of blessings, Abram?" Emma asked in her soft, shy voice.

"*Ya*, and you too. Are you sure it's not too much with your two *kinner*? This passel can be more of a hindrance than a help at times."

Emma shook her head. "The midwife said it was good for me to be active. And if they can give a bit of a hand with some dusting and such, I'd be grateful. And you can go have a bit of spare time to breathe."

The screen door eased open behind Emma, and Little Joe toddled out to grab hold of his *mamm's* dress.

"Uh…he's gettin' big," Abram offered, still a bit uncomfortable with the size of Emma's belly.

"I know, and Rosemary is too. I think she favors Joe. She's down for a nap now. Anyway, come on, children. I'll give you each a job to do!"

Abram lifted John out of the wagon and caught a brief hold on Mark's shirt. "Behave." He bent to hiss in his *bruder's* ear, then ruffled his hair with affection.

The whole brood disappeared into the house, and Emma waved good-bye. Abram waved back, then climbed into the wagon, his jaw set with determination.

Fern stepped into the lush herb garden adjacent to the back kitchen door. She let her fingers trail with delight over the leaves and flowers: echinacea, licorice, milk thistle, valerian, and so many more that she knew by touch and smell. She prayed as she walked; as far back as she could remember, growing things in God's creation and the work she did in her grandmother's kitchen were as linked with praise as anything else she could imagine.

Dear Lord, she prayed, *how amazing it is that when You rose from the dead, Mary recognized You as the gardener of the place. Ach, how true it is that You like to garden our souls. You've called us Your " field," and I pray that You would continue to do a great work in the garden of my mammi's life. Give her strength; bless her health... And, Gott, please, for Abram Fisher, help him with this task of taking care of things. Maybe let him be more willing to accept help, and guide my thoughts in regard to this man. Amen.*

Chapter 7

Abram set the brake on the wagon and stared for a long minute at the large, pretty house. Ezekiel Yoder had left his young wife more than well-off, having married late in life after building up a fine leather tooling business.

His jaw tense, he decided that maybe he was a bit *narrisch* coming here in the first place. He let his mind rove back to the time he'd first been to this house, shortly after Ezekiel had died. He'd been asked to fix box sills on the downstairs windows so that Tabitha might grow pansies to brighten the front of the house. He'd actually been a little leery of her then, thinking she might want to be more than friends—like most of the women he'd encountered in his life. Instead, he'd discovered an intelligent friend, one who was willing to listen to him without chiding. They kept their friendship private, though; Abram did not want to set tongues wagging about him and Tabitha, who was more or less happy in her widowed state. He jumped down and approached the steps only to look up in surprise when the front door eased open with a cozy squeak.

"Abram Fisher! You've caught me cleaning and everything's a mess. But come in—what's wrong?"

He sighed. She knew him well.

He mounted the steps, then let her close the door behind him. He let her take his hat, and his gaze swept the beautifully carved furniture and the light-blue walls. It was a homey room, and against his will he thought of Fern. He'd love to give her a home like this... He nearly groaned aloud at his wayward thoughts and dropped onto a nearby couch. Tabitha joined him there.

She spoke with a laugh. "It must be bad if you can't even get it out."

He looked at her pretty, smiling face. "Women," he managed.

Her smile grew to one of delight. "Women? Or... woman?"

He rolled his eyes. "Okay...woman."

She clapped her hands. "Who?"

He put his face in his hands and mumbled, "Fern Zook."

"Fern? Why, she's *wunderbaar*! Beautiful eyes, kind, loving...she'd be a great mother."

He shook his head. "No, no, no."

"But why?"

He looked up, then stretched his legs out tensely. "I don't want any woman. I want to farm—to keep things simple."

"Well, *Gott* never meant for things to be simple—I should know."

He touched her hand. "You miss Ezekiel?"

"Always. And believe me—loving someone is worth the pain of losing them."

"I just don't know," he said. "Look, I don't want to bother you. I've got some errands to get done. I only wanted to talk for a minute."

"Well, my advice is to seek her out."

"We'll see." He rose and offered a hand to help her up. As they walked into the hall, they were both startled by a quiet knock at the door.

Fern stopped at the screen door. She couldn't help but recognize the shadowy figure of the man standing behind Tabitha Yoder. She clutched the bottle of stinging nettles, wishing wildly for a moment that she might shatter the glass. Instead, she turned and spun off the porch, intent on walking as far away as possible, even as she told herself that she had no right to think anything of what Abram Fisher did with his spare time. He'd never given her any indication that he was interested in her.

"Well, there goes *Gott's* intervention," Tabitha said with a smile. "You know what she's probably thinking... Go after her!"

He nodded, confused by the sudden apparition of all of his thoughts. "Right." Then he stepped out the door into the bright sunlight of day.

He could see Fern's straight back fading into the distance of the dirt road, and he couldn't help himself when he clambered onto the wagon seat with haste and tugged on the reins. He drew up beside her within moments and set the brake, hopping down to catch up with her.

"Fern... Fern, wait."

She kept going, swinging one arm and ignoring him completely.

"Fern!" Something whispered in his mind and he found himself hollering to her as she stirred up the dust on the dirt road with her furious steps. "Fern...tell me about the windows!"

She stopped and spun on her heel to stalk back to him. He swallowed as he admired her blazing green eyes.

"Who do you think you are, Abram Fisher? Who?"

And then he found himself praying that the answer to her question would come to him...

Chapter 8

The sun playing on the shades in his chestnut hair was momentarily diverting as he removed his hat to wring it between his strong hands. She stood close enough to smell him, to breathe in that mysterious male scent that was uniquely him. His dark-blue eyes were intent but hesitant, and she clutched the brown glass bottle in her hand a bit tighter.

He was beautiful, like some towering oak, but with enough vulnerability in his stance to make him approachable. And she wanted to approach him…to shake him, startle him, touch him. She couldn't believe he was bringing up the windows. She pursed her lips and almost turned to go when he spoke.

"I don't know who I am right now, Fern." His deep voice was threaded with tension. "I don't know what I want, what I'm doing, but I know that you…you matter…in this world."

She arched an eyebrow at him, trying to still the beating of her heart. "And?"

He reached out long, calloused fingers to touch her wrist, his thumb rubbing against her rapid pulse, making her hand feel small and delicate in his much larger one. "And…those windows. I made you cry…"

She pulled her hand away from the tempting pressure of his grasp. "And here you are at the Widow Yoder's… Did you make her cry too?"

He frowned. "Look, I was—paying a visit to a friend, all right?"

She took a deep breath and felt all of her anger drain away. She bowed her head. "Abram Fisher, I don't know what's come over me. It's all right for you to…visit… anyone you want. I have no right—"

He lifted her chin, and she felt unbidden tears drip from the corners of her eyes. She reached her tongue to lick at the salty fall and found him tracing the track of her tears with a gentle finger. Somehow she found her voice, feeling convicted suddenly to tell him the truth.

"The windows…" She smiled through her tears. "It's silly, really."

"Not if it pains you so," he said in a soft voice.

"*Ya*… I guess that's true." She sniffed. "Two years ago an *Englischer* came through selling roofing and windows and such."

He dropped his hand to her shoulder. "I remember. I think *Daed* sent him packing."

"Well, we didn't. *Mammi* thought it was a *gut* investment. So the *Englischer* stayed and did the work with some of his men. One of the workers, Henry, took a liking to me, I guess. I was out in the garden one evening, and he—well, he kissed me and… I thought he really cared for me. But I heard him laughing with the other workers the next day, telling them that he'd kissed the plump Amish girl and left her wanting more…" Her lip trembled. "It was my fault; I should not have let him kiss me. And I am pl-plump."

Abram slid his hand from her shoulder back to her hand, twining his fingers through hers. He took a step closer, and she could feel the press of his long legs against her skirt.

"Fern," he whispered hoarsely. "Do you know how beautiful you are? Enough of life is full of sharp edges and spare lines."

She forgot that they stood in the middle of a traveled road in broad daylight, and felt sheltered by his shadow. He said her name and she waited, melting inside, as he moved closer, the brush of his mouth as light as feather down…

"Abram!"

He broke away with a muttered word as Matthew burst from the field at the side of the road, gasping for breath.

"What is it?" Abram stepped away from her, and Fern wrapped her arms around her chest as she anxiously watched Matthew sink to his knees in front of his older brother.

"Matt…what's wrong?"

"Emma Mast… Her baby's comin'. And the midwife's not there."

"I'll go get my *mammi*," Fern said, moving toward the wagon.

"Ca-can't," the young boy gasped. "The baby—it's coming now, right on the kitchen floor. You'll have to come, Fern."

Fern felt Abram's gaze sweep over her. "Can you do it?" he asked urgently.

"*Ya...ya.* Let's go." She caught her breath and began to pray.

Chapter 9

Emma had somehow managed to corral all of the kids into one of the bedrooms.

"I—told them—to do coloring books," she panted as Fern sank down on the kitchen floor beside her. "Said—we'd have—a contest. I should have gotten into bed...but it all happened so fast this time." She moaned faintly, and Fern put her hand on the other woman's shoulder.

"Shh, Emma. Save your strength." She glanced up at Abram and Matthew.

"Matt, can you stay with the *kinner*? Tell them everything's all right. And take that plate of cookies with you and a pitcher of juice. You did a great job finding me." Fern smiled as she spoke.

Abram patted his *bruder's* shoulder as he passed, loaded down with the food and drink and a stack of paper cups.

"Maybe I should go look for Joe," Abram suggested. He wasn't squeamish, but he was embarrassed as could be for Emma's sake.

"You'll stay right here, Abram Fisher," Fern said. "I may need you… *We* may need you, right, Emma?"

Emma managed a tight smile. *"Ya…it's all right."*

Fern rose and went quickly to the sink to wash her hands; Abram followed, mixing his hands up with hers as they got at the water.

"Hold your hands with your fingers up," she instructed. "Let the water run down your elbows. And don't touch anything if you can help it."

He did as he was told, standing awkwardly nearby as Fern returned to Emma and gently raised her skirts.

"Ach, Emma, we got here right on time with the Lord's grace; I can see the head. Your *boppli* has dark hair." Fern's voice was full of happy encouragement. "Now, do you have any blankets or sheets ready for the babe?"

"Last—room on the left."

Abram was already on his way. He scooped up a pile of small bedding and hurried back, handing the items off to Fern and then going to the sink to rewash his hands before she could tell him to do it. He came back in time to see Emma's grimace of pain and a small head emerging; he looked at the plastered ceiling.

"Abram, come here, please," Fern said low. "The cord's around the baby's neck."

He moved forward and dropped to his knees beside Fern. Suddenly everything felt all right, normal even. He was helping his best friend's wife and child, and Fern was there…her competent hands guiding his to hold the infant's wet head while she carefully unwrapped the cord. Abram held his breath, and the slippery, tiny body was cradled in his hands. The little girl opened her mouth and let out a mewling cry that set him laughing with joy.

"It's a girl, Emma, and she seems fine." Fern took the baby from him to lay against Emma's abdomen, then went to work with some scissors and thread that she pulled from her apron pocket. "*Mammi* says to always be prepared," she murmured as she cut the cord.

Then she looked at Abram with her big green eyes, and he felt something strange turn over in his chest. She was so beautiful, so capable... How had he ever thought her pushy? He wanted to kiss her, right there on the Masts' kitchen floor. He had the deranged notion that if he did, a garden might spring up around them, filled with the scent of roses and heather...

"*Danki*, Abram. *Danki!*" Joe was shaking his shoulder, and he realized sheepishly that Fern had risen and moved away while he still knelt beside Emma.

He got to his feet and shook his friend's hand, then clasped him close in an emotional hug.

"I wanted a girl," Joe mumbled. "But it didn't matter, really—just so she's healthy."

"Well, let's make sure that Emma and the baby stay healthy by getting them into bed. I've still got a few more chores to do," Fern said.

Abram gently helped Joe carry his wife to the bedroom and listened to Fern's sweet-toned voice through the thin wall as she gave the news of the baby to the other children. His chest was tight with emotion as the *kinner* replied with a roar of approval, and he almost laughed aloud when he heard Fern shush them. She would make a wonderful mother.

* * *

"Matthew told me he left a note for the midwife; she should come soon to check you and the baby out," Fern said as she surveyed a very content Emma nursing her newborn.

"We don't know how to thank you and Abram for coming."

Fern smiled. "*Derr Herr* allowed this time, and you can tell your daughter that He willed that she be born in the kitchen, the heart of the home."

Emma smiled back. "So you were with Abram when Matthew found you?"

Fern flushed and concentrated on tucking the bedclothes more neatly about her patient's legs. "*Ya*…we were talking."

"Abram doesn't normally talk much—except to Joe. I think it's nice for you two."

"*Ach*, Emma, there is no 'us two.' I wouldn't want anyone to think—"

Emma grinned. "Do you think I'd say anything inappropriate about the woman who helped bring my daughter into this world?"

Fern looked into the other woman's eyes and knew that she had found an unexpected friend.

Abram watched the jubilant movements of his friend as he swung his young son up in the air and felt faintly envious. Joe and Emma's farm might be small, but it was a place of love and security. He wondered at himself that he had thought Joe trapped—perhaps it was he himself who was trapped, kept by his own fears from taking the risk to love.

"So let me get this straight. You went to Tabitha's to

visit and Fern saw you there?" Joe laughed out loud as
he set his toddler down.

"*Ya*...so now she thinks..."

Fern slipped out the back door of the Mast house to
hang the sheets she'd hand washed on the clothesline.
She couldn't help but hear Joe's laughter and smiled
at the sound. Then she heard the rumble of Abram's
deep voice and found herself listening without meaning to do so.

"Now she thinks that there's something... I care for
Tabitha a great deal..."

Fern stilled like a doe on a frozen pond. He was
talking about how he felt for Tabitha Yoder, and Joe
was laughing as if it were a joke—Fern seeing them
together. The barking of the family dog alerted her that
a buggy was coming, and she looked with tear-filled
eyes to see the midwife pull up. She blindly stuck the
last wooden clothespin on the line and slipped inside
the house, swiping at her eyes to say a quick good-bye
to Emma. She made the excuse that she had to get a
remedy to someone, then prayed that *Derr Herr* would
forgive her the lie. Then she quietly left the house by
way of the back door and cut across the small cornfield
to reach the familiar back road. She never wanted to
see Abram Fisher again.

Chapter 10

Abram finally managed to get all the kids loaded back in the wagon and set off for home, but he couldn't stop thinking of Fern and wondering why she had left so suddenly. His mind strayed to the amazing moment when his mouth had brushed hers, and he felt a thrill go through his chest. Then he heard a suppressed whimper and anxiously turned to look at his siblings behind him.

"What's wrong? Who was that?"

"It's John," Matthew informed him. "I think he has a bellyache. He had an awful lot of those cookies at the Masts' house."

Abram shook his head. So much for time to think on sweeter things.

"John? Are you all right? Do you want to come up here and sit with me?"

John wailed aloud then. "I think I'm gonna throw up. I want *Mamm*!"

There was a general scramble to get as far away from John as possible, and Abram felt the wagon shift. "Sit down where you're supposed to!" he ordered over his shoulder just as he heard the unmistakable sound of retching, followed by simultaneous cries of "Yuck!" He shook his head and pulled the wagon over to the side of the road. He couldn't let his *bruder* be sick alone.

Fern walked hard, trying to concentrate on putting one foot in front of the other. Finally she found a place in her spirit that was willing to pray.

Dearest Fater, help me not to be hurt by what a man does or says to me. Help me to focus on the job of healing that You have blessed me with and make me truly able to serve others before myself.

Then she reached into her apron pocket and felt the bottle that was meant to aid the Widow Yoder, and she knew what she had to do. She turned in the direction of the woman's home with determination, knowing that she was getting a chance to have her prayers answered sooner rather than later.

The afternoon had nearly waned to twilight as she marched up the steps to knock at the door.

Tabitha Yoder appeared in a moment, looking beautiful as ever, and Fern had to swallow to find her voice.

"I—I'm sorry I left so abruptly earlier; I've got your stinging nettles." She offered the bottle, hoping the other woman would not want to make conversation, but she was disappointed.

"*Sei se gut*, won't you come in, Fern?"

Fern decided that she could either live out what she prayed for or hide, and she was not one to hide, so she went in to have a glass of lemonade.

After a brief discussion of the other woman's sinus ailments, Fern rose to excuse herself when Tabitha caught her eye with a slight smile.

"So, did Abram catch you?"

Fern felt her face fill with color. She wished she could pretend that she didn't know what Tabitha was talking about. "He—he wanted to speak to me, *ya*."

"You're a lucky girl," the widow observed.

"I really must be going. Thank you for the lemonade, and I hope your sinuses get better." Fern started for the door, and her hostess followed.

"Fern, I meant what I just said. To have that man pursuing you is wonderful."

Fern could only nod, speechless, as she headed out into the evening air.

Abram had begun to wonder how many times a person could throw up when John could finally stand a few sips of water and curled up in bed. Abram got the rest of the *kinner* bedded down, then told Matthew he was headed to the creek for a quick bath. He grabbed a bar of his *mamm's* oatmeal-and-honey soap, a thick towel, and some clean clothes, and headed down the narrow path that led to the water. He hoped nothing disastrous would happen while he was gone, but he was half-prepared for the event nonetheless.

He hurriedly stripped off his soiled clothes and walked into the cold creek water, savoring the refreshing feel. A few lightning bugs were putting in an appearance as he soaped his chest and then his hair. Quickly he submerged, then sloshed out to dry ground to towel off and don clean clothes, glad that so far he had heard no screaming coming from the direction of the house. He was halfway there when he heard someone else coming up the path.

Several keen sensations assailed Fern at once—the firmness of a male chest, a spicy masculine scent, and an innate awareness that it was Abram Fisher whom she sought to steady herself against. She tried to draw back, but a firm arm curved around her back and she dropped her hands to push against him.

"Fern," he whispered.

She looked up into his shadowed, handsome face and almost melted against him. But then his remembered words burned through her like a hot brand, and she stamped a small foot in the area of his own bare feet.

"Ow!" He half laughed. "What's the matter? Tell me where you went today; I wanted to drive you home from Emma and Joe's."

"Let me go!" Her anger had increased at his casual words, and she pushed against him in earnest. She couldn't still the rapid play of her heart beneath her blouse—she told herself that it was fury, not passion.

"Fern, what's wrong?" he asked softly, tilting his head closer to her.

She shook her head to break the spell of his closeness. It didn't matter that his question sounded earnest. The man had said what he said; she had heard him—he had feelings for Tabitha Yoder. He was simply having a joke at Fern's expense. "Exactly how many women did you go about kissing today, Abram Fisher?"

There. That stilled him, though she thought for one wild minute that she could feel his heartbeat echo in time with her own, some thrumming tattoo dancing in her brain, heating her skin.

"I only kissed you, Fern," he said finally, almost confusedly. "Though I hardly would call what we had time to share a true *buss*. Can we try again?"

She squirmed against him. "*Nee*."

He let her go, so abruptly that she almost fell. "I don't understand."

"You do," she snapped, not wanting to hear any more of his honeyed words. She needed to get home.

"Fern…today, the baby, us together… I thought… What's wrong? What happened?"

"Why don't you ask the next girl you feel you want to kiss, Abram Fisher, because I will not be speaking to you again."

She spun on her heel, nearly tripping over an exposed root, then hurried along the path, knowing he stared after her.

Chapter 11

Abram did something that night that he hadn't done since he was a child; he slid out of bed and dropped to his knees on the hardwood floor to pray. Though he knew he could talk with *Derr Herr* anywhere, the position seemed to matter. Tonight he needed guidance beyond the ordinary. He had no explanation for Fern's behavior, unless she had seen him offer a friendly hand to Tabitha and in truth believed that the other woman was someone he was in love with. And yet, what right did he have to question what Fern did or didn't do? He realized that he wanted that privilege, but had no idea how to go about it.

Fater Gott, I surely have changed over the last few days. Yet You are one who never changes. Help me to manage these new feelings for Fern. Bless her and her life. Help me to get along all right with the kinner and the farm until the folks get home. Give me the right words of comfort and kindness to say to everyone, but especially to Fern. Let me serve her one day, Fater, as I seek to serve You. Amen.

He rose from his knees, feeling a peace inside, along with a resolute decision to go tomorrow and ask Fern what she was feeling. He had just put his head to his pillow and drew the light cover over his bare shoulder when the night was cut by an ear-piercing scream.

Abram's eyes flew open and he jumped from bed, knocking his knee against the bedside table. He hobbled out of his room in the direction of the screams, knowing it was one of the boys who cried. He burst into Mark and Luke's room, prepared for anything from a hippopotamus to a bed fire.

Luke sat in the middle of his bed howling like a banshee, while Mark danced around making vain efforts to hush his brother.

"What is going on?" Abram struggled not to raise his voice.

"My mole!" Luke wailed. "I had him under the bed in a cardboard box. But Mark took him out and now he's gone. His name's Moldy. What are we going to do?"

Abram sagged against the door frame. "A mole? Do you know how big a fit *Mamm* would have if she knew you were keeping one of those pests in the house? Why, she'd—"

A scream from across the hall made Abram nearly jump. He rushed to Mary's room and flung open the door. The little girl stood in the middle of the bed, looking petrified.

"Abram," she cried. "There's a mole under my bed!"

"Of course there is," he muttered, then bent to look for the errant pet.

* * *

Fern knew that her grandmother wondered at her quiet behavior during their warmed-up supper, but for once the older woman didn't seem to question overly much. So Fern washed up their few dishes, then cast about for something to do that would not involve thinking of Abram Fisher.

Her grandmother called from her bedroom, and Fern hurried to the cozy, first-floor room with its nine-patch quilt and carved wooden furniture. A single kerosene lamp burned on the bedside table, illuminating the well-worn Bible open on the bedside table. Her grandmother had slipped into her nightgown and was sitting up in bed, her long, gray braid undone.

"I remember how you used to come in here every night for prayers and a story when you were a little girl."

Fern smiled as she sat down in the rocking chair next to the bed. "I did, didn't I? You made me feel so loved. You always have."

"But," her grandmother said, eyeing her shrewdly across the top of her reading glasses, "it is a man who makes a woman feel loved the best at times. Your grandfather did that for me."

Fern nodded, wanting to avoid treacherous ground in the conversation. But her grandmother wanted to talk.

"The licorice plants are coming in thick this year," she said.

Fern smiled. "I know. I used to love to taste the leaves."

"*Ya*, we've had many a *gut* taste from our herb garden, eh? But there are some things in life that we must taste that cannot be grown but by the Master Gardener."

"Like what?" Fern asked softly, pleased and comforted by her grandmother's insightful mood.

"Ach, a taste of faith, for example."

"What would that be?"

The old woman smiled, the light catching on the faded blue of her eyes. "A taste of faith is a taste of love. It's one step nearer to the Master, to understanding His heart, His desire and plan for our days."

"You make it sound so beautifully simple." Fern thought of her tangled emotions about Abram and longed for the peace she heard in the dear voice. Perhaps such wisdom was meant only for the old, the truly wise of heart.

"Fern, is there something that troubles you, child?"

Fern thought. She didn't want to break the moment with burdens of her own, so she shook her head, then rose. She went to the bed and laid her cheek close to her grandmother's while the old woman wrapped her with arms of love and comfort. It was more than enough to bring balm to Fern's troubled soul, and she slipped from the bedroom with a tender smile on her lips.

Abram surveyed the tired faces of his younger siblings as they sat down to breakfast on Saturday morning. He was tired too, having spent half the night looking for the mole, which had probably made its way back outside where it belonged. But he was determined to get the kitchen into some kind of order before approaching Fern. He knew his *mamm* would be disappointed to see the messy state of things, and he planned to make sure that everyone worked together to get things in running order.

He glanced down at a short list he'd made before breakfast. "Mark…dishes."

"Awww… Abram, why can't I—"

"Not another word. Matthew, you put the dishes away once they're dried, and water the plants on the window-sills if you think you can revive them."

Matthew nodded readily.

"John and Mary, the floor. Get everything off of it and put it where it goes, including crumbs. You can use the small broom and dustpan."

The children nodded, and he began to relax.

"And, Luke…" He glanced at his *bruder,* whose bottom lip still trembled over the loss of his mole. "You'll help me scrub the floor and countertops and table. We, uh, might find a trace of that mole."

Luke's face brightened considerably.

"All right. Let's work, and then we'll take a little walk." Abram rose with a clap of his hands.

"Where will we go?" Mark asked.

"Never mind…"

"I bet I know."

"Dishes," Abram said. "Now."

Chapter 12

Saturdays were always busy at the Zook house, because everything needed to be done by one thirty so that Fern and her grandmother could get to Our Daily Bread in time for their weekly hour of prayer. This Saturday was no exception, with two callers needing medicinal help. The first was Esther King with her nine-month-old daughter, Abby. Fern glanced at her grandmother before she even opened the door to the telltale wailing of the child.

"Teething," she murmured.

Esther was a first-time mother and a bit nervous; Fern sought to reassure her once she'd taken a peek inside the baby's mouth and saw the reddened gums.

"She's teething, Esther. A bit frustrating for you, I know, but there are several things we can do to help. First"—Fern accepted a bottle of diluted oil of cloves from her grandmother—"this will act as a numbing agent. Second, and perhaps even better…celery."

"Celery?" Esther repeated blankly.

Fern went to the deep freezer and pulled out a plastic bag full of large pieces of celery. She opened it and brought a chunk of the frozen vegetable to Abby. She put it in the baby's mouth and rubbed it gently against the sore gums. Almost like magic, Abby stopped her crying.

"A frozen carrot will do too, but some think there's actually an enzyme in the celery that helps the gums."

The women basked in the sound of silence as Abby gnawed cheerfully on the celery.

"Just make sure it's a big enough piece that she can't get it all in her mouth and choke," Fern said.

"Ach, it's such a relief to see her not in pain." Esther smiled, then shyly offered a plastic bag to Fern. "Crocheted washcloths. I thought you could use a few extra."

Fern looked in the bag at the deep, pretty colors and gave an exclamation of delight. *"Danki*, Esther. They're beautiful."

Fern saw mother and daughter out and returned to wrapping the gingerbread for the prayer time when someone knocked heavily on the door. For a heart-stopping moment she thought it might be Abram, but then she pushed the thought aside. She opened the door with a firm look, only to gasp in horror at the sight of James "Lanky" Miller bleeding all over her doorstep. He was holding a can, and when she realized the blood was coming from his big hand, Fern had a numbing premonition of what might be inside.

"Cut my finger off, girlie. It's right here." He thrust

the can toward her and she took it automatically, smelling the kerosene he must have used to soak the finger in.

"Uh, Lanky, you've got to get to Dr. Knepp. We can't—"

"Doc's not home; his missus neither. It's you or nuthin'."

Fern swallowed and glanced down at the swimming finger. *"Nee*, it's the hospital for you, but I'll try to stop the bleeding as much as I can."

"Hate hospitals, all them white walls...though I got my *buwe* in the buggy. Suppose he could drive me."

"Fern, don't try to stop the bleeding," *Mammi* Zook called. "Time matters if they'll try to get it reattached."

"Right," Fern agreed, extending the can back to Lanky with haste. "The hospital's only a fifteen-minute buggy ride away. Keep tight pressure on it...the site of the wound, I mean."

The man tipped his hat and turned, sloshing kerosene out onto the porch as he went. Fern closed the door, wishing she could have been more help. She leaned back against the door and muttered a quick prayer for Lanky and his finger.

Abram considered that things were going relatively well. The children, for once, were quietly engaged in their kitchen work, and he was on his hands and knees finishing scrubbing the hardwood floor with pine oil soap. He was working out in his head what he'd say to Fern and how exactly he'd accomplish it with a wagon full of kids and her grandmother present. But he was determined.

Mary was picking up crayons around the corner, and Abram had just about reached her with his scrub brush when he caught sight of a small black creature peering at him from between the little girl's shoes. He closed his eyes for a second, telling himself he was imagining the appearance of Moldy, when Mary saw the apparition too. She screamed and teetered backward, sending the mole running and upsetting the scrub bucket.

He rose with Mary in his arms. "Luke, we've sighted your mole."

"Let's mousetrap him," Mark said with gusto.

Luke started to wail, which tipped John off as well. "No traps! You'll hurt him," Luke cried.

Abram gave Mark a quelling glance as he rocked Mary to and fro. "*Nee*, no mousetraps. But maybe a safe trap." He could barely hear his own voice over the noise of the two boys, and his head began to throb—definitely not a *gut* way to begin the process of dating.

"I'm not going to go today, Fern."

"What?" Fern looked up from packing her Bible in a hand-sewn bag.

Mammi Zook relaxed back into a bentwood rocker in the sitting room adjacent to the kitchen. "I said I'm not going. Think I'll have a bit of a nap instead. You'd best hurry on; you'll be late."

Fern went to her grandmother's side and placed a hand on the old woman's forehead. "Are you ill?"

"*Nee*, Fern. Run along with you."

Fern bent to kiss the wrinkled, rose petal-soft cheek. "All right. I won't be long. You rest."

Chapter 13

Our Daily Bread had been an Amish store since the 1950s. Owned and operated by the Lapp family, it was untouched by the tourist trade, being a discreet distance from any main road. The Amish in Paradise liked to joke that it was their Walmart, selling everything from farmware to household goods and fabric. Ann Lapp had continued the tradition set by her husband's grandmother, that on Saturdays at two o'clock local women would gather in the store's upstairs storage room to meet for a time of fellowship and prayer. It was a peaceful highlight of Fern's week and provided a chance to catch up with women she might not otherwise see.

She entered the store to the good-natured greetings of various men, who liked to gather downstairs for their own time of talk, and made her way through the good-smelling place to the back stairs. She could hear the drift of feminine voices as she climbed and soon arrived at the upper room. Hiram Lapp always made sure that there were folding wooden chairs set up in a circle and plenty of tables for food.

Fern unwrapped her gingerbread and smiled as Eve Bender and Hannah King came over to greet her. Both women were good friends; Eve was a bit older than Hannah and Fern, but her beautiful face belied her age.

"Mmm, gingerbread from Esther Zook's recipe." Hannah laughed. "I can't wait."

"Where is your *mammi*?" Eve asked.

Fern pushed away the worry she felt at the question. "*Ach*, she decided to stay home and have a bit of a rest."

"Is she well?" Hannah put a concerned hand on Fern's arm.

"She says so, but I don't know. I'm trying to convince her to go see Dr. Knepp sometime soon. So, what did you ladies bring?"

Fern was soon absorbed in the general time of talk and catching up before Ann Lapp called for everyone's attention and they all sat down to share prayer requests and concerns as well as items for praise. Fern was wishing that she could somehow share how she felt about Abram Fisher, but the thought made her embarrassed. She decided to continue to pray about the man alone.

After a hurried, hushed conversation with Hiram Lapp, Abram made his way as fast as he could through Our Daily Bread. He climbed the stairs and sought through the circle of bowed, *kapped* heads for Fern. Thankfully she was sitting nearby, in front of a flour barrel, and he sidled up to it to tap her gently on the shoulder.

"Fern," he whispered. "Please come with me."

She opened her eyes wide with surprise, then made to shoo him away, but he caught her hand in a tender grip. "Now, please."

She rose, and he heard the telltale rustle of listeners as she went with him, but he didn't have time to worry about it. He led her downstairs and through a surprisingly silent store, then out to the wagon full of quiet *kinner*.

"Abram Fisher, what is going on?" She glared up at him in the sunlight, and he bowed his head, dropping her hand.

"Fern, I went to your home a bit ago. Your grandmother… I thought she was sleeping, but she'd passed away. I'm sorry."

He watched disbelief become replaced with a calm practicality on Fern's pretty face. "We've got to go for Dr. Knepp," she said, her voice quiet and detached.

"Fern, I stopped there on my way. He's gone for the day. Anyway… I'm sure. She wasn't breathing."

"Take me to her, *sei se gut*."

Fern entered her home quietly while Abram and the children waited outside in the wagon. She tiptoed across the floor to where her grandmother sat in the rocker, her eyes closed and a peaceful expression on her face. Fern automatically did the things that she knew should be done—checking for a pulse and respirations, looking at the arms for signs of mottling. Finally she dropped to her knees beside the chair to lay her head gently in the dear lap, knowing she was truly gone.

She sat for a long moment, blaming herself for not taking her grandmother to the doctor sooner. And yet she remembered the rose tea, the secret of the rose tea…

Could her grandmother have known even then that this time was close?

A soft knock sounded on the door, and she looked up. She could see the stocky, balding figure of Bishop Smucker through the screen door.

"May I *kumme* in, child?"

Fern rose and swiped at her cheeks with the backs of her hands. News of a death spread fast in the community; someone from the store must have told the steadfast leader.

She opened the door to the kind, elderly man and he entered, placing a bracing hand on her shoulder as he glanced at her grandmother.

"As the Lord wills, Fern. *Ya?*"

Fern nodded, knowing it to be true.

"I sent young Abram home with his bunch of *kinner*, and I stopped at the phone shed to notify Dean Westler. He'll be here later this afternoon, once the women have come and helped tend to things."

Fern looked away. Dean was an *Englischer* and the only *ausleger* the Amish of her community had used for longer than she could remember. He was familiar with the Amish customs and was a quiet, gentle man. Fern had seen him attend to many a preparation; she just hadn't expected to need his services so soon, despite her grandmother's age.

Soon Esther Zook's closest women friends began to arrive. Eve Bender caught Fern close in a tearful hug, and Fern was relieved at the strength of her friend's shoulder.

"Everything will be all right," Eve whispered.

Fern smiled through her tears, then turned away as a group of women carried her grandmother into the bedroom, where Fern knew they would bathe the body and dress it in white before the undertaker arrived. The body would then be embalmed for two viewings, the funeral service and then the final viewing at the burial. It seemed like an arduous amount of emotional strain to climb through, but Fern remembered the gentle conversation she'd had with her grandmother the previous night and felt some comfort.

She accepted a cup of herbal tea from Hannah King and took a place in the rocker where her grandmother had sat. It was her job now to greet and mourn with others of the community, who came bearing words of comfort and good food.

Hannah pulled a kitchen chair close to Fern and spoke softly. "They said it was Abram Fisher who came and got you—I didn't see."

Fern dipped her head from her friend's gaze. She knew Hannah wasn't being nosy; the two had often discussed their similar desires for husbands to appear in Paradise.

"Ya. It was Abram, but I think the bishop sent him home."

"Too bad. He would be *gut* comfort, I bet."

"Ach, Hannah, I don't know. We—we had been… talking. But then…"

The other girl reached to pat her hand. "No explanations needed. Just don't shut him out if you can help it. Remember, some of your plants must surely be more stubborn to grow than others."

Fern couldn't help but smile despite her sadness.

Abram rubbed the back of his neck. He was worn out with explaining to the kids about Esther Zook's death. Mary was afraid that *Mamm* and *Daed* might die in Ohio, and she got John worrying too. Even Mark seemed pensive, while Luke occupied himself with a last look under the beds for Moldy. When everyone but Matthew was finally asleep, Abram went into the boy's room and sat down on the edge of his bed.

"What are you reading?" Abram asked.

"An *Englisch* book—I know *Mamm* might have a fit. But it's Mary Shelley's *Frankenstein*."

Abram smiled. "A monster tale, then?"

"Ya, but it's more than that. It makes you think about things—like what happened to Esther Zook today. I mean, I know that it will happen to all of us sooner or later; I just don't think I'm ready."

Abram cuffed him lightly on the shoulder. "You don't have to be ready tonight. I guess that when that time comes, *Gott* prepares the person somehow. I mean, some sort of clue maybe, so that the person can maybe help others around them get ready so they won't hurt as badly."

"Are you going to see her?" Matthew pushed his glasses up on his nose and stared at his big brother.

Abram had to laugh. *"Ya,* if you'll keep a watchful ear for any mole problems or the like."

"I will," the boy promised solemnly.

"Danki, Matthew. Enjoy your book."

Chapter 14

Fern looked out of the window at the sound of some-one turning into the drive. She thought it might have been the undertaker's hearse returning the body, but it was an Amish buggy that drew rein in the light of the lanterns burning on the front porch. Although tradition normally would not have left Fern alone in the empty house, she had insisted, knowing that she wouldn't be alone for long. Her grandmother's sister, Rose, had sent word that she would be coming to take up the reins of the household until after the funeral.

Fern went out onto the porch and watched the wom-an's progress from the buggy with a grim beating of her heart. Rose was the antithesis of her name, and was probably ninety if she was a day.

"Fern Zook. So Esther's gained her rest, hmm? Tell Billy he can go on back home." *Aenti* Rose gestured with her gnarled cane to the morose-looking young man driving the buggy.

Fern felt a rush of sympathy for Cousin Billy. "Wouldn't a cup of tea be nice—"

"Nee." *Aenti* Rose mounted the steps and tilted her gray head, staring up at Fern with eyes as dark as agate.

Fern watched Billy turn the buggy with a feeling of despair, then reminded herself that it would only be for a few days. "Won't you come in?"

"You're here alone? Take my bag, for goodness' sake."

Fern took the heavy black bag and followed Rose into the house as the woman made a disdainful perusal of the cozy home.

"Hmm… Esther and her herbs. I suppose she taught you everything she knew?"

"I can only hope so," Fern said demurely, leading her *aenti* to the large bedroom. She was loath to see her grandmother's sanctuary marred by the attitude of her older sister, but *Mammi* had no use nor need for earthly comforts now.

"Considering the hour, I will retire now. I expect breakfast to be served at five o'clock. I am too old to bother with cookery. I like a coddled egg."

You are a coddled egg. Fern bit her lip at the irreverent thought and nodded.

"And gracious, let Alexander out of the bag!"

Fern looked down at the bag she held and realized with something of a shock that it was moving. She cautiously opened the top and a black streak of cat leapt up at her face, then dived to the floor to encircle *Aenti* Rose's skirt with a loud purr.

"Mmm…isn't he a pretty one?" Rose crooned. "Now, back to breakfast. I also will take—"

She was interrupted by a soft knock at the front screen door.

Fern crossed the room, knowing it was a bit late for callers, but grateful for any diversion from her disagreeable relative and her cat. She pushed open the door and saw Abram Fisher, his hat in his hands.

"Fern… I'm sorry for the lateness of the hour. The kids took awhile to get to bed."

"Exactly who are you?" *Aenti* Rose questioned.

Fern had forgotten everything, even her anger toward the man, when she looked up into his anxious and beautiful face. Now she spun round to her aunt with a frown.

"*Aenti* Rose, you must know the Fishers next door. This is their eldest son, Abram."

The old woman sniffed. "I meant, who is he to you?"

Fern drew a calming breath. "He found *Mammi* and came to tell me, and brought me home. I am…most grateful."

"Well then, don't leave him to catch a summer chill. Come in, Abram Fisher. You must meet my cat."

Abram didn't move from his seat at the kitchen table when the cat slowly climbed from his lap to balance on his shoulder.

Aenti Rose gave a delighted, slightly toothless smile, which made the wrinkles in her face look like deep ravines. "*Ach*, smart *buwe* to recognize a fine place to perch. Nothing like the broadness of a man's shoulder, eh, Fern?"

Abram didn't look at Fern, knowing the older relative for what she was. Everyone had an *Aenti* Rose in their family, it seemed to him. He'd had an *Aenti* Josephine who had made him want to crawl under the table at times with her odd remarks. As for the cat...the thing probably smelled the mole. He cleared his throat.

"Is there anything that I can do for you, that you might need?" He was pleased to see a flush color Fern's pretty cheeks. She might be grieving, but she still felt alive, and he thought that took a lot of internal strength.

"We're fine," *Aenti* Rose asserted. "At least I am. This girl will probably moon about for a few days, but the Lord's will is not to be fretted over."

Abram twitched his shoulder and sent the cat spluttering onto the table into *Aenti* Rose's teacup, sloshing tea over the old woman in the process.

"*Ach*, Alexander. You naughty sweet. Now I must change. I will rejoin you shortly, Abram Fisher."

She hobbled from the table with her cat following and closed the door to the bedroom behind her.

Fern looked at him. "You did that on purpose," she whispered.

He shrugged. "A broad muscle twitch, that was all."

She looked down at her tea, and Abram reached a hand outward on the table, palm up.

"Fern, I am so sorry about your *mammi*. I know how dearly you loved her...at least, I think I do. I'm sorry now for the time I've missed not really seeing you... just tending to the land. I was afraid of what a woman in my life might mean."

He watched her pale lashes flutter, then lift. "A... woman in your life? Am I...that?"

"*Ya*," he said hoarsely.

"But I overheard you talking at the Masts' house."

"So that was it—Tabitha Yoder?"

"Yes, you said that you cared for her…and I saw you two together."

"Fern, no one really knows, but Tabitha is a *gut* friend of mine…nothing more. I guess I've told Joe about her, but that's all. She's only a friend." He looked into Fern's eyes and saw a wash of joy come over the green pools.

"A…friend?"

"Ya, I promise." He was struggling for something else to say when she reached a tentative finger to the contours of his palm. His heart started to beat harder as he watched her slow exploration.

She traced the long fingers slowly, up and then down, and the calluses on the lean hand from years of work; then she pushed up the cuff of his sleeve a bit and found his pulse beating amid the thick veins on the underside of his wrist.

"Fern…" Her name sounded like a plea from his lips, and she looked up to find his face flushed, his eyes gleaming a sleepy, heated blue.

"What do you want from me, Abram Fisher?"

"I want… I want…"

The bedroom door opened with a heralding creak, and Abram slid his palm away while Fern put her hand in her lap, feeling as though her fingertips burned where she'd touched him. Her grandmother would have been so pleased…

Aenti Rose approached the table. "Now, let's talk some more to this fine young man."

Chapter 15

Fern lay in her bed. The events of the day swirled around in her mind like yellow paint dropped in white. She could not believe that her grandmother was gone, yet she knew in her heart that there had been some subtle spiritual preparation for the event, and she could be grateful to *Derr Herr* for that. *Mammi* herself seemed to have had some inclination of her impending trip to heaven, as she'd celebrated with the rose tea.

Then Fern thought of touching Abram's hand—it still gave her delicious chills, and she thought how strange it was that such a new pleasure in life should come on a day of death. Yet that was the way of things; she knew this especially to be true of the land, her garden.

She thumped her pillow and rolled over, thinking of all that she did not know...her grandmother's remedies, even those that were written down in a large book with a careful hand. There was more to healing than simply words on paper, and it was that guidance and tutelage that she would miss. She sighed into her pillow. Certainly there was no mentoring woman to be found in *Aenti* Rose…yet Fern could pray for others, and she fell asleep on the wings of those prayers.

Fern awoke to the muffled sound of the cock crowing and grabbed her wind-up alarm clock. Nearly six thirty! She could only hope that *Aenti* Rose was fatigued by her journey and had slept past her normal waking hour. Fern dressed hurriedly, careful to wear all black in observation of mourning for her grandmother, did her hair, added her *kapp,* and flew down the stairs.

Aenti Rose was nowhere to be seen, but the table was well set with many of the things to eat that had arrived at various points the day before—sticky buns, fruit salad, warmed-up sausage-and-bacon breakfast casserole, as well as fresh scrambled eggs and fried potatoes and boiled eggs.

Fern glanced toward the closed door of her grandmother's bedroom, then jumped when the front screen door banged open. *Aenti* Rose hobbled in briskly on her cane with Alexander in close attendance.

"Well, I can see that I'll be doing my own work around here. Esther may have trained you to be lax, but I'm not of a similar mind. My land, girl, the cat and I have already been out for a morning walk!"

"I'm sorry," Fern apologized sincerely. "I suppose I was overly tired from yesterday."

Her aunt waved her silent. "I hear a car coming. Must be the undertaker. Good thing I saw some buggies up the way. We'll need the men to carry the body in." She turned back to open the screen door, and Fern saw two buggies pull up behind the hearse.

Fern fastened her apron more snugly about her waist and realized that she hadn't much to do. It was the *gut* way of Amish deaths that the community arose as a whole to offer care and support. Two men would dig the grave by hand this morning for the afternoon burial. Someone else would go to the cabinetmaker and pick out the simple pine coffin with its two openings on top—one to cover the lower two-thirds of the body and the other to open on hinges so that the face of the dear one might be viewed. The bishop would manage the funeral service at the house that afternoon. No, there was little for her to do. Even the expense of the death was taken care of by the community.

She moved through the day as if it were some distant dream. At the funeral she listened to the words of Bishop Smucker as he extolled the righteousness of the Almighty. Fern had read that it was the *Englisch* way to eulogize the life of the deceased, but the Amish focused on the praise of *Derr Herr,* with only occasional mention of the one gone from their midst.

And then, in the beautiful summer afternoon, she was at the grave site and found herself longing to see Abram in the gathered crowd.

"Stand still," Abram ordered for the third time as John squirmed under the wet comb.

"You don't do it like *Mamm,*" the little boy complained.

Abram shook his head. He had no idea how his mother, in fact, got the whole bunch ready for church meeting, let alone for a burial service. And they were going to be late if Luke and Mark didn't show up soon. They'd had to miss the actual preaching because Abram had spent a full hour tramping the fields trying to find his brothers and had then decided that they'd come home eventually, though he was haunted by images of broken arms and legs.

Mary sat stiffly in her black and dark blue, the only two colors acceptable to wear for a burial, except for the light straw of the men's summer hats. Matthew had braided her hair and pinned it under her black bonnet after getting himself ready. Abram shot his brother a look of appreciation as the boy swiped at a spot on one of his shoes.

"Matt, go have one more holler around for those two. We have to leave. I'll get my hat."

Abram arrived with the three children in time to join the end of the line filing past the coffin with its open-hinged top half. This was the last chance to view Esther Zook before the actual burial, and he caught a firm hold on Mary's little hand. It was not the Amish way to shield children from the death and burial process, but he hoped that his baby sister wouldn't burst out crying. There was still no sign of Mark and Luke, and he could only dream that they weren't stuck in some mess of Mark's creation.

They reached the coffin, and Abram gazed down into the sweet, serene old face. The undertaker used no cosmetics, nor was there a need to with the aged beauty of one like Esther Zook. There was dignity about death, Abram considered as he slowly filed past the coffin; a somber mystery and majesty that was a keen reminder of the all-powerful hand of God.

He crossed with Mary, John, and Matt to the other side of the open grave and looked up to find Fern smiling at him. He smiled back, longing to murmur something comforting to her, but only silence was appropriate. So he tried to speak with his eyes instead— encouragement for her heart and praise for her beauty, the gentle curves of her pale skin against the black of her bonnet, and the luminous glowing of her green eyes... And then he heard it.

From the other side of the white-picket-fenced enclosure of tombstones came the tumultuous whoop and holler of children. "Whoop! Whoop! Whoopppeeeee! *Hiya!*"

Abram looked up and thought he might be losing his mind at the strange apparition headed for the graveyard. A giant sow with a rope around her neck galloped full-tilt toward the fence. Two boys were on her great back, screaming and holding on for dear life. Abram's heart sank to his shoes. He'd found Luke and Mark.

When the sow crashed through the fence, there was no use pretending that it wasn't happening. Everyone at the graveside had turned to watch in silent fascination as the pig made straight for them, gamboling over tombstones and kicking grass clods up in the air. At the last possible second the sow veered off from the group, but not before everyone had a chance to identify the two riders... Mark had a grin on his face and Luke held on, deathly pale. To add to the mayhem, *Aenti* Rose's cat, which had apparently followed his owner to the burial, screeched and took off like a black streak after the pig. Alexander leapt straight into the air and landed square on the sow's long rear end, sending it flying over another tombstone and then squalling as it flattened the other side of the fence and cut across a field, leaving the group at the graveside in stunned silence.

It had all happened in seconds, but to Abram the scene had played out in sickening slow motion. He willed himself to look up and face his community. At first he couldn't believe it when he heard it, but Fern started to laugh, light and free like crystal tinkling. The *Englisch* undertaker coughed, then joined in, and then the bishop slapped his thigh and burst out in a loud guffaw. Everyone laughed then, and Abram found himself being patted on the back in commiseration. Somehow the flying fleet-footed pig had turned the gathering into a joyous one.

Abram's heart was full when Fern passed him afterward and leaned close to whisper, *"Mammi* would have loved to see that."

Chapter 16

Aenti Rose was still in attendance a week after the burial, and Fern began to fear that the woman might stay permanently, especially after she remarked that she enjoyed the bishop's preaching at the church service the day before.

Fern sought refuge in her garden. She wished at times that she might make it larger, but its space was enough now that she could hardly manage it alone. She was cutting back echinacea and wondering when she'd get to see Abram again when her aunt came out into the garden.

"Deborah, I've got a proposition for you."

Fern discreetly shooed Alexander away from a yellow butterfly and turned to her aunt.

"It's obvious," the old lady continued, "that you cannot live in this house alone and carry out your...work, as you call it. I would like to invite you to return to the mountains with me instead. There are many marital prospects there, although some are a bit older and have children already. You will make a fine wife, I believe, with proper instruction. And while it would be nice to think that you'd have a chance with men hereabouts, even young Abram Fisher, you must acknowledge that your looks are somewhat of a detriment."

The old woman paused for breath, and Fern eyed her with a raised brow. "My looks…are a detriment?"

"Well," Rose blustered, "when I was your age, I was as slender as a willow."

"And had twice its bark," Fern muttered.

"What was that?"

"Nothing. *Aenti* Rose, while I appreciate your offer, I must refuse. And further, I'd like you to consider how… how I actually might be attractive to a man."

"With an emphasis on *might*, my dear."

Fern twirled a stem of echinacea thoughtfully. "Perhaps, but perhaps not."

"Well, suit yourself. In any case, I'm phoning for Billy to come and pick me up today."

"*Danki, Aenti.* For all that you have done. I've appreciated it," Fern said humbly.

The old lady nodded and turned, and Fern gave a final shoo to the stubborn cat.

Abram inhaled deeply as he walked through the cornfield with Joe. The *kinner* were back at the Mast house admiring the new baby, whom they'd named Deborah in honor of Fern. Abram regretted that the avalanche of chores he'd been trying to keep up with had kept him away from her. He chuckled to himself when he thought of Mark's face after the pig incident at the burial. The boy had clearly expected to go over his brother's knee but had received laughter instead.

"What's funny?" Joe asked.

"Mark…"

"You were just like him when you were his age, you know?"

"I was not."

"Ya, and I should know, because I was your help-less accomplice."

They both laughed, then Abram cleared his throat. "Joe, I've been thinking lately…"

"About?"

"Fern."

"Ach, well."

"She's sort of behind my eyelids when I go to sleep…"

"And when you wake up?"

"Yeah."

"So marry her."

"See, that's it. It sounds so easy when you say it, but I don't even know if she'd be willing to date me. And now, with her grandmother gone, she doesn't really have anyone to talk to about this stuff."

"Women talk to other women. Is that really what's wrong?"

"Nee…you know me too well. The trouble is that I can't picture how I'd be at it…a husband, a father… You've got it down pat."

Joe laughed. "Marriage is always a true struggle, but it's worth it. And it seems like you're on the right track with Fern…two whole people coming together to make one."

"What do you mean, 'whole people'?"

"I don't know. I guess some can marry because one has troublesome needs and the other can fill them. I think it's better when you're real and she's real, and then you have the marriage."

"Again...it sounds so simple."

Joe clapped him on the shoulder. "Simple as pie."

Chapter 17

On Tuesday, Fern saw her *aenti* off with little regret, then returned to her garden. The zucchini were running wild, and she picked thirteen of them and carried them to the back door in a small wheelbarrow. She decided she'd make zucchini bread to take to Abram and the *kinner*. She was still a bit nervous about going to his house unannounced, but supposed a bold step here or there wouldn't hurt.

She went into the house and was struck by the sense of emptiness now that her *aenti* had left. It seemed that even plunking the zucchini on the table made a disheartening *thud*. She was relieved when she heard a buggy pull up.

She went out onto the porch and was glad to see Eve Bender step down from the buggy.

"Thought you could use a bit of company."

"I'd love nothing more," Fern said with a smile.

She let her friend into the kitchen, and Eve glanced at the zucchini. "Going to make bread? I can help."

"Ya, if you'd like. I—I'm making it for Abram Fisher and his family."

Eve gave her a conspiratorial grin. "So the prettiest girl I know has managed to snag the attention of the beautiful but remote Abram Fisher. Are you going to tell me the story?"

Fern felt herself blush. "I don't know what to say. I don't really know how to handle a man's attention, as you call it. And I didn't snag him…at least, I don't think so."

Eve laughed as she deftly peeled the zucchini. "The most important thing to know about courting and marriage, my friend, is that your life is not his life."

"What do you mean?"

"It's good for you to have all this." Eve gestured with one arm to encircle the herbs and the kitchen. "This is you. Abram has his land too. Now you may find a way to bring those two pieces together somehow, to serve each other and the community—but to know yourself first is the most important thing."

"So it's like two wholes make a stronger whole?"

"I believe so."

Fern sliced the zucchini thoughtfully. Her friend's simple words touched her and made her consider once more how grateful she was for her grandmother's influence in her life.

"Danki, Eve," she said quietly.

Her friend leaned over to hug her close. "My pleasure."

Abram saw Fern coming down the lane with a basket over her arm and made haste to douse his face and hands with fresh water. He'd been cleaning stalls and looked a mess, but there was no help for it. The children saw her coming too and ran out to greet her, laughing and talking. Abram hung back, watching her face light up with a bright smile.

"I brought some zucchini bread. I hope it's all right that I came by." She sounded shy, and Abram was surprised.

"Come over anytime. I've been working around here and wanted to give you some time to be with your *aenti.*"

Fern giggled at his dour face. "She went home."

"*Ach*…well…nice."

"Can we have some bread now, Fern?" Mark asked, jumping up and down.

"Of course."

Abram led her into the relatively clean kitchen and fetched a knife and plates and the crock of butter. Fern doled out generous slices, and the children were quiet as they sat at the table.

"Would you like some?" she asked Abram. He shook his head and grabbed her hand instead.

"*Nee*, let's go out on the porch and sit a bit. And you *kinner* can have seconds."

He was pleased with the look of happiness that shone on Fern's face at his suggestion. He led her out the door and onto the porch swing. "Sorry about the coveralls," he said, ruefully brushing away some stray flecks of hay.

"I like them."

He glanced at her sideways. "Really?"

She nodded. "I guess I like anything you wear."

He caught her hand in his. "Fern Zook, you know how to talk to turn a man's head."

She shrugged. "It's just the truth."

He leaned closer to her, breathing in her fresh scent, and placed gentle lips to the bare skin of her neck. He felt her shiver in response, and she turned to look at him. There was both innocent invitation and desire in the depths of her green eyes. He was half-afraid of being interrupted, but he moved his mouth closer to hers, then softly kissed her full on the lips.

"That—that was wonderful," he managed, half-laughing with the joy of the kiss. He looked at her anxiously then. "Was it wonderful?"

"*Ya*," she said. "I wish—"

"Abram, I wanna give Fern a present."

It was Mary, holding something close in her arms, and Abram could only be grateful that he'd actually gotten one kiss in. He couldn't wait until his parents came home. "What's the present?" he asked, faintly anxious that it wouldn't be something odd or disgusting.

"Well, you know Sparkle had her babies a few weeks ago… I thought I'd let Fern have Mayflower so she won't be alone since her *mammi* died." Mary lifted the dish towel from her arm to reveal a beautiful soft gray kitten with a white chin and bright green eyes.

When Fern cried out in pleasure, Abram wished he'd thought of the gift himself.

"*Ach*, you darling! *Danki*, Mary. You are so right. Now I won't have to be alone. And I love her name… Mayflower." Fern cradled the animal to her breast and smiled at Abram. "Isn't she beautiful?"

He looked deep and meaningfully into her eyes. "Yes, she surely is."

* * *

A little later Fern walked home, barely noticing the summer storm clouds gathering as she stared down with pleasure at her new companion. She was traipsing through the field when suddenly there was the loud sound of cracking wood, and the ground gave way beneath her feet.

Chapter 18

Matthew came running into the kitchen. "Abram, it's a letter from *Mamm* and *Daed*."

Abram took the letter from his brother's hand and sat down at the table to read, with Mary on his lap munching zucchini bread.

To: Abram Fisher
Paradise, Pa.

Dear Abram,
We hope that all is well with you and the *kinner*. *Fater* has improved and we think that we are not needed so much, though Elizabeth would love to have us stay. But we are missing home and have decided to come back at the end of next week. It

surely will be good to be home. We appreciate how much work you've done so we could take this trip.

We love you, *Sohn*,
Mamm and *Daed*

"What's it say?" Mary pulled on his arm.

Abram let the letter sink in and thought with dismay of all of the work to be done in the next few days. *"Mamm* and *Daed* are coming home early, that's all."

The kids whooped and hollered until Abram spoke sternly. "I know, I know. But we have a heap of work to do around this place before then. So we might as well start now."

Sounds of disapproval met his response, then Mary spoke up suddenly. "Look, Abram, on the porch. It's Mayflower. Why would Fern give her back?"

Abram strode to the screen door and caught the kitten up in his hands to make sure it was the right one. Then he glanced out at the ominous clouds threatening and the large drops of rain starting to fall.

"She wouldn't," he muttered, feeling uneasy. "She wouldn't give it back."

Fern was praying desperately. She realized that she'd fallen through an abandoned well and felt completely foolish. Everyone knew where the wood-covered unused wells in the area were and usually avoided them with ease. But she could smell wood rot in the jagged fragments that nearly pierced the skin of her face as she clung to the edge of the ground. She was relieved that the kitten had somehow jumped free; she'd seen her go off like a shot and could only hope she'd head back to the Fisher home.

After several useless tries to pull herself up, she loosed one shoe and let it fall, wanting to gauge how deep the well was. She listened and heard an ominous splash after a good four seconds and knew that she could not let go.

She remembered a phrase from the Bible…*to Him who is able to keep us from falling…* She'd never thought of those words in such a literal sense before, but now she repeated them over and over as her arms and fingers began to grow numb with the strain. The grass and dirt she held were quickly turning into mud from the rain as she lifted her head and screamed for help.

Abram told the *kinner* to stay in the house until he returned, then he set out in the teeth of the storm to trace Fern's route home. He had no doubt she was in some kind of danger; he could feel it within himself, but he didn't know if she'd gone down the lane or cut across the field. He paused, the wind whipping around him, and prayed to God for guidance. Then he heard the faint cry of a female voice. He turned in the direction of the field.

"The old well!" he said aloud, then took off running. He saw the jagged edge soon enough and Fern's white-tipped fingers grappling in the mud. He threw himself on his belly and inched forward.

"Fern," he called over the pounding rain. "I'm here… Hold on."

"I'm…not trying to let go."

He laughed with relief at her spirit and moved until

his hands touched hers. He locked his fingers around her wrists.

"Abram…you can't pull me up. I'm too heavy!"

"Are you, then?" he said, lifting her up inch by inch.

When she finally lay full on the ground, he lay head to head with her, winded but not tired, though his arms shook with the thought that he might have lost her. He grinned into her muddy, beautiful face and then laid his hands on either side of her head, pushing her soaked bonnet down and off, and kissed her. He tasted the earth and reveled in its aliveness, then he silently praised God as he deepened the kiss, slanting his head and feeling her delicious response.

Fern sat at the Fishers' kitchen table wrapped in blankets and one of Abram's *mamm's* robes. She drank the hot chocolate that Matthew had made for her and relished the weight of Abram's arm around her shoulders and Mayflower's tiny body in her lap.

Mary sat across from them, eyeing them dreamily. "Are you two gonna do it now?"

Fern looked up in alarm as Abram laughed. "Maybe."

"Do…what?" Fern asked.

"Ach, that's a family secret," Abram teased, nuzzling her neck. "I'll have to let you in on it one day soon."

Fern smiled at him as Mayflower suddenly jumped down from her lap. The cat scuffled about by the stove for a moment, then returned to her new owner. Fern jumped when she saw a mole, perfectly unharmed, then joined in the laughter as Luke told the story of the small creature.

Fern looked around at the children, then at Abram, and knew that what her grandmother had told her would hold true for a lifetime…a taste of faith was a taste of love.

Later, when the *kinner* were all in bed, Abram found the words to whisper against Fern's temple, half afraid, half joyous.

"Will you marry me, Fern Zook?"

He was delighted when she lifted her mouth to his with a shy smile.

"Ya."

To: Henry and Martha Fisher
Middle Hollow, Ohio

Dear *Mamm* and *Daed*,
Hope this letter catches you in *gut* time before you leave. I wanted to let you know that everything is going well with the *kinner* and the farm, but I do have a surprise for you… Fern Zook has agreed to marry me in the fall. (She says hello and hopes you'll be happy for us!) A lot of things have happened since you've been gone, but finding Fern has been the best. Please come home safely to a soon-to-be new member of the family.

With love,
Abram

* * * * *

ACKNOWLEDGMENTS

I would dearly like to thank my fellow authors in this collection; my editor, Natalie; my copy editor, LB Norton; and my agent, Natasha Kern. Thank you to my family, to Brenda Lott, and to my dearest husband, Scott Long. I would also like to thank Dean Westler for his humor and insight.

About the Author

Kelly Long is the author of the Patch of Heaven series and the historical Amish Arms of Love. She was born and raised in the mountains of northern Pennsylvania. She's been married for twenty-six years and enjoys life with her husband, children, and Bichon. Visit Kelly on Facebook, Fans-of-Kelly-Long, and Twitter, @KellyLongAmish.

A SPOONFUL OF LOVE

AMY CLIPSTON

For Stacey

Chapter 1

Hannah King glanced at the clock over the sink. One hour before the guests would arrive. A mental list clicked off in her mind: clean the downstairs bathroom and sweep the back porch. The bed-and-breakfast had to be perfect before the *Englisch* guests arrived.

After scrubbing the bathroom sink and counter, Hannah headed outside. She breathed in the cool autumn air and smiled. This was her favorite time of year. She propped the screen door open, grabbed the broom from where it leaned against the house, and began to push errant leaves back toward the lawn below. She was finishing up when she felt something breeze by her face, followed by a clatter in the kitchen.

"Hello?" Hannah peered through the doorway. "Who's there?" She scanned the kitchen and gasped when she spotted an overturned glass on the floor and a small bird circling above the table.

Wielding the broom like a tennis racket, Hannah swung at the bird, hoping to send it toward the open screen door. "Get out!" She looked around in search of another implement to corral the poor creature.

The bird fluttered past her arm and she swung the broom, narrowly missing the window above the sink.

"Shoo!" Hannah cried. "Go back outside!"

"Hannah?" her *mamm's* voice called from the doorway. "*Was iss letz?*"

"A bird." Hannah took another swing. "Please help!"

But her *mamm* ignored her, crossing the floor to look into the small bathroom just off the kitchen. "What's this water?" She put her hands on her wide hips and eyed the mess. "The toilet is overflowing."

"Oh no." Hannah groaned and then swung at the bird, which flew into the window.

"Let me try." Her *mamm* held out her hand. "You take care of the toilet."

Hannah hesitated; she wanted to handle the situation on her own. But with guests coming, she couldn't let her pride get in the way of a positive first impression. "*Danki.*" She reluctantly handed her *mamm* the broom, then moved to the bathroom where the pipe behind the toilet was spraying water, which was pooling on the floor.

What else can go wrong?

Hannah turned off the water flow valve while her *mamm* continued to swat at the bird. A moment later she heard a knock at the door and grimaced. "The O'Malleys must be early."

She wiped her hands on her apron, straightened her

prayer *kapp*, and opened the front door. An *Englisch* couple, middle-aged and well tanned, stood on the stoop, smiling broadly.

"Hannah King?" The man extended his hand. "Greg O'Malley."

"*Ya*, I'm Hannah. Nice to meet you. You're a little early, but it's no problem."

"I'm sorry." The woman held out her hand, and Hannah shook it. "I'm Robin. We got an earlier start, and traffic was light on the turnpike."

A thump followed by a crash sounded from the kitchen, and the visitors raised their eyebrows.

Hannah ignored the noise. "Please come in."

The *Englisch* folks stepped into the house, pulling large suitcases with wheels that scraped along the wood floor.

Hannah asked them to sign the guest book in the living room, then handed them a set of keys. After taking their credit card information, she led the guests into the kitchen, where her mother stood by the closed bathroom door. "Robin and Greg, this is my mother, Rachel."

Her *mamm* smiled, despite her crooked prayer *kapp* and apron. "Welcome to the Paradise Inn."

"Thank you." Robin turned to her husband and grinned. Hannah wondered if this was a special occasion for them.

"You may go upstairs," Hannah said. "I'll be right behind you." After the guests started up toward the bedrooms, she turned to her *mamm*. "Did you get the bird out?"

"*Ya*." Her mother pushed a wayward strand of brown hair behind her ear. "But I knocked over a chair or two in the process."

"*Danki* for coming over when you did." Hannah touched her *mamm's* hand.

"You go tend to the guests. I'll take care of the bathroom next."

Hannah hurried up the stairs.

"This is rustic, but lovely." Robin looked around the sparse hallway.

"Thank you." Hannah knew pride was a sin, but she felt it just the same when folks commented about their home. "This house has been in my family for three generations." She pointed toward the end of the hall. "I think you would be most comfortable in the large bedroom." She flung open the door to reveal the four-poster bed, two bureaus, and a sitting area with a little sofa.

Robin smiled at Hannah. "It's perfect."

"Would you like something to eat?" Hannah fluffed up the bed pillows.

"No, thank you," Greg said and patted his stomach. "We had a big breakfast on the way here."

"Okay. Breakfast is served at eight," Hannah said. "Oh, and your stay includes one Amish supper. Would you like it tonight?"

"That sounds wonderful. I'm excited to eat food someone else has cooked!" Robin nudged her husband's side.

Hannah picked up a pile of brochures and maps from the dresser. "Here's some information about the area attractions. Feel free to ask me if you need anything else."

"Wonderful," Robin said. "We hope to see all kinds of authentic Amish places while we're here."

"*Gut.* Well, you settle in." Hannah smiled as she skipped down the stairs, mentally planning the supper menu. But first she needed to help her mother finish cleaning up the mess in the bathroom.

Stephen Esh tossed his duffel bag onto the seat of the taxicab and climbed in beside it. The knots in his stomach had loosened some since leaving his home in Sugarcreek, Ohio, that morning. He'd never been to Lancaster before and was interested to see how it differed from his home community. Reaching up, he lifted his straw hat and smoothed his hair, hoping that he didn't look as disheveled as he felt.

"Where to?" The cabdriver looked at Stephen in the rearview mirror.

Stephen frowned. *That's the ultimate question.* The truth was, he had no idea where he was headed, but he knew his goal—a new start.

"I need to know a destination, son," the cabbie said.

Stephen looked out the window at passengers leaving the bus station with luggage in tow. He imagined they all had places to be. "Are there any hotels around here?"

The cabbie grinned. "This is a tourist area. There are plenty of hotels, motels, and bed-and-breakfasts. What did you have in mind?"

"Are there any Amish hotels?"

"You mean run by Amish folks?"

"Right."

The cabbie cranked the engine, revving it to life. "There's an Amish-owned bed-and-breakfast called Paradise Inn."

"That sounds perfect," Stephen said. *Paradise sounds like just what I need.*

The cabbie merged into traffic. "How long are you in town?"

"I'm not sure." Stephen absently watched the passing traffic. "I'll see where the Lord leads me."

"Are you visiting friends or family?"

"No. I don't have any friends or family here." Stephen met the driver's curious expression in the mirror. "I'm looking for a fresh start."

Leaning back in the seat, Stephen sighed. Leaving home had been his only choice.

Chapter 2

The cab stopped in front of a two-story, white clapboard house. Stephen noticed a burgundy minivan parked near the path leading toward the front door. A rock driveway led out to the road where a modest sign by the mailbox read PARADISE INN.

"Here we are." The cabdriver looked over his shoulder and told him the fare.

Stephen paid. "Thanks. Keep the change." With his bag on his shoulder, he started up the driveway. The minivan rumbled down the driveway, and the couple inside waved as they passed.

Stephen nodded as he continued up the path to the front door and knocked. After a minute he peeked in the small window nearby. Seeing no movement, he glanced toward the road and wondered if he should've asked the taxi driver to wait. Yet he assumed the Yankee couple who had left in the van were guests. If so, then the proprietors should be at home.

"Hello?" He rapped on the door again. "Is anyone home?"

The house remained silent, and Stephen decided to investigate the property. He headed to the back, where he found a smaller house, a couple of barns, a henhouse, and a fenced pasture. Beyond the barn was an apple orchard, and the bright red apples were a beautiful complement to the cool fall weather.

A movement caught his eye. A young woman was hanging laundry on a clothesline spanning from the back porch to the peak on the largest barn. She was clad in a traditional Amish frock and apron, and seemed to move without thought as she hung out the sheets.

Suddenly she noticed him standing there and gasped. "You startled me." Then she smiled. "May I help you?"

At first Stephen couldn't speak. He was mesmerized…the slender frame, angelic face, and sandy blond hair sticking out from under her *kapp* were hauntingly familiar. He blinked.

"May I help you?" she asked again.

"I'm looking for a place to stay," Stephen said. "Do you have any rooms available?"

She hoisted the laundry basket onto her hip. "I do. Follow me."

"*Danki*." He climbed the steps and moved through the back door into the kitchen.

The woman placed the basket on the floor and then handed him a piece of paper. "These are our rates. How long will you stay?"

Stephen read the price list and shook his head. "I'm not sure."

She lifted her eyebrows, causing a wrinkle to pop up above her eyes. Here he was trying to escape the painful memories from home, and the woman before him could have passed for...

"I'm looking for work." He studied the prices. "Why do some rooms cost more?"

"The price is based on the size of the room."

He nodded. "What's in your smallest room?"

"A single bed, a bureau, and a small desk."

"I'll take it." He held out his hand. "I'm Stephen Esh." When he touched her hand, he was overcome by the impulse to not let go.

"*Willkumm* to the Paradise Inn. I'm Hannah King. Follow me, I'll show you the room."

While climbing the stairs, he felt one of the steps shift and squeak under his weight.

"You have a loose stair."

"*Ya*," she said with a sigh. "I know."

"I can fix it if you'd like." He was already feeling anxious and wanted to get his hands busy on something productive.

"*Danki*, but I'll see to it." She stopped at the end of the hallway. "Here's your room."

"It's perfect." He took a quick peek inside before he turned back to her. "I saw a Yankee couple leaving in a van. Are they guests here?"

"*Ya*. They're from New Jersey."

He dropped his duffel bag on the floor and stepped over to the bureau to examine a few brochures. He glanced at the bed and noted that it looked comfortable. He hoped he'd get a good night's rest. It would be the first in a long time.

Stephen could feel Hannah's eyes on him. He wondered how she saw him. Probably as a normal guy, maybe even an eligible bachelor. But the Lord knew that wasn't the case.

Hannah took in Stephen Esh's height and broad shoulders. He had a handsome face and a pleasant demeanor, but his steely blue eyes had a sadness about them. She also noticed dark circles under his eyes and wondered if he'd slept well. She'd never had a guest complain that the beds weren't comfortable. She made a mental note to ask him later.

"Will you be eating supper with the other guests tonight?" she asked as she walked toward the door.

"That'd be nice." It had been a while since he'd visited with Yankees. He enjoyed hearing about their way of life. He would never leave his faith because he loved being Amish, but he'd never met a Yankee who wasn't friendly and easy to talk with. The corner of his mouth lifted, and he shrugged. "Could I possibly pay you to make me something for lunch?"

"You don't need to pay me. I have plenty of food, and I love to cook. Come to the kitchen after you settle in."

Hannah pulled out the fixings for chicken salad. The morning had been a little too exciting, what with the bird, the bathroom, and her newest guest with the sad eyes. She assumed he was a bachelor, since he was clean-shaven, and she knew from his clothing and his speech that he was an Amish man from Ohio. What was he doing so far from home? Hannah knew it was best to keep her distance from the guests, so she pushed that thought aside and focused on cutting up the chicken. One thing she knew for certain was that her *mamm* was not going to be happy that a single man was here for an extended stay. Never mind what the bishop would say.

But she was the manager of the inn, and it provided the financial support she needed to care for her parents. That and the extra eggs they sold to neighbors who weren't raising their own chickens. Although her family had operated the bed-and-breakfast for nearly a decade, Hannah had taken over its management a year ago when her *daed* had a stroke. He had loved to talk with the people who came to stay here, showing them around the property and telling them about the Amish ways. She and her mother were still adjusting to his new condition.

She put the sandwich, chips, and a pickle onto a plate, then filled a glass with water. The faucet was still dripping. She would have to remind her brother to fix it when he came by later.

Hannah fetched the laundry basket and headed outside to finish hanging the clothes. She hummed to herself while she worked, and the crisp fall air tickled her nose. She was finishing up when the storm door squeaked open.

"*Danki* for the lunch."

Stephen made his way toward her, his hands shoved in his pockets. Her heart leapt unexpectedly, but she stuffed down this unfamiliar reaction. "*Gern gschehne.*"

"I cleaned up. The plate and utensils are in the drain board."

"You didn't have to do that. *Danki.*"

He gestured toward the kitchen. "I worked for my uncle's plumbing company back home, so I know everything there is to know about pipes and faucets. I'd be *froh* to fix the leaky faucet for you."

"*Danki*, but you don't need to." Hannah wondered why he was so anxious to do all these home repairs.

He jammed a thumb toward her parents' house. "That's the *daadi haus*?"

She nodded.

"Do you live there?" Stephen asked, but then cleared his throat. "Sorry, I don't mean to pry."

"That's okay." She pointed to the inn. "I live here on the first floor. My *bruder*, Andrew, is married and has his own farm a few miles away." She picked up the empty laundry basket and made her way to the back door.

Stephen followed.

"I need to find some work. Do you have a list of Amish businesses around here?" he asked as they entered the kitchen.

"*Ya*." Hannah grabbed a few flyers and brochures from a stack she kept on the counter for her guests and handed them to Stephen. "I have some work to finish up before I start supper." She grabbed a stack of white sheets from the hall closet and climbed the stairs, her mind distracted by this mysterious guest.

She figured he must be trying to keep busy. The question was why?

Chapter 3

Stephen sat at the kitchen table and studied the information Hannah had given him. The sting of homesickness settled in his gut. Stephen was the younger of two sons, and his older brother had just been baptized into the community. He wanted to know how his parents and brother were doing and if they'd listened to the message he'd left on the answering machine earlier this morning. He was certain they felt betrayed by his decision to leave after they'd tried to talk him out of it. However, he had to do what was best for the community. And himself.

It had been six months since the accident, but the memories still haunted his dreams at night and his thoughts during the day. Although he'd confessed his transgressions before his congregation, he knew it was best for him to leave. He couldn't stand the memories.

He would write his parents a letter once he found a job, put their worries at ease. With the help of a small map, he sketched a list of businesses he'd hit first thing in the morning.

His thoughts drifted back to Hannah. She was certainly unlike any of the young women he knew back in Ohio. He glanced out the window toward the *daadi haus*, and then the quiet sound of water dripping interrupted his reverie. Although Hannah had told him not to worry about fixing the sink, he had to keep busy or his mind would start spinning. He trotted up the stairs and grabbed the tools he'd stashed in his bag.

On his way out the bedroom door, he spotted Hannah smoothing a quilt over the double bed in the room across from his. She met his gaze, and he nodded. She quickly smiled before looking down. He spotted a light-pink blush on her ivory cheeks. It was endearing, the way she blushed when he smiled at her. He wondered if she was spoken for, then immediately reminded himself that he had no business considering another *maedel*. He had no job, no home, and a bucket-load of heartache to mend.

Once Stephen was gone, Hannah turned toward the doorway, annoyed at the silly blushes she couldn't control. It embarrassed her to think that her guest might think she was acting coy. She finished dusting the room, swept, and then stowed the supplies in the hallway closet.

Coming back downstairs, she froze when she stepped into the kitchen and saw Stephen leaning over the sink with the faucet in pieces and a bag of tools beside him. "What are you doing?" She bit down on the corner of her bottom lip, trying to keep the frustration out of her voice.

He looked over his shoulder. "Fixing the leaky sink. It was dripping so loud it echoed in here."

"Stephen." She took a deep breath. "You don't need to do repairs for me."

"It's not a problem." He pointed toward the stairs with his screwdriver. "I'm going to fix that loose step too. I like to keep busy; it...helps me."

Hannah studied him. He certainly was persistent. What was he trying to forget? "My brother plans to come by and fix a few things soon. He'll take care of these repairs."

"I don't mind helping you now." He continued working on the faucet.

"You're a guest, not a worker here."

"By the way, would you mind giving me a list of your neighbors? Maybe one of them needs a farmhand."

Hannah couldn't believe the man's persistence. But what could she do, shy of snatching his tools away from him? She fetched a notepad and pen and wrote the names and locations of surrounding farmers.

Stephen left the sink and moved closer to Hannah, and she caught a whiff of his earthy scent. Her shoulders tightened. She ignored her response and handed him the list. "The neighbors are nice. You can tell them I sent you."

"*Danki.*" He smiled.

"*Gern gschehne.*" Hannah crossed to the laundry room, grabbed an empty basket, and flew out the back door. After closing the door behind her, she took a deep breath to slow her racing pulse. She hoped that the remainder of his stay wouldn't be so distracting. She walked to the clothesline and felt the bedsheet hanging there. Still a bit damp. She knew it hadn't been out long enough, but she'd been anxious to get out of the house. She couldn't believe Stephen was fixing the sink when she told him not to. She couldn't decide if she was more offended or thankful.

"Hannah Mary!" Her *mamm* rushed down the path and into the yard, holding up the length of her dress. "I'm *froh* you're outside."

"*Was iss letz?*" Hannah felt panic rise within her. "Is *Daed* okay?"

"Your *daed* is napping." She looked toward the door. "I saw a man out here earlier. Is he a guest? Does he have a wife?" The tone of her voice did nothing to hide her disapproval.

"Yes, he is, and no, he doesn't. His name is Stephen Esh." Hannah glanced toward the door to make sure Stephen couldn't overhear them.

Her *mamm's* eyes rounded. "Why is he here alone?"

"He hasn't said. He's looking for work, so I think he's planning on settling here."

"Where's he from?"

"I didn't ask him, but from his clothes I think Ohio." Hannah felt her irritation rising. All these questions made Hannah feel like her *mamm* didn't trust her with the business, or the guests.

"Has he said how long he's staying?"

"I don't know that either. You know we don't require the guests to give us firm departure dates."

Her mother straightened. "The perception of you and a bachelor alone at the inn will be frowned upon, especially by the bishop. You need to stay at the house while he's here."

"*Mamm*," Hannah began, "I'm certain the bishop would understand that Stephen is a paying guest and nothing inappropriate is going on. Also, we have other guests right now. I won't be here alone with him."

Hannah's mom assessed her daughter's face. "Bring him over to meet your *daed* and me."

"*Ya, Mamm.* I will. But right now I need to go gather up the eggs. Mrs. Smucker is coming by later to get her share. Call me if you need help with *Daed*." Hannah walked away feeling like a child.

Chapter 4

Stephen sat at the large kitchen table across from the New Jersey couple and pierced another bite of roast beef. The food reminded him of the delicious meals his *mamm* made and caused his homesickness to intensify. He put his fork down and drank some of his meadow tea.

"This is delicious." Robin wiped her mouth with a napkin. "These mashed potatoes and gravy are the best I've ever had."

"This is much better than anything you've ever made, Robin," Greg said with a crooked smile, clearly teasing her.

"You said you liked my store-bought meals." Robin swatted him with her napkin. "Frozen lasagna and garlic bread was a hit last weekend with our bridge club. They almost believed I'd slaved all day making it."

Stephen glanced at Hannah, hoping to catch her re-action to the conversation. She smiled, and his heart turned over in his chest as he thought of Lillian. He missed Lillian's beautiful smile, a feature people often commented on. Perhaps God had put Hannah in Ste-phen's life to allow him to say good-bye to his Lillian—to gain some closure.

Stephen watched Hannah gather more rolls from the oven. He couldn't help studying her delicate features and ivory skin. The more he looked at her, the more he saw that she didn't look as much like Lillian as he first thought. She had bigger eyes, and they were brown in-stead of blue like Lillian's. And she was much taller than Lillian.

"Do most Amish families stay in one house and never move?" Robin scooped more mashed potatoes onto her plate.

"*Ya*, we stay close to relatives. Some build homes for their children on their land." Hannah refilled the guests' glasses, never losing her pleasant expression. "They normally stay nearby so they can visit often and attend church together."

Stephen supposed Hannah fielded questions like this all the time. The guests' inquiries didn't seem to bother her in the least.

"This meat is excellent. Is that rosemary I taste?" Greg said.

"It is. That's something my mother always added."

"*Appeditlich*," Stephen echoed. "Reminds me of *mei mamm's* cooking."

"What does *apple—*" Robin laughed. "I can't say it, Stephen. What does it mean?"

"*Appeditlich.* It means delicious. I was echoing what you said."

"Oh." Robin lifted her tea glass. "Are you from this area too?"

Stephen shook his head. "I'm from Ohio."

"Are you visiting for a while?" Greg asked.

"*Ya.* I'm going to see where the Lord leads me." Stephen glanced at Hannah and found her studying him. Although he longed to tell her the truth about his past, he shuddered at the thought of her reaction. He never should've taken the buggy out in that pouring rain. If only he'd waited until the rain stopped...

"How do your appliances work without electricity?" Robin buttered a dinner roll.

"Are they gas powered?" Greg asked.

Hannah nodded. "*Ya.* Powered by propane."

Stephen admired how Hannah kept her expression pleasant and her demeanor professional.

Once dinner was over, Hannah refused Robin's help with the dishes and insisted the guests go on their way and enjoy their stay in Paradise.

Stephen carried his dishes to the sink. "I can help clean up."

"Don't be *gegisch.*"

"I don't mind at all." Standing close to her, he could smell her lilac shampoo. He gathered up the rest of the dirty dishes and placed them in a stack on the counter. "Do you always cook for your parents?"

"Sometimes *mei mamm* cooks, but I try to help as much as I can since she has to care for *mei daed.*" She turned on the faucet and waited for the water to warm.

"Your *daed* is *grank*?"

"He had a stroke a year ago." She kept her eyes on the sudsy water.

"I'm sorry." He gathered up the utensils. "*Mei daadi* had a couple of strokes before he passed away."

"He did?" Hannah's eyes widened. "Did it affect his speech? Was he paralyzed?"

"His right side was paralyzed after the first stroke, and his speech was slurred. The second stroke was minor, but the third impaired his speech permanently." He shook his head. "It was hard to watch his health deteriorate."

"*Ya*, it is difficult." Hannah looked away for a moment. He could tell she wanted to say more. A moment later she said, "It's as if I'm mourning *mei daed*, but he's not in heaven yet."

"I understand. I did a lot of little projects around *mei daadi's haus* to help make things easier for him, like walking down the stairs. Everything took enormous effort. He was very active before the stroke." Stephen studied Hannah's eyes. He felt an instant connection with her. He'd never met anyone with whom he could share the depth of his feelings about his grandfather's illness. Not even Lillian.

"You must have been close."

"We were. He passed away five years ago." He smiled. "I used to help *mei mammi* plant flowers so *mei daadi* could enjoy his favorite pastime—sitting on the porch and watching the birds and butterflies. We planted a butterfly garden in the corner of the yard, and *Daadi* loved it."

"I love growing flowers too. I've thought about planting a butterfly garden."

"I know it's not normal to hear that a guy likes to

garden, but it's the truth. *Mei mammi* taught me all she knew about plants. *Mei daadi* insisted we had the most colorful garden in Sugarcreek, but I'm not certain that was true."

"If you're still here closer to spring, maybe you can help me plant a butterfly garden."

"I'd be glad to."

"That would be *wunderbaar*." She paused for a moment and then smiled. "Tell me more about your life in Sugarcreek. Do you have a big family?"

"I have an older *bruder* named Jacob." He thought of Hannah's brother. "How often does Andrew come by to help?"

"As often as he can." She shrugged. "He's busy with his farm and family."

He nodded toward the bathroom. "I noticed the toilet is running."

She raised her eyebrows. "I'll mention it to Andrew."

Another easy job I can do to keep my mind off Lillian.

"I'd like to get a ride to town tomorrow," Stephen said. He placed the utensils next to the sink. "Do you have a regular driver?"

"*Ya.*" She wiped her hands on a towel. "His name is Curt." She pointed toward the large barn through the kitchen window. "There's a phone in the barn, and Curt's number is pinned to the bulletin board. Tell him that you're staying here."

"*Gut. Danki.*" As he headed out to the barn, Stephen sent up a little prayer asking God to heal his heart so he could move on with his life here in Paradise.

Chapter 5

Later that evening Hannah watched her *daed* gingerly lower himself into the chair at the head of the table. As he sank down, his right arm bobbed lifelessly at his side, and Hannah swallowed a sigh. Although his debilitating stroke had claimed the use of the arm and slurred his speech nearly a year ago, Hannah still found herself startled by his disabilities.

Her father lowered his head, and Hannah and her *mamm* followed suit. Hannah silently asked God to bless her family as well as the *Englisch* couple and Stephen. She also asked God to heal the sadness she saw in Stephen. When she heard her father shift in his chair, she knew prayer time was over and it was time to eat.

"What have you found out about Stephen Esh?" Her mother slapped a mound of mashed potatoes on her *daed's* plate.

Hannah picked up the platter of roast beef and served herself a slice. "During supper he said he didn't know how long he'll be here. He said the Lord will guide him."

Mamm shook her head as she cut up *Daed's* roast beef. "I don't like that a single Amish man is staying at the inn for an extended period of time." She pointed the knife at Hannah. "I'll ask your brother to stop by and introduce himself." She smiled as if satisfied with her idea. "Maybe Andrew should stay at the inn to make sure Stephen is behaving appropriately."

Hannah shook her head. "That's *narrisch, Mamm.* Andrew has more important things to do than chaperone me. Stephen doesn't make me feel uncomfortable." *Except when he smiles and I blush like a schoolgirl.* "He's been a gentleman. He even helped with the dishes tonight."

Her *mamm* furrowed her eyebrows. "Why would he offer to help with the dishes?" She glanced at Hannah's father. "This young man doesn't sound normal. Don't you think we should be concerned about Hannah's safety?"

Daed shrugged and scooped up a spoonful of mashed potatoes. Even before the stroke, he'd rarely taken her mother's worries seriously. Although her father's personality had changed in many ways after the illness, he still didn't get upset or excited by her mother's accusations.

Hannah bit back her rebuttal. She had done just fine this past year. Dozens of guests had come and gone without any complaints or problems.

"What does he plan to do while he's here?" Her *mamm* filled her own plate with food.

"He wants to go to town tomorrow. I'm certain he'll find a job and soon earn enough to get his own place. Once he's gone, you won't have to worry anymore."

"I worry about you all the time, Hannah. I always worry about my *kinner* and my *grandkinner*. A *mudder* never stops worrying."

Out of the corner of her eye, Hannah spotted her father shaking his head. He may have suffered a stroke, but he still had his sense of humor.

"What kind of work does Stephen do?"

"He said he worked for his uncle's plumbing company." Hannah ran her index finger along the side of her glass. "He seems handy. He's already fixed the sink and offered to do more jobs around the inn. I keep telling him that Andrew can do it. I don't want to have to pay him, and we certainly need the money he's paying to stay at the inn."

She glanced at her *daed* and remembered how he once took care of the farm and the inn. Like Andrew, her father used to be able to keep a farm going and fix everything from the faucet to the floorboards. Now he could barely walk from the family room to the kitchen without stumbling.

"You're right. We need his money more than his help." Her *mamm* frowned. "Ask him to stop with the repairs the next time you see him."

"I already did. He insists."

Her mother sniffed. "I'll have Andrew speak with him."

The message was clear. Whatever Hannah couldn't handle, her brother would.

Her mother went on to talk about how she had run into Eve Bender at the market earlier when she went to

pick up a new pack of needles. She prattled on about
how tall Eve's fifteen-year-old sons, Elias and Amos,
were getting and how polite they were to carry her gro-
ceries to the buggy.

"Hannah," her mother said, her expression lifting.
"I ran into Sarah Glick at the market too."

"Oh?" Hannah wondered why that was so exciting.

"Her son Jason was asking about you." *Mamm's* grin
widened. "I wonder if he's going to invite you to a singing."

"Jason's nice." She'd had a crush on Jason Glick
when she was twelve, but he'd never shown any interest in her.

"He's handsome too."

Hannah wished her mother would stop playing
matchmaker. She listened to her *mamm* talk about other
members of the community during the rest of the meal.

When the meal was over, Hannah helped clear the
table. She heard the scrape of a chair on the linoleum
and noticed her *daed* struggling to stand. She dropped a
dish into the warm soapy water and rushed over to him.

"Let me help you." She took his left arm, but he
pulled it away.

"I'm fine," he mumbled. "Just want to go to the
schtupp and read *The Budget*."

Although she was determined to help him, Hannah
nodded. "Call me if you need me."

"*Ya*," he said, his voice gravelly.

This was her father's nightly routine. However, she
hadn't seen him struggle as much as he did tonight. He
moved slowly, and his frown illustrated the effort each
step took as he shuffled toward the small family room.

She watched until he was safely in his favorite chair in front of a small table.

Hannah gathered up more dishes and moved to the sink beside her *mamm*. "*Daed* is having a hard time, *ya*?"

"*Ya*." Her mother focused on scrubbing a pot. "I need to talk to Fern Zook about him. I've heard she has some *gut* herbal remedies for strength and balance."

Fern lived with her grandmother, a homeopathic healer, and many sought her out before going to an *Englisch* doctor. But Hannah suspected her father needed more than an herbal remedy.

"There could be another reason why he's getting weaker, *Mamm*." Hannah brought the glasses to the counter. "The doctor said *Daed* may have had some mini-strokes."

"No, no." Her mother shook her head. "He just needs some new herbs. I'll go to Fern soon."

Hannah could see her *daed* staring down at the paper on the end table. She was always amazed that he found ways to do his favorite things despite his disability. Although he was losing his bodily strength, he still harbored a great spirit. "I'm worried about him."

"You fret too much."

Hannah raised her eyebrows at the irony of that statement. "He may need a wheelchair."

Her *mamm* grimaced. "Your *daed* would never agree to a wheelchair. He's determined to remain independent. Stop talking *narrisch*."

"But his safety is more important than his independence." Hannah tapped her fingers on the counter for emphasis. "We need to tell him we're worried about him. He's a reasonable man."

"No. Fern will know how to help him. A wheel-chair would break his spirit, and I couldn't live with that." Her mother rinsed the last of the utensils. "Don't be so negative, Hannah Mary. Your *daed* will be just fine. Remember the verse from our devotions the other night? 'I wait for the Lord, my soul doth wait, and in his word do I hope.'"

"*Ya, Mamm.* You're right." Hannah forced a smile, but she would ask God for direction on this. While the Scripture verse offered comfort, it didn't address the issue at hand, which was her father's safety. Yet Hannah knew that once her mother had her mind made up, there was no use arguing.

Later that evening Hannah curled up in bed with her Bible to continue reading 1 Kings. Her eyes moved over chapter 7, which was today's chapter.

The reading was about a widow who provided a room for Elijah. The widow fed him and took care of him, and in exchange, Elijah saved her sick son from death. The story spoke to her. What was God trying to tell her?

Then a thought hit her: Had God sent Stephen to Hannah, like He'd sent Elijah to the widow?

A shiver danced up her back. Closing the Bible, Hannah dismissed the thought. Why would God send Stephen to her? What could Hannah offer this stranger? The idea was preposterous. She was content—no, more than content, she was happy—to run the inn and help support her parents. Right? She had never dreamed of living her life any other way.

Hannah snuggled under the sheet and quilt while the meaning of the Bible story swirled in her head. Then she remembered the prayer she'd said for Stephen before supper. Did God want her to help Stephen overcome his sadness? Her pulse leapt at the thought. She was open to doing God's will, but He'd have to tell her exactly what to do. *And what is making Stephen so sad, Lord?*

Chapter 6

Stephen stared out Curt Wilson's van window and clenched his jaw. After visiting several farms and businesses, he hadn't managed to get one job offer. His grand plan to settle into his new surroundings was proving more difficult than he imagined. Perhaps he should have stayed in Sugarcreek, continued working at his uncle's plumbing company, and somehow learned to stomach the daily reminder of the pain he'd caused. Is that what a real man would have done? Persevered? Was he a coward?

"Do you want to go anywhere else?" Curt asked, giving Stephen a sideways glance from the driver's seat.

Stephen studied the piece of paper with a big X crossed through every farm and business listed. "No, I don't think so. I may have made a big mistake by coming here."

Curt turned down the radio and looked at him. "Don't give up. The Lord wouldn't have led you here if He didn't have a plan for you."

Stephen hoped the older man was right. He again looked out the window at the vast patchwork of farms beyond the winding road and thought of Lillian. He had to make peace with what had happened. Hadn't he been taught that the Lord forgives us in the moment of our transgressions? Why was it so hard for him to forgive himself?

You are My beloved son.

Stephen looked over at Curt, who had turned up the radio and was singing and tapping on the steering wheel. He obviously hadn't heard anything.

Lord, is that You speaking?

Stephen remained quiet until the car turned into the driveway at Paradise Inn. What would Hannah think of him when he told her he wasn't able to find work? Probably that he was a failure, and she'd be right. He'd failed at protecting Lillian when he took the buggy out in the pouring rain. It was his fault that she was dead.

Stephen pushed the memory away. He had picked up supplies in town so that he could fix the toilet and caulk the shower in the upstairs bathroom. He wondered if he should ask Hannah's brother for permission first instead of going ahead with more repairs after Hannah had asked him not to. He wished he'd thought of that sooner.

He turned to Curt. "Do you know Hannah's brother, Andrew?"

"Yes. I drive for him too."

"Does he live nearby?"

Curt pointed toward the intersection and slowed to a

stop. "He's a few miles away. Do you want me to take you to him?"

"*Ya*. I'd like to meet him."

After a few more twists and turns on the two-lane roads, the van bounced up a rock driveway toward a large, white two-story house. A sprawling white barn sat behind it with a herd of three smaller barns nearby.

Curt stopped the van by the large barn. "Do you want me to wait or come back later?"

"I'll ask Andrew where to find a phone shanty and call you when I'm finished," Stephen said, opening the door.

"Sounds good." Curt smiled. "Have a good visit."

"*Danki*." Stephen climbed from the van, adjusted his straw hat, and walked toward the house. As he approached the front steps, he heard a voice call behind him.

"*Wie geht's!*" A tall man with light hair, a beard, and brown eyes approached from the barn.

Stephen immediately noticed the family resemblance—the high cheekbones and light complexion.

"*Wie geht's*," he echoed, walking toward the man. "I'm looking for Andrew King."

"I'm Andrew." He stuck out his hand.

Stephen shook Andrew's hand, and the warmth in the man's eyes made Stephen feel an immediate kinship with him. "Nice to meet you. I'm Stephen Esh. I'm staying at your parents' bed-and-breakfast."

"*Willkumm* to Paradise. How long are you staying?"

"I'm not sure. I'm visiting from Sugarcreek, Ohio."

"I was in Sugarcreek a few years ago when my *fraa* went to visit her cousin. It's a nice place."

Stephen nodded. "*Ya*, it is. I was out running errands

today, and I wanted to meet you. Hannah speaks very highly of you."

"Would you like to come in?"

"*Danki*." Stephen followed Andrew up the porch steps to the house.

"My *fraa* and the *kinner* went to see her *mamm*, so it's quiet today," Andrew said while walking into the kitchen.

Stephen admired the spacious room. "How many *kinner* do you have?"

"Two. *Mei sohn* is three, and *mei dochder* is five." He moved over to the counter. "Anna Ruth left *kichlin*. Do you like chocolate chip?"

"*Ya*." Stephen sat at the table and ran his fingers over the smooth wood. "This is a nice table. My *daed* was a carpenter. He did work like this."

"Anna Ruth's *daed* is a carpenter too." Andrew set a dish of cookies on the table. "He made the table as our wedding gift." He returned to the counter and poured two glasses of meadow tea.

Stephen continued to run his fingers over the table and thought of his *daed*. Homesickness stung inside him. "Your father-in-law does great work."

"*Ya*, he does." Andrew placed the glasses of tea on the table.

"*Danki*." Stephen sipped the cool tea. "You have a nice farm."

Andrew sat down across from him. "It's a lot more work than I ever imagined when we bought it, but it's a labor of love." He broke a cookie in half before taking a bite. "What brought you here?"

Stephen shook his head. "I needed to make a new start, and the Lord led me here."

Andrew nodded. "That must have been a tough decision."

"It was." Stephen fetched a cookie from the plate. "But I'm doubting it now." He placed his marked-up list on the table. "I haven't been able to find any work so far."

Andrew peered down at the list. "You visited each of these places?"

"I did. I'll have to start hitting Yankee businesses tomorrow."

"What skills do you have?"

"I worked for my uncle's plumbing business and helped out in my *daed's* carpentry shop." Stephen wiped his hands on a napkin.

Andrew was silent as he tapped his fingers on the glass in front of him. "I imagine you've noticed my parents' inn and farm need some attention."

Stephen smiled. "That's why I came here. I picked up supplies to fix the toilet on the first floor and caulk the shower. But I didn't feel comfortable doing the jobs without your permission, since I'm only a tenant."

"*Mei schweschder* and *mamm* have their hands full." Andrew sighed. "Since *mei daed* had his stroke, he can't handle the upkeep, and *mei mamm* has to care for him. I wish I could do more, but I have my hands full here too."

Stephen thought of the chores he used to do on his parents' farm and a wave of guilt hit him. "Farming is a lot of work."

Andrew broke another cookie in half. "Would you be interested in working at my parents' inn and farm for a wage?"

"Absolutely." Stephen couldn't believe his good fortune. *Thank You, Lord.*

"*Gut.* I'll pay you to care for the bed-and-breakfast, the grounds, and the animals." He stopped and looked at Stephen. "Don't feel pressured to accept. I just thought it might help us both, since you need a job and my parents need help."

"I'll do it." Stephen stood up and extended his hand.

"*Wunderbaar!* You're helping my family. I'm very grateful."

"I am too." Stephen grinned. For the first time since he arrived at Paradise, he felt that God had made His purpose clear. He vowed to do his best for them, and he hoped the job would ease the pain in his heart.

Hannah stepped into the inn's kitchen after helping clean her parents' house. She placed the bucket and mop in the laundry area and then crossed to the refrigerator while contemplating her supper menu. Andrew and his family were joining her and her parents tonight at the *daadi haus.* Her *mamm* insisted she invite Stephen so they could meet him. She was examining choices in the freezer when she heard a loud noise coming from the bathroom off the kitchen. She moved quickly toward the source of the racket.

Looking in the bathroom, Hannah found Stephen crouched over the commode while working on the mechanism in the tank. "What are you doing?"

"I'm fixing this pipe. Did I startle you?"

She nodded and wondered again why he was so determined to fix everything that was broken here. Whatever he was running from, she wished she knew how to help.

"I'm sorry, Hannah. I dropped the wrench."

"Oh," she said. "I didn't see you get back from town."

He wiped his hands on a red rag. "Curt dropped me off, and I started working on the toilet. I'm going to caulk the shower upstairs when I finish here."

"Caulk the shower?" She shook her head with confusion. "I thought you were going to find a job. Did you visit those businesses I recommended?"

"I did." Stephen ran the back of his hand over his forehead. "I made a few extra stops too."

"Did you find a job?"

"I did." He nodded.

"When do you start?"

"I already have." He made a sweeping gesture, motioning around the bathroom. "I'm in charge of keeping up the bed-and-breakfast and the farm. Andrew hired me." He stood up, causing her to stare upward to meet his eyes.

"You spoke to Andrew? Did he come see you while I was at my parents' house?"

"No, I went to see him after I finished getting rejected by just about every business in this town." Stephen crossed his arms over his wide chest. "I wanted your brother's permission before I made more repairs around here. Andrew said he regrets he can't help you more. When I told him what I could do, he asked me if I'd like the job."

Hannah was silent while she absorbed the news. A knock on the back door interrupted her thoughts. "Excuse me." She hurried to the door and saw Jason Glick through the screen. "Jason, what a surprise. Please come in."

"*Mei mamm* asked me to come by for eggs." He stepped into the kitchen.

She pulled two cartons from the refrigerator. "Please have a seat. I baked some cookies early this morning."

"*Ach*, no, *danki*." He handed her money and took the cartons. "I need to get back to the store."

Stephen appeared in the bathroom doorway, wiping his hands on a rag. He nodded at Jason. "Hello."

"How rude of me." Hannah felt her hands grow clammy. "Jason, I would like you to meet Stephen Esh. Stephen, this is Jason Glick. Jason and I went to school together."

"Nice to meet you." Jason shook Stephen's hand. "I've known Hannah since before she could walk, isn't that right?" Jason smiled at Hannah.

"That's true."

Stephen nodded slowly while he held his mouth in a thin line.

"Stephen just moved here from Sugarcreek, Ohio. Andrew hired him to do repairs and take care of the grounds here at the inn." Hannah looked around the kitchen. "Andrew hasn't had the time to help us, so there are a few things that need attention."

"Oh." Jason raised his eyebrows. "That's *gut* that you can help out the King family." He turned to Hannah. "I know that you've needed some help since your *daed's* stroke. How's he doing?"

"He's doing *gut, danki* for asking." She fidgeted with the corner of her apron. "May I at least get you a drink?"

"No, no." Jason waved off the offer. "I really need to get going. Nice to meet you, Stephen."

"*Ya.*" Stephen straightened his back.

Jason touched the brim of his hat. "Hannah, would you walk me outside?"

She followed Jason onto the porch.

"I volunteered to come and get the eggs because I've…been thinking of you." He reached up and rubbed the back of his neck. "I'd like to see you again." He smiled, revealing a dimple in his left cheek. "Maybe you could let me take you to the next singing?"

"Oh." Hannah's eyes widened as her mind reeled. "*Ya.* I'd like that."

"*Wunderbaar.*" Jason started toward the porch stairs. "I need to get back before *mei mamm* thinks I ran off. I'll see you Sunday."

Hannah waved as Jason guided his horse and buggy down the driveway toward the road. She stood on the porch until his buggy rounded the curve, thinking about the afternoon's events. She had never received attention from any men her age in the district, and over the span of one week, she was spending time with two! Perhaps she could finally find a lasting relationship like some of her close friends had. She hoped a future with a husband and family was part of God's plan for her life. But then what would become of the inn?

Before she had time to dwell on this, she remembered her *mamm's* invitation for Stephen to join the family for supper. Taking a deep breath, she walked into the house to ask him.

Chapter 7

Hannah listened while Stephen shared a story about repairing a bench leg before church service only to have it collapse because he hadn't secured it well enough. Her brother laughed and recounted one of his own blunders at the *daadi haus*.

"*Mamm* opened the door and the knob came off in her hand." Andrew was laughing so hard his face was turning red. "There she was, holding the doorknob and looking so startled and confused."

Mamm tried to suppress a smile, but couldn't. Her *daed* even nodded.

Hannah looked toward the end of the table where her niece and nephew were gazing at the whoopie pies perched on the counter. She gathered up the empty platters and bowls and touched Anna Ruth's arm. "I'll get the coffee if you get the desserts."

Her sister-in-law brought the pumpkin whoopie pies and apple roll-ups to the table. "I changed up my apple roll-up recipe," Anna Ruth said. "I hope you enjoy them."

Hannah placed the sugar bowl and mugs on the table and filled the mugs with coffee.

Her *mamm* reached for a whoopie pie. "Hannah, did I see a visitor stop by earlier this afternoon?"

"Jason Glick came by for eggs."

"I'm not surprised." Her *mamm* grinned. "Sarah said he wants to ask you to a singing."

Hannah's cheeks heated. Why did her *mamm* have to embarrass her like this in front of her brother and Stephen?

"I'm so *froh*! He's a nice young man, and he has a *gut* job at his parents' store."

Andrew scooted his chair back and walked over to the percolator to refill his cup. "*Daed*, tell Stephen about the history of the bed-and-breakfast. He was asking me some questions earlier."

Stephen listened while Hannah's *daed* slowly shared the history of the buildings and land. Although the older man struggled with each word, Stephen never frowned or appeared impatient. Hannah's heart warmed at the respect and patience he was showing.

"It's a *schee* bed-and-breakfast," Stephen said when her *daed* was finished speaking. "I'm glad Andrew asked me to work here."

Her *mamm's* eyes widened. "What's this?"

Hannah held her breath, wondering if her *mamm* was about to make a scene.

"Stephen is working for me." Andrew pushed his chair back from the table. "He's going to be the groundskeeper and take care of any repairs in the bed-and-breakfast."

Her mother looked at her *daed*. "Did you know about this, Saul?"

Her *daed* shrugged. When he struggled to stand, her *mamm* reached for his left arm.

Andrew came around the table and took the right one. "I'll help him, *Mamm*." He turned toward his children. "Lizzie, please help your *mammi* bring the dishes to the counter. Joshua, you may go play with your toys in the *schtupp*." He helped his father walk to the family room before crossing to the back door and grabbing two flashlights. "Stephen, let's go outside."

"Sure." Stephen met Hannah's gaze. "*Danki* for supper." His eyes let her know there was a lot he wasn't saying, but she found herself confused. Was he bothered to know that Jason had asked her out? Jason had never shown any interest in her before. Was he only asking because he'd found out an unmarried man was staying with her? This was all so confusing. She wished she could talk to her mother about it, but they'd grown more distant since *Daed's* stroke.

"*Gern gschehne.*"

Anna Ruth looked down at her daughter. "*Danki* for helping, Lizzie. You did a *gut* job bringing the glasses to the counter. You may go play now." She pushed in the chairs around the table and started putting away the leftovers. "Stephen seems like a nice man. I imagine you're both *froh* to finally have reliable help."

Hannah looked at her mother, who was wiping down the counters. "He is. I don't know much about him, but he's certainly friendly and quick to offer help. I was surprised to hear he went to see Andrew today. Even more surprised that Andrew hired him to work here." Hannah tried to keep her tone of voice level.

Her *mamm* scrubbed the bottom of the soup pot with such force that Hannah thought it might break. "Andrew had no right to hire Stephen without consulting your *daed* and me first."

Anna Ruth dried a clean dish. "Andrew had the family's best interest in mind, *Mamm*. He feels bad he can't come over more often."

"Hannah and I can handle it. Stephen needs to find a job elsewhere."

"*Mamm*, you know we need the help. Anna Ruth is right." Hannah pulled the broom from the closet and leaned on the handle. "Remember the bird that flew in the house? And then the toilet overflowed, right when the O'Malleys were arriving? And the time the pipe burst upstairs? It's *gut* to have a handyman around every day."

"That's true." Anna Ruth took another clean dish from the rack. "And you and Stephen are getting along just fine."

Hannah studied her sister-in-law's expression. "What are you saying?"

Anna Ruth smiled. "He likes you, Hannah."

"That's very inappropriate." Her *mamm* glowered. "A young bachelor and an unmarried *maedel* shouldn't be living together. What would the bishop say?"

"We're not 'living together,' *Mamm*. He's a guest at our inn. And besides, he doesn't like me in that way."

Anna Ruth shrugged. "He spent a lot of time at dinner watching you."

"Anna Ruth!" Her *mamm* dropped the sponge and put her hands on her hips. "Please don't encourage this."

Anna Ruth blanched as if Hannah's mother had hit her. "I didn't mean to insinuate that Hannah should have an inappropriate relationship. I just thought it was sweet how Stephen looked at her." Her expression softened. "*Mamm*, you know Andrew wouldn't have hired him if he had any doubts about Stephen's character."

"I don't think it was Andrew's decision to make. His *daed* and I own this property, and Hannah runs it for us." Hannah's mother wagged a finger at her. "You must tell me if Stephen's not doing a *gut* job or if he makes any advances toward you. We will have no tolerance for that."

"*Ya, Mamm*." Hannah picked up a dish and glanced toward Anna Ruth, who shook her head.

Her *mamm* handed Anna Ruth a clean dish and then smiled. "Besides, Jason Glick wants to date you. You should concentrate on him, Hannah Mary."

Hannah thought about Jason. He was handsome, kind, and had always showed her respect when they were in school together. Once she had dreamed of being his girlfriend. But now that he'd finally asked her to a singing, she felt a hint of hesitation.

Chapter 8

Andrew leaned against a fence post. "I should've told my *mamm* about your new job before supper, but I didn't get the opportunity. I'll explain everything to her later. She tends to overreact about things, but I know how to handle her."

"That's fine." Stephen rested his arm on the slat in the fence and tried to swallow the sick feeling in his stomach. He knew jealousy was a sin, and he had no right to feel that way about Jason Glick, a man he didn't even know. Yet every time he'd looked at Hannah sitting across from him, he'd found himself wishing he were the one taking her to a singing instead of Jason, who was clearly the perfect match for Hannah in the eyes of her mother.

Had he lost his mind? He wasn't a member of this community, and he wasn't even baptized. But Hannah brought to life feelings he thought he'd never experience again. He couldn't take his eyes off of her at dinner.

He turned his focus to his new job. "I fixed the toilets in both bathrooms today. I also caulked the shower upstairs and fixed the squeaky steps."

"*Wunderbaar!* I've been meaning to fix those things for a while." Andrew motioned toward the house. "But *mei fraa* keeps me busy at the farm."

"I'm certain she does." Stephen thought of his parents. "*Mei mamm* kept *mei daed* busy, but *mei bruder* and I always helped out when I was home."

"Are you close to your *bruder*?"

Stephen shrugged. "*Ya,* we're close."

"Did he support your decision to move away?"

Crickets chirped, and in the distance Stephen heard a cow lowing. He rubbed his chin, considering his answer. He was still haunted by the betrayal in Jacob's eyes when he'd shared that he was going to leave Sugarcreek. Although Stephen wanted to be honest with Andrew, he feared Andrew's reaction if he told him what had happened to Lillian. "No, not really."

Andrew raised an eyebrow. "Oh."

"Jacob said I was running away from my problems instead of facing them." Stephen shook his head. "But *mei bruder* isn't like me. He's made different choices."

"Stephen, you can be honest with me." Andrew said the words slowly and with emphasis. "Are you running from something?"

Stephen breathed in deeply, then blew the air out of his mouth. "Six months ago my fiancée died in an accident. It was late, and I was taking her home. It was raining, and a pickup truck swerved into my buggy. She died instantly."

"*Ach*." Andrew grimaced. "I'm sorry."

"We were planning to be married soon, and I was going to build a house on my parents' farm."

"I can't imagine—"

"There's more." He peered over the fence toward the pasture to avoid Andrew's eyes. "She was pregnant with *mei kind*."

Stephen looked up, expecting Andrew to shake his head and show his disapproval.

Instead, the other man steadied his eyes on him, his face expressionless.

Stephen took another deep breath and continued, "The day before, Lillian and I had admitted our sin to our bishop, and we planned to confess to the church the next Sunday. Lillian was baptized, but I wasn't. I was going to be baptized immediately and then we were going to be married." Stephen felt tears well in his eyes.

He swiped his cheek. "After she died, I confessed to the community and asked her parents to forgive me, but I couldn't bear to be baptized. I didn't feel worthy of God's holy sacrament."

Stephen paused, remembering her parents' sobs when they heard the news. "Her parents said they forgave me. And I tried to put my life back together, but every day I was reminded of what I did. I was torturing her parents by their having to see me at church and around the community. I couldn't live with the pain in their eyes any longer." Stephen was quiet for a moment, willing the muscles in his throat to relax. "The only way for me to make peace was to leave. So I came here. I knew Lancaster was a large community, and I figured I'd find work easily." He took out his handkerchief and wiped his nose. The truth hung between them. "Do you want me to leave now?"

"No." Andrew shook his head. "I understand why you felt you had to leave, but God and your community forgave you, Stephen."

Stephen nodded. He'd heard those words a dozen times, but they did nothing to ease the heavy burden weighing down his heart.

"You're welcome to stay here as long as you want." Andrew patted Stephen's shoulder. "You should feel worthy to be baptized. You need to pray about that."

Stephen nodded. His bishop in Sugarcreek had also tried to convince him of this, but in his heart Stephen didn't feel that it was the right time.

"Andrew!" Anna Ruth called from the back porch. "Joshua's ready for bed."

"Coming!" Andrew jammed a thumb toward the house. "That's my cue to go." The moon overhead gave them enough light to make their way to the barn. After Andrew retrieved the horse, Stephen helped him hitch it to the buggy. Anna Ruth appeared on the porch with her mother-in-law and the children in tow.

Stephen told them good night and waved as the buggy bounced down the driveway.

Hannah stepped out onto the porch and pushed a stray lock of hair under her *kapp*. "Did you and *mei bruder* have a *gut* talk?" Her brown eyes sparkled in the moonlight.

"*Ya*. We did." He motioned toward the door. "I'm going to go say *gut nacht* to your parents."

Stephen found Saul reading a Bible propped on a small table, and silently marveled at the older man's faithfulness. He managed to spend time with the Word despite his disability.

Saul looked up and raised his eyebrows.

"*Gut nacht*, Saul." Stephen held out his hand. "I enjoyed dinner. You have a *schee haus* and family."

"*Danki*." Saul patted Stephen's shoulder. "*Gut nacht*." His words were slow and garbled, but Stephen understood.

Stephen then joined Hannah and her *mamm* on the porch.

"*Gut nacht, Mamm*." Hannah hugged her mother. "I'll see you tomorrow."

Stephen thanked Rachel for supper and then fell in step with Hannah while they walked to the inn.

After saying good night, he slowly climbed the stairs and made his way to the small bedroom. As he untied his shoes, he contemplated the evening. He'd shared his past with Andrew and had been relieved at his new friend's reaction and glad to simply speak the truth. He was certain that when Hannah found out, she wouldn't be interested in keeping his company. She deserved someone who hadn't made so many serious mistakes. Someone more like his brother, Jacob. Someone like Jason Glick.

Stephen stood in front of his bedroom window and peered down at the *daadi haus*. Closing his eyes, he opened his heart up to God. *Please, Lord, lead me where You want me to go and show me Your plan for me. I am Your servant.*

Chapter 9

The following Friday afternoon Hannah mixed dough for chocolate chip cookies while the smell of wood stain permeated her senses. Stephen had stained the banister earlier, then went outside to start mending the back fence. She marveled at how focused he was on his work and more than once had been tempted to ask him why he never sat still. But that was his business, not hers.

The screen door opened and slammed shut, and her *mamm* stood in the doorway with a wide grin on her face. "Hannah, there was a message for you. Jason called."

"I'll go listen to it right now." Hannah started wiping her hands on her apron, but her mother held her hand up.

"I erased it by accident. I'm sorry. I meant to save it, but I was so excited that he called you I hit the wrong button." She sounded sincere.

"What did he say?"

"He called to say hello and tell you he was looking forward to seeing you Sunday. He wanted to come by to see you, but they've been busy at the store."

Hannah felt the lunch she'd finished an hour ago churn in her belly. "Anything else?"

"No, that was it." Her *mamm* jammed her hands on her wide hips. "Aren't you excited?"

"I am." Hannah pulled out a baking sheet and some wax paper. "*Danki* for telling me." She wondered why she wasn't more excited and then pushed the thought away.

Her *mamm* scrunched her nose. "What's that smell?"

"Stephen restained the banister." Hannah motioned toward the stairs. "It looks *gut*. You should go see it."

"Why on earth did he do that?"

"It needed attention, *Mamm*. I can't remember the last time it was done. I hope it's dry before the new guests arrive."

Hannah's mother looked at her but didn't say anything.

"Do you need my help with *Daed*? I'm almost done here once these cookies are baked."

"Hannah…" Her mother paused and looked at the linoleum floor. "I worry that you're handling too much here at the inn. I was thinking about going back to balancing the books. Last month our numbers were a little off. Maybe you were preoccupied with all the chores." *Mamm* shifted her weight and examined the dirt under her fingernails.

Hannah stopped in her tracks and looked at her mother. "Why didn't you tell me this sooner? If the numbers didn't balance, you should have told me." She felt perspiration beading on the back of her neck. Her mother never seemed satisfied with Hannah's efforts. "I'm able to handle the business just fine, *Mamm*. Thank you for your concern."

Her mother looked unconvinced, but she shrugged and said, "Well, we'll talk about this later. I just came over to tell you about your message. I think Jason really likes you. Your *daed* rarely called me when we were dating. Of course, back in our day it was quite a hike to the nearest phone shanty."

Hannah knew her mother was rambling because she was uncomfortable.

"Jason and I aren't dating, *Mamm*." Hannah began scooping spoonfuls of dough onto a cookie sheet. "He only asked me to a singing."

"You'll be dating soon." Her *mamm* craned her neck to look into the kitchen. "Where's Stephen?"

"He went to town for supplies. He's been busy today. He repaired the Sheetrock in the laundry room and replaced the broken window upstairs. He started working on the fence, but ran out of nails."

"Is he doing a *gut* job?"

"*Ya*." Hannah pointed toward the laundry area. "He said he wants to build a set of cabinets for my supplies, so when *Englischers* ask to see my wringer washer, I don't need to be embarrassed by the clutter." She couldn't stop her smile. Stephen had great ideas for making the bed-and-breakfast more efficient. She scooped the rest of the dough onto the cookie sheet and then slipped the sheet into the oven.

"That's *gut*." Her *mamm* walked to the back door and pushed it open. "Andrew also left a message saying he'd stop by today. I'll see you later."

From the window, Hannah watched her mother go back inside the *daadi haus*, then she put her hands on the counter and lowered her chin to her chest.

Lord, when is what I do going to be enough for my mamm?

Hannah was washing the mixing bowl when she heard the *clip-clop* of horse hooves. She peered out the window and saw her brother's buggy rattling down the rock driveway toward the barn.

She hurried outside and waved as Andrew walked to the porch. "Hi, Andrew. How's it going?" She hugged her arms to her chest as the cool autumn breeze engulfed her.

"Fine, *danki*." He gestured toward the door. "Is Stephen here?"

"No. Curt drove him to town for some nails. He's working on the fence. He's done a lot around here the past few days."

"I'm *froh* he's doing *gut* work for you." Andrew's smile faded. "Stephen is a *gut* man. I'm glad he's here. He's been through a lot and needs a *freind*." His mouth formed a thin line. "But be careful not to get too close to him. He's not ready for anything more than friendship."

Hannah studied her brother's serious expression. "What has he been through?"

"Just trust me, Hannah."

The following Saturday afternoon Hannah led two new guests, Larry and Melissa McDermott, down the stairs after showing them their room. When they reached the kitchen, Hannah handed Melissa a brochure and a map of the area.

"Here's a listing of some popular tourist sites and

also some Amish businesses that are off the beaten path." Hannah felt someone's eyes on her. Turning, she found Stephen watching her while he replaced the door-knob to the laundry area. She focused on the guests and tried to ignore her self-consciousness. "Let me know if you have any questions."

Melissa studied the brochure. "I'm so excited to finally be here. My sister talks nonstop about Lancaster County. I can't wait to go shopping."

Larry sighed. "I knew if I didn't bring you here, you'd drive me crazy."

Melissa grinned at her husband and then turned back to Hannah. "Do these stores have those little jars of jelly?"

"*Ya*, I believe they do."

"Great! They make good gifts." Melissa touched her husband's arm. "Let's go find some lunch."

"That's a fabulous idea." Larry nodded. "I'm starved. Let's check out the Bird-in-Hand Restaurant your sister raves about. I'd like to try that ham loaf."

Melissa followed her husband toward the door. She suddenly stopped and gasped. "Hannah, you don't have electricity, do you? How will I charge my cell phone?"

Hannah bit back a smile. "Don't you have a charger in your car?"

"You're right!" Melissa snapped her fingers. "Silly me! Thank you, Hannah." She followed Larry out the front door, which closed with a loud *click*.

Hannah turned to Stephen and, as if on cue, they both laughed.

Stephen stepped over to her. "Do you get the same absurd questions from all of your guests?"

"I do. Shouldn't an *Englischer* know she can charge her cell phone in her car?"

Her heart warmed when she found his smile reached his eyes for the first time since he'd arrived at the inn. She hoped she'd see it more often. She looked at the kitchen clock and clicked her tongue "*Ach.* I missed the prayer meeting again today."

"Where's your prayer meeting?"

"We hold it on Saturdays at a store in town called Our Daily Bread. It's an Amish store owned by Hiram and Ann Lapp. *Mei freinden* and I talk, pray, and catch up on town news. I've missed the last few meetings because I've been so busy here."

Stephen gestured toward the door. "Want me to take you? I can hitch up the horse and get you to town in about fifteen minutes."

"*Danki,* but we won't make it in time. The meetings start at two sharp. Besides, I have work to do here."

"We'll make it a date for next Saturday. I promise I'll have you there in time to pray and hear all the latest."

A date? Her stomach flip-flopped, and then guilt settled in her stomach for getting so excited. *What about Jason?*

"That sounds *wunderbaar.* I left the dust cloth in my bedroom earlier." She walked past him and her hand accidentally brushed his, her hand heating at the touch.

She looked back and found him watching her, his blue eyes intense. She thought of what Andrew had said about Stephen's need for friendship. The urge to give him encouragement gripped her. "You do *gut* work. I'm glad you're here to help run the inn."

"*Danki.*" His eyes studied hers, and she nodded.

Hannah stepped into her bedroom and hoped she could be the friend Stephen needed.

Stephen shook his head with amazement. A weight had lifted from his shoulders when he'd shared a little laugh with Hannah.

Stephen knew he was treading on dangerous ground. His attraction to Hannah was palpable. He could feel the energy sparking around him when she was close, and his skin tingled when her hand brushed his. Her laugh was a sweet melody reminding him of his favorite hymns. Yet he couldn't pursue her since he wasn't baptized. He'd made that mistake with Lillian, and the results were heartbreaking. Besides, Hannah had a suitor, a man she'd known all her life.

Hannah appeared in the doorway and held up the dust cloth. "I found it."

What a schee *smile!*

"I'm *froh* you found it."

She started for the stairs. "I'm going to work in the bedrooms."

He watched her go. "Hannah."

"*Ya?*" She faced him, her eyes wide with anticipation.

"Is there church tomorrow?"

"*Ya.* The service will be at the Bontrager farm." She hesitated, and a shy smile turned up her rosy lips. "Would you like to come?"

"*Ya*, I would like that a lot."

"*Gut.*" She disappeared up the stairs, and calmness filled him at the thought of attending church with Hannah and her family.

Chapter 10

Hannah sat across from Stephen at her parents' table the following morning. He studied her discreetly. Hannah's royal-blue dress looked to be her best frock. Stephen admired how her brown eyes shone in the glow of the propane lamp.

Hannah scraped fried potatoes onto her plate. "You need to come by and see the bed-and-breakfast, *Daed*. Stephen has been working hard fixing it up."

"I haven't done much, Hannah." Stephen shook his head at the compliment.

Hannah listed off all the jobs Stephen had completed. When the elderly man smiled and nodded at Stephen, he felt warm with a sense of accomplishment. Might God have led him to this family for a purpose? If that was true, then perhaps Stephen had a reason for being despite the tragedy of Lillian's death.

"*Ach*," Rachel said. "Look at the time. We better go or we'll be late."

"I'll hitch up the horse." Stephen took his dirty dish and utensils to the counter and headed outside.

He had the horse and buggy ready by the time Hannah and her parents exited the house. Saul stumbled, nearly falling down the steps, and Stephen rushed over and took the man's arm. "Let me help."

"I can handle it." Rachel nudged Stephen out of the way. "He's used to leaning on me."

Stephen made for the buggy and held his hand out as Hannah approached. "May I help you up?"

Hannah took his hand. "*Danki*, Stephen."

Heat sizzled through Stephen's veins as he lifted her. It occurred to him that he was happiest when he was helping others—particularly helping Hannah and her family. He'd have to spend more time thinking about that later.

Hannah settled onto the rear bench.

"Stephen," Rachel snapped from the other side of the buggy, "would you please help Saul get in?"

"Of course." Stephen hurried around to the other side and assisted Rachel into the rear bench seat next to Hannah, then lifted Saul into the front.

Hannah and her *mamm* discussed recipes during the ride to the Bontrager farm. Stephen watched Saul stare out at the passing scenery, his expression blank.

Stephen leaned over to him and lowered his voice. "Is this what they always discuss on the way to church?"

Saul chuckled. "*Ya*." His mouth slanted to the left, distorting some of his words. "Food or gossip."

Stephen laughed.

Hannah bent forward. "What are you two scheming up there?"

"It's guy talk." Stephen raised his eyebrows and smiled. "We can't tell you."

She wagged a finger at him. "No fair."

"*Ya*," Saul said slowly, struggling for each word. "It is."

Stephen laughed again.

"That's the farm up ahead. You can see the buggies there." Hannah leaned over the seat and pointed toward a rock driveway.

Stephen breathed in her perfume-scented soap and enjoyed the warm aroma of lilac again. *It must be her favorite.*

He got behind a line of buggies rolling toward a large white barn. As he guided the horse toward the farm, he considered what this church service meant to him. Going to church was a step toward being a member of the community. It was similar to making a commitment to a new life. Stephen wasn't ready to make a commitment, but he was ready to explore this new community. Hannah's community.

Hannah leaned closer to him. "Are you ready to meet the rest of the district?"

"*Ya.*" Stephen nodded as the buggy wheels hit the rock driveway. "I am."

Hannah took Stephen's warm hand and climbed out of the buggy. "*Danki.* I want to introduce you to *mei freinden.*"

"I'd like that."

Jason trotted over. "*Wie geht's!*"

"Jason, you remember Stephen Esh?"

"*Ya, gut* to see you again." Jason gave Stephen a quick nod and then studied Hannah. "How are things at the inn?"

"It's been busy." She began telling Jason about the guests who had come to stay recently.

Stephen interrupted them. "I'm going to help your *daed* get settled for service."

Hannah watched him walk to the other side of the buggy, touched that he took such care with her father.

Jason gestured toward the Bontragers' house. "Would you like to head inside?"

"Oh." Hannah looked back to where Stephen was helping her *daed* out of the buggy. "I was going to wait for Stephen."

"He'll catch up." Jason started telling her about his parents' store and how much business had picked up.

Hannah turned back toward her parents' buggy and found Stephen watching her, his expression unreadable.

"Stephen!" Andrew waved as he exited the barn.

"Hi, Andrew. *Wie geht's?*"

"I'm doing well. How are you?"

"Fine, fine." Stephen's eyes searched the sea of people and found Hannah and Jason standing together on the porch. He couldn't deny they'd make a fine couple. They were certainly better matched than he and Hannah were. Jason didn't likely have a past that haunted him.

"How was the ride over?" Andrew's question broke through Stephen's thoughts.

"*Gut.* Your *daed* was funny in the buggy."

Andrew raised his eyebrows. "*Mei daed* was funny?"

"*Ya.*" Stephen shared their conversation. "I bet he had a great sense of humor before his stroke."

"He did. I miss that. I appreciate how you take the time to talk to him. Some folks don't count him in their conversations since he can't speak well anymore."

"Everyone counts, *mei freind*." Stephen's eyes roamed back toward the porch where Hannah and Jason now stood with a group of young people. He longed to be a part of that group, and he wanted to be the one standing with Hannah.

"You're right. Everyone does count." Andrew pointed toward the house. "I'd like to introduce you to some of my *gut freinden*."

Stephen walked with Andrew to the house and tried to commit to memory the dozen or so names that Andrew rattled off while introducing him around. He shook hands and repeated the name of his hometown several times. When he turned toward the porch again, Hannah and her group of friends had disappeared.

"It's time to head inside." Andrew pointed toward the line of people moving into the house.

When the congregation moved to the backless benches for the service, Stephen made his way to the section that was filled with young unmarried men. He scanned the crowd until he located Hannah sitting next to a young woman who was stifling a yawn.

Although he tried his best over the three hours to concentrate on the bishop's words, Stephen's thoughts kept flowing back to Hannah and her family. His gaze frequently found its way back to her. She was sitting up straight and seemed to be listening attentively.

Stephen was pulled back from his thoughts when the bishop recited some verses from the book of Acts: "Be it known unto you therefore, men and brethren, that through this man is preached unto you the forgiveness of sins: and by him all that believe are justified from all things, from which ye could not be justified by the law of Moses."

The words hung over Stephen like a black fog. His stomach churned and he suddenly felt sick. Everything in his body rebelled against the words, and bile rose in his throat. He stood, and the minister stopped speaking. Every set of eyes in the room turned toward him. He looked at Hannah and found her watching him with her eyebrows careening toward her hairline.

He hopped up from the bench, pushed past the young men in his row, and rushed outside. With his head hanging low, he staggered down the porch steps and toward the barn, where he dropped to his knees. He tried in vain to swallow back the lump in his throat.

Deep in his heart Stephen felt that the words from the Scripture just didn't apply to him. He didn't feel worthy of God's love, and the cross couldn't possibly cover his sins.

He didn't deserve to be a part of the congregation, and he wasn't one of God's children. He'd committed a sin far too terrible to deserve any love at all.

Hannah waved and greeted her friends Fern Zook and Eve Bender on her way to the kitchen after the church service. Hannah and Anna Ruth each grabbed a pitcher of water from the counter to serve to the members of the congregation who waited for lunch.

"It was a nice service." Hannah carried the pitcher to the family room, where the benches were converted into tables.

"*Ya*, it was." Anna Ruth stopped at the edge of the room a few steps away from a table of young men.

"How are things going with Stephen working at the bed-and-breakfast?"

"Everything is *gut*." Hannah smiled. "Stephen is doing *wunderbaar* repairs. He fixed the barn door and is working on the pasture fence."

Anna Ruth raised her eyebrows. "He's been working hard. I had a *gut* feeling about him after we all had supper the other night."

Hannah thought about the accounting mistake and considered that having Stephen around would relieve her of many of the stresses of trying to make do with little to no maintenance. His help would allow her to focus more on the business side of running the inn. She refocused and noticed a big smile on Anna Ruth's face.

"And before you ask, Stephen and I are only *freinden*."

"It's *gut* to have a *freind*." Anna Ruth started toward a far table, holding the pitcher up high to avoid spilling the water.

Hannah glanced toward the table of young men and spotted Stephen next to Andrew. He fit right in, laughing and joking with the other young men.

Hannah made her way down the line, refilling water glasses. She stopped to pick up Jason's glass.

"*Danki*. Can we talk later?"

"*Ya*." Hannah placed his full glass on the table. "I'll look for you after lunch."

"*Gut*. I look forward to it."

Hannah didn't look, but she could feel Stephen's eyes on her. She wondered what he was thinking.

"Stephen, I'd like you to meet Bishop Smucker." Andrew gestured toward the older man while they stood together on the porch later that afternoon. "Bishop, this is Stephen Esh. He moved here recently from Sugarcreek, Ohio, and he's working at my parents' inn and farm."

Stephen and the bishop shook hands. "It's nice to meet you," Stephen said. "I enjoyed the church service."

Bishop Smucker was short and stocky. He was slightly balding with a long gray beard and his handshake was firm. "*Willkumm* to Paradise. Are you planning to stay?"

Stephen nodded. "I believe so."

"*Gut.* If you ever need someone to talk to, don't hesitate to come see me." He stared at Stephen, causing Stephen to shift his weight on his feet. The bishop must have been alluding to his rushing out of the service. He was certain everyone was curious about his erratic behavior.

"*Danki.* I'll keep that in mind."

The bishop walked away to speak to another member of the congregation and Stephen stared after him, wondering if the older man could see the burdens weighing down his heart. *Does he sense the guilt I'm carrying?* He made a mental note to go visit the bishop soon.

Hannah stepped out onto the Bontragers' porch after lunch and spotted Jason standing with a group of men next to the pasture fence. He waved before walking toward her.

She met him at the bottom of the steps. "Hi."

"Hi." He nodded toward the fence. "Let's go for a walk."

Hannah fell in step with him and wondered what he wanted to talk about. She looked toward the barn and saw several of the young men playing a game of volleyball. Would Stephen see them walking off together? Did it matter?

Jason stopped when they were away from the rest of the church members.

"The youth gathering is at Katie Beiler's tonight." Jason stuffed his hands in his pockets. "Are you still planning to go with me?"

"*Ya.* I'd like that." She looked closely at his face and noted again how handsome he was. His hazel eyes were full of mischief, his confidence evident.

"*Wunderbaar!*"

Jason discussed the logistics of when they would leave for the gathering, but Hannah glanced around distractedly, wondering what Stephen might be doing. Her eyes stopped short when she found him talking to Becky. He wasn't going to ask her to tonight's gathering, was he? Her jealousy surprised her. Her brother's warning hung in her mind. She'd have to find out what Andrew knew…and soon.

Chapter 11

The next morning Hannah greased a loaf pan for the banana bread she was making. She hummed as she worked and reflected on the events of yesterday.

After the service she'd ridden with Jason over to the youth gathering. She'd had a good time with her friends, but she'd found she was less excited about being with Jason than she thought she'd be. She pondered the thought while scraping the batter into the pan.

Hannah slipped the banana bread into the oven and then remembered she hadn't checked the answering machine yet. She hurried out to the barn and saw there were no messages. She walked back toward the house, thinking of Jason and examining her feelings for him. He was friendly, and she felt comfortable with him, but…there was just no spark. Jason was handsome and kind, but he didn't cause her heart to race like a stallion.

Not like Stephen.

The thought caused Hannah to gasp. How could she allow herself to feel that way about Stephen, whom she had only met a few weeks earlier? And when her brother had warned her not to pursue him? Was she just imagining these feelings? But her cheeks heated whenever he stared at her, and when he touched her accidentally, her heart would lurch. More than anything, though, she was attracted to the kindness and care he showed her father. Stephen understood better than anyone what it was like when someone you loved had a stroke. Their connection was undeniable. And so were her feelings.

Hannah climbed the porch steps and remembered the Scripture story that had haunted her for the past few weeks—the widow at Zarephath. She couldn't escape the feeling that God had sent Stephen to the Paradise Inn for a purpose. But what was that purpose? And what role did she play?

The questions swirled through her mind as she reached the screen door. She stopped when she heard muffled voices in the kitchen. She hadn't heard anyone arrive.

Hannah found Stephen handing a map and brochures to an *Englisch* couple in the kitchen.

"Here is some information about the area. You'll find a list of the more popular sights that most folks like to visit. It also lists a few Amish-owned businesses that are off the beaten path."

"Oh, excuse me." Hannah rushed over to the couple. "You must be Mr. and Mrs. Morton. I'm Hannah King. I'm so sorry I wasn't here when you arrived. I was out in the barn checking the messages."

"It's no problem at all," the woman said. "I'm Lucy. Nice to meet you."

"I wasn't expecting you for a couple of hours."

Lucy patted her husband's arm. "This one wanted to leave early. Hannah, this is my husband, Rick."

"It's nice to meet you. Let's get you checked in." Hannah took their credit card information, had them sign the guest book, and then gave them their keys. "I'm certain you want to get settled. Head up to the second floor. Your room is the first on the left. I'll be up in just a moment."

"Thank you." Lucy pulled her suitcase toward the stairs, and Hannah could hear her exclaiming to her husband about the house and the apple orchard.

Hannah smiled at them as they retreated up the stairs and then turned to Stephen. "Thanks for greeting them. I didn't even hear their car."

Stephen shrugged. "I was glad to help. I've heard your speech so many times I could recite it in my sleep."

"I imagine you could." Overwhelmed by his thoughtfulness, she touched his arm and felt electric pulses flow through her hand. "I truly appreciate your help here. I've realized I can't efficiently run this place and care for my parents on my own." She self-consciously withdrew her hand and rubbed it down the front of her apron.

His smile faded. "*Gern gschehne*, Hannah. I'm glad I'm here too."

She looked into his deep blue eyes and wondered if he truly cared about the Paradise Inn. If so, did he also care for her? She wanted to ask the question, but she was afraid of his response. What if he said it was only a job to him? Hearing those words would crush her.

"I need to get outside to do a few things." He pointed toward the stairs. "I think you need to get upstairs to show the Mortons their room. You go take care of our guests."

"Oh! You're right."

Our guests. She thought about the word while she climbed the stairs.

Stephen took his time measuring and cutting the wood he'd purchased at the supply store earlier in the day. He swiped the back of his hand across his brow before he began to build the ramp that would connect the back door of Hannah's parents' house to the outside world. After witnessing the trouble Saul had exiting the house for church, Stephen had decided a ramp would be of great help to Saul. Once he completed the one for the *daadi haus*, he would build one for the Paradise Inn as well to encourage Saul to visit.

Stephen hummed as he drove nails into the plywood. The ramp soon began to take shape, and he smiled to himself. He hoped his crude design, which was similar to the one he'd built for his grandfather, would be sufficient.

He looked toward the inn and imagined Hannah telling the guests the history of the building. He was surprised by how appreciative she had been when he'd greeted the guests. It was a simple task, but she acted as if he'd saved the business. His heart warmed at the thought of helping her. Perhaps someday they might be more than friends, but he wouldn't push the issue. He'd let her set the pace in whatever direction God led their relationship.

The back door opened with a bang, and Stephen found Saul studying him with furrowed eyebrows.

"*Wie geht's*, Saul? How are you feeling today?"

Saul pointed toward the ramp. "What's this?"

"It's a ramp." Stephen stood and wiped his brow again. He was sweating despite the crisp fall air. "I thought it might help you get out of the house more." He gestured toward the inn. "Maybe you can come join me for lunch one afternoon, *ya*?"

Saul smiled. "*Ya*."

Rachel appeared in the doorway. "What's all the noise out here, Stephen?"

Stephen made a sweeping gesture toward his project.

"Why do we need a ramp?" Rachel raised an eyebrow. "He's not going to use a wheelchair, if that's what you're implying. You get around just fine, right, Saul?"

"Ramp is *gut*." Saul shuffled past her and into the house.

Stephen tried in vain to stop his grin. He admired how straightforward the older man was. It seemed the best tactic for handling Rachel.

Rachel scowled. "He doesn't need a ramp."

"He thinks he does. He said it was *gut*. I told him the ramp would help him get out of the house more."

Rachel peered at him with suspicion brewing in her brown eyes. "Did Andrew tell you to build this?"

"No, he didn't."

"Was it Hannah, then?"

"No, it was all my idea. I've been thinking about it since my first Sunday here, when I saw how Saul struggled down the stairs before church." Stephen leaned against the railing. "I thought it would be a nice way to help him be more mobile. I imagine he feels cooped up in the house. *Mei daadi* liked to get out after he had his strokes. Just being outside, feeling the breeze and seeing the flowers, made him *froh*."

"He's not cooped up." Rachel paused, obviously thinking about something. "He likes to read."

Stephen reached for the hammer. "I'm glad he likes to read, but I think he needs a ramp. His health may continue to fail. I did little projects like this for *mei daadi*, and he appreciated them. It helped his quality of life."

"This really isn't necessary, Stephen."

He used the hammer as a pointer and gestured toward the ramp. "I'm going to finish my project now. I'll build one for the inn when I'm done."

Rachel stood for a moment watching him, and then she disappeared into the house.

Stephen's eyes were wide as he looked toward the door after Rachel had gone. He'd hoped she would thank him, but he knew he was building the ramp for the right reasons. He had a feeling Hannah would approve, despite her mother's reaction.

Later that afternoon Hannah was preparing to put a Dutch Country meat loaf into the oven when her *mamm* appeared in the kitchen. "*Wie geht's?*"

Her mother pointed out the window over the sink. "Did you see what Stephen is doing at my *haus*?"

Hannah added water to the mixture in the pan. She then looked out the window and spotted Stephen painting a wooden structure that was attached to the back porch stairs. "Is that a ramp?"

"*Ya*. Did you know he was building a ramp for your *daed*?"

"No. How thoughtful." She turned to her *mamm*.

"When he came in for lunch, he said he was fixing the fence around the chicken coop, but I hadn't looked out the window or paid much attention outside." She stuck the meat loaf in the oven. "I've been worried that *Daed* is going to fall and hurt himself. The ramp is a fantastic idea."

"He didn't ask me first."

"His heart is in the right place." Hannah touched her *mamm's* sleeve. "Stephen has really been a help to our family. I'm so glad Andrew hired him."

Her mother frowned. "Do you have feelings for him, Hannah Mary?"

"He's *mei freind.*"

"Remember what I said about how things can be perceived. You're living under the same roof, and you're unmarried. If the bishop disapproves…"

"*Mamm*, please." Hannah grimaced. "We're *freinden.*"

"I'm warning you, *dochder.* Maybe he'll be able to save some money and move out on his own soon." Her *mamm* lifted her arms in a dramatic gesture and started for the door. "I'll see you later."

Hannah shook her head as her *mamm* disappeared out the back door. How could she think anything inappropriate would happen between her and Stephen? They knew what was considered appropriate behavior.

Hannah peered out the window to watch Stephen paint the ramp. What a wonderful and thoughtful man. He seemed to be an answer to her prayers—her helpmate who would care for her parents and the bed-and-breakfast she loved so much. Hannah needed to do something nice for him as a way to say thank you.

She looked toward the pantry as an idea nipped at

her. She rummaged through the shelves and made a shopping list. She would make him something special and surprise him.

Chapter 12

Hannah inhaled the warm scent of soft pretzels as she pulled them from the oven Friday night. She'd looked forward to this for the past couple of days. Baking Stephen her grandmother's famous soft pretzels seemed the best plan.

She removed the six pretzels from the baking sheet and brushed them with butter before sprinkling coarse salt on them. She was setting out napkins when the back door opened and Stephen stepped in.

He hung his hat and jacket on the peg by the back door. "What smells so *appeditlich*?"

"A surprise for you."

"A surprise for me?" He moved to the table and grinned. "Soft pretzels."

She bit her lower lip. "Do you like them?"

"Like them?" He chuckled. "I love them, Hannah. How did you know?"

"Just a *gut* guess, I suppose." She pointed toward the sink. "Wash up and have a seat."

He scrubbed his hands and dried them on the dish towel. "Why did you make me a surprise? Do you need me to replace the roof?"

She laughed. "No, I'm not trying to bribe you. I wanted to thank you for all the *wunderbaar* work you've been doing."

"It's a very nice way to say *danki*. But you didn't need to do this."

"I wanted to. You went above and beyond your job duties this week by making those ramps. I appreciate that you're taking care of *mei daed* just like you took care of your *daadi*."

Hannah stared up at him, and her heartbeat accelerated. The feelings bubbling up inside her were nothing like what she felt when she was with Jason. With Stephen, she felt as if her heart might burst with excitement and fear all at once. Was this what it felt like to fall in love?

She wrenched herself from her trance and took a step back. "I hope you like the pretzels. It's my favorite recipe from *mei mammi*."

"Sounds *wunderbaar*." He sat at the table.

Hannah sat across from him and passed him the plate of pretzels. "Would you like coffee?"

"*Ya*, please." He took a pretzel and broke off a piece before popping it into his mouth. "Hannah, this is amazing."

"*Danki*." She poured two cups of coffee and handed one to him. "*Mei mammi* was known for making some of the best food in the district. At church service, her dishes always disappeared first. She taught me well."

"When did she pass away?"

"Three years ago. I still miss her." Hannah broke off a piece of pretzel while wondering about Stephen's mysterious past. "Do you miss your family?"

"*Ya*, I do." He took another pretzel from the plate.

"Do you think you'll go home for a visit?"

"I don't know."

He kept his gaze on the pretzel, and she wondered if he was avoiding her eyes. He broke off a piece and bit into it.

"These pretzels are spectacular, Hannah. You should sell these to your guests."

She raised her eyebrows. "You think so?"

"Absolutely." He sipped more coffee. "They'd probably buy them by the trunk full. You'd have to spend your days making pretzels, and I'd take care of the guests as well as the grounds."

She chuckled. "I'll be a pretzel baker."

"That's right." He lifted his mug in agreement.

"You're *gegisch*, Stephen Esh. I don't think I'll make a living as a pretzel baker, but I'm *froh* you're enjoying them." She savored the taste of the butter and salt while trying to think of a way to get him to tell her more about his life in Ohio. Finally she decided to ask a direct question, hoping it wouldn't shut down the conversation completely. "So why did you leave Sugarcreek?"

Stephen rubbed his chin, and at once Hannah regretted asking. "If it's too personal, then forget I—"

"No, it's okay. It's time I told you the whole story. You have a right to know." Stephen sat up straighter and took a deep breath. "Seven months ago my fiancée died in an accident."

"*Ach*, Stephen." Hannah reached for his hand and

then pulled it back, knowing the gesture was too personal. "I'm so sorry. No wonder you have a hard time sleeping. Your heart is broken."

"*Danki*." He cleared his throat. "I was taking her home one night, and it was raining. A pickup truck swerved into my buggy. Lillian died instantly from the impact. We were going to be married, and I was going to build a house on my parents' farm."

"The Lord will comfort you." Hannah shook her head as tears filled her eyes. "He'll cover your grief with His love."

He studied his coffee mug. "There's a reason why we were going to be married right away."

Hannah tilted her head. "What do you mean?"

He kept his eyes focused on the mug. "She was pregnant with *mei kind*."

Hannah's mind absorbed his confession. *Lillian was pregnant.* Although Hannah had shown interest in a few young men, she'd never once considered being intimate with them before marriage. She wondered what kind of person Lillian was to commit such a sin, then she realized she was judging Lillian. Judging someone was a sin, which meant Hannah was no better than Lillian.

Stephen's eyes probed hers as if waiting for her to comment. "You must think that Lillian and I are terrible people."

Hannah cleared her throat as the guilt from her judgment choked her words. "Well, that's not a choice I would have made, but sin is sin in the eyes of God. None of us is perfect, and it's not my place to judge either of you."

Stephen raked his hand through his hair. "The day before the accident we had admitted our sin to our bishop, and we planned to confess to the church at the next service." He looked into her eyes, his shame evident. "We knew we had made bad choices. But we were trying to make things right."

Hannah nodded slowly, taking in his words. She could feel his grief, and her heart ached for all he'd lost.

The worry in his face transformed to a frown. "Lillian was baptized, but I wasn't. I was going to be baptized immediately and then we were going to be married. After she died, I couldn't bring myself to be baptized. I didn't feel worthy of it. I confessed to the community and apologized to her parents, but I had to leave." He paused and blew out a deep breath. "Everything I looked at and everything I touched reminded me of her. But worst of all, I couldn't stand the grief in her parents' eyes every time they saw me at church. They had to look at me and remember that I'd lived while she'd died."

Hannah brushed away a tear. "But, Stephen, you must know that the Lord appoints when we live and when we die. You couldn't control that."

"I think I could have." He grimaced. "I never should've taken her out in that pounding rain. I knew it was dangerous, but I thought I could get her home safely. I was wrong, and I can't forgive myself. I should've waited for the rain to let up, but I was impatient. I wanted to be alone with her so we could make plans and talk over our future."

"I can feel your pain, Stephen. It's obvious that you're hurting so much that it's choking your heart. But God forgave you, and your community forgave you. Now it's your turn to forgive yourself."

"If it weren't for my stupidity, Lillian would still be alive today."

"How do you know that? Everything happens in God's time. You can't predict what could've happened if you hadn't taken her out in the rain."

Stephen stared at her.

"You can't change God's plan, and you can't doubt it." Hannah ran her finger over the table's wood grain. "When I was six, my cousins and I found a litter of newborn kittens in *mei mammi's* barn. The mother cat was very docile and she didn't protest while we held the kittens. I was hugging and kissing the tiniest one, and I accidentally dropped it."

She sniffed while the memories flooded her. "I can still remember how devastated I was when *mei mammi* told me the kitten had died. I felt so guilty, and I cried and cried. But *mei mammi* reminded me it was an accident and it was also God's will that the kitten didn't make it."

Stephen ran his hand down his face and nodded.

Hannah leaned forward. She wished she could take his hand in hers to console him. "Is it our place to question His will? I know a kitten doesn't come close to comparing to your beloved Lillian, but you can't let that burden weigh down your heart anymore." She smiled. "Stephen, you're the kindest man I know. You've lavished buckets of tenderness on my parents and our land, but you don't have a spoonful of love for yourself."

His shoulders slumped. "I know you're right, Hannah. It's just hard."

"Let God heal your heart. If you give Him the chance, He will carry your burdens. And you're worthy to be baptized. God loves us all equally, and you're one of His children."

He sipped more coffee and then met her gaze. "Remember when the bishop read from the book of Acts?"

"*Ya*." Hannah recited the verses. "I like that passage very much."

"I don't feel that it's true for me." He took another pretzel from the plate.

"What do you mean?"

"I don't feel worthy of Jesus' forgiveness."

Hannah shook her head. "We all sin and fall short of the glory of God, but Jesus died to save each of us."

He chewed the pretzel, the heavy moment passing. "Okay, it's your turn to talk."

"*Ach*." Hannah shrugged. "I don't have anything to share. I've spent my life here on this farm. There's not much more to tell."

"I'm certain there's more." His eyes probed hers. "Is Jason Glick your boyfriend?"

Hannah considered the question. Although Jason wasn't her boyfriend, it was apparent by the attention he'd given her that he wanted to be. Hannah was more attracted to Stephen than Jason, but Stephen wasn't baptized like Jason was. And Stephen offered no promises. "No, Jason isn't my boyfriend. We're getting to know each other."

They talked about their plans for the weekend, and she discussed the guests who were supposed to arrive in the coming weeks.

Soon the pretzels and coffee were gone, and Hannah saw that it was almost eight o'clock. "I didn't realize that it was so late. *Danki* for having a snack with me."

Hannah placed the dishes in the sink. When she

turned, she nearly walked into Stephen, who was standing close to her. He cupped his hand to her cheek, and she sucked in a ragged breath. He moved his fingers down her cheekbone, sending shivers dancing down her spine.

"Hannah." His whisper was a beautiful hymn to her ears. He leaned down to her, and she held her breath. Just as their lips closed in to make contact, the back door opened with a slam, and Hannah jumped backward, colliding with the counter.

Her mother stood by the door with her hands on her hips. "Hannah Mary! What's going on here?"

"*Mamm*, what are you doing here?" Hannah gritted her teeth. Her *mamm* just ruined a perfect moment. When would she treat Hannah as an adult and allow her to live life at her own discretion?

Bishop Smucker stepped into the kitchen behind her mother, and Hannah swallowed a gasp. She smoothed her apron and touched her prayer *kapp* as her cheeks heated. "Bishop Smucker. What a surprise."

"Good evening." The bishop fingered his beard.

Stephen nodded at the bishop and slipped his hands in his pockets.

"The bishop was in the area and stopped by to say hello." Her mother studied her. "Did we come at a bad time?"

"No, not at all." Hannah eyed her *mamm*. "We were having a snack before bed. I made soft pretzels and coffee to thank Stephen for his hard work."

Her mother and the bishop looked at each other and then back at Stephen and Hannah. *Have they been talking about Stephen and me?*

"Hannah, may I speak with you alone?" Her mother

pointed toward the hallway leading to Hannah's room. "The bishop would like to talk to Stephen."

Hannah hesitated.

"Hannah." *Mamm's* voice was urgent. "Let's go now."

Hannah nodded at the bishop on her way down the hall.

Her mother followed behind her and closed the bedroom door. "Why are you having a snack and coffee so late? Won't the caffeine keep you up the rest of the night?"

"This can't possibly be about the pretzels and coffee." Hannah sank onto the edge of her bed. "Why are you and the bishop really here?"

"You're right." Her *mamm* sat on a chair across from Hannah. "The bishop came to check on things at the inn. He's spoken to Stephen at church, and even though he thinks Stephen is a nice young man, he's heard things."

"Heard things?" Hannah shook her head. "What do you mean?"

"There have been concerns in the community about Stephen and you being here alone."

"Why would someone go to the bishop about Stephen?" Hannah stood. "Who would do that?"

"I warned you."

"I know you did, but there was no reason to warn me." She studied her mother's eyes. "Who talked to the bishop about Stephen and me?"

"I don't know. The bishop only told me that there was some concern, and he wanted to remind Stephen about behaving properly."

Hannah tried to remember who had stopped by recently. "There were several people who bought eggs during the past few weeks, but I don't remember anyone making any comments."

"No matter who it was, you have to be mindful of how your behavior is perceived by others. You're both unmarried. Don't you think it's inappropriate for you to be sharing a late-evening snack alone?" Her mother's eyes bored into hers. "I know I interrupted something between you two, Hannah Mary. I'm not blind."

Hannah couldn't lie. Her *mamm* had interrupted something—Hannah's first kiss. And she couldn't deny that she'd wanted it to happen.

"What about Jason?" Her *mamm* tilted her head. "Do you forget about Jason when Stephen is around?"

"I don't know." A lump swelled in Hannah's throat. "I'm confused. Jason is kind, and I've liked him since I was a child. But Stephen is—"

"Stephen is a stranger. You've known Jason your whole life, and we know his family."

"But I don't know if I love Jason. He seems overconfident, and I noticed him looking at other girls at church and the singing. I don't know if I trust him to be more than a friend."

"Love is a feeling that grows over time. You're *freinden* now. You'll grow to love him as you get to know him better. That's how it was with your *daed* and me, and that's how it should be."

Hannah considered her mother's words. She wished that the answer were clearer about which one God had set apart for her. She knew one thing for certain—she'd wanted Stephen to kiss her, and she hadn't felt that way when she was with Jason.

Her *mamm* started for the door. "I need to get back home and help your *daed* get ready for bed." She looked back at Hannah and smiled. "If your heart is troubled, then pray. The Lord will lead you to the right answer. *Gut nacht,* Hannah."

"*Gut nacht.*" Hannah watched her mother leave the room. Although she was troubled by the bishop's visit, she was thankful for the opportunity to share her feelings about Jason and Stephen. It was the first time she and her mother had truly talked since her father's stroke. She was confused by her mixed emotions, but she knew her mother's advice was right. She had to pray.

She closed her eyes. *Please see me through this confusion, Lord, and lead me to the right choice.*

Stephen turned to Bishop Smucker. "What would you like to talk about?"

The bishop nodded toward the back door. "Let's go for a walk."

Stephen followed the older man outside and toward the barn. His mind reeled with questions while they walked. He didn't think he'd done anything improper since arriving in Paradise. Yet the disapproval on Rachel's face warned him that this might not be a friendly visit.

The bishop stopped in front of the barn and faced Stephen. "How are you getting along in Paradise so far?"

"Very well." Stephen leaned against the barn wall.

"*Gut.*" The older man folded his arms over his chest. "I wanted to stop in and see how you were doing. A couple of members in the community voiced a concern about your being here."

"Why were they concerned about me?" Stephen stood up straight.

"Hannah is a sweet *maedel*, and they were worried about how folks may view her if she's alone with you at the inn."

"We're not alone. There are guests coming to stay all the time. In fact, the inn hasn't been empty since I arrived."

"My instincts about folks are normally correct, and you seem like a *gut* man. However, I've known Hannah since she was born. I grew up with her *daadi*. If your relationship at the inn seems improper, she has to live with the consequences. Do you understand what I'm saying?"

Although frustration struck inside him, Stephen nodded. "I do."

"There may be guests in the inn, but if you're seen alone together, it could be damaging to Hannah. You were alone with her tonight, and a scene like that could be misconstrued by others. Rumors can spread like wildfire in a close community."

Stephen frowned. He knew rumors all too well, since he'd experienced them firsthand after Lillian died. Although the members of the community said they forgave Stephen, he heard whispers about the sin he and Lillian had committed.

"If you know you're going to be alone with Hannah, you need to find an appropriate chaperone. It would've been smarter if you'd shared your snack at Rachel's *haus* instead of being alone with Hannah. I'm certain the rules were similar in Sugarcreek."

"The rules were the same." Stephen kicked a stone with the toe of his boot.

The bishop frowned. "If you choose not to follow the

rules, then I may have to ask you to move out of the inn and stay somewhere else."

"I understand."

"*Gut.*" The older man smiled. "I'm glad we could have this talk, Stephen. *Gut nacht.*"

Stephen looked toward the inn and wondered how Hannah's talk with her mother was going. He thought back to the conversation they'd shared earlier, and he hurried over to the buggy. "Bishop, may I ask you a question?"

"Of course." The bishop dropped the reins and climbed back down. "What's on your mind?"

"Do you believe we're completely forgiven if we confess our sins to God and our community?"

"*Ya.*" The bishop raised his eyebrows. "Why do you ask?"

"What if you confessed, but the sin was still heavy on your heart? How do you overcome that burden?"

The bishop paused as if to collect his thoughts. He then placed his hand on Stephen's shoulder. "Well, son, I would imagine you'd need to ask God to remove that burden for you. I also think you'd have to find a way to forgive yourself."

Stephen nodded slowly. "Right."

"I can tell by your expression that you're struggling with something. You must trust that God loves you, no matter how terrible you feel your sin is." The bishop squeezed Stephen's shoulder. "Jesus died on the cross to forgive our sins. None of us is truly worthy of His love, but we're saved because of that love. God chose us, not the other way around."

Stephen mulled over the words, but he still didn't feel worthy of being forgiven. A long silence fell between them. Stephen's shoulders slumped with the heavy load of the bishop's words.

"Why don't we pray together?" The bishop folded his hands.

Stephen nodded and closed his eyes.

"Heavenly Father, *danki* for giving Stephen and me the opportunity to talk tonight. We ask that You lay Your healing hand on Stephen's head and help him to forgive himself for the burdens that are troubling him. You have the power to open our hearts. Please lead Stephen to find peace through Your Son, Jesus Christ, our Lord. Amen."

"Amen." Stephen looked up at the bishop. "*Danki.*"

"*Gern gschehne.* I better get going." He climbed into the buggy. "You have a *gut* night."

"You too. Drive safely." Stephen headed back into the house while the buggy wheels crunched on the rock driveway. He contemplated the bishop's words on his way up to his room. The words made sense, but what did he need to do in order to release the guilt?

Chapter 13

Stephen breathed in the sweet smell of the ripe apples while picking them from the trees in Hannah's family's orchard and dropping them into a bucket below his ladder. Although it had been a couple of weeks since he'd talked to the bishop, the older man's words still echoed in his mind. He pondered the bishop's suggestion to forgive himself, and he prayed daily for God to help him find that forgiveness. He was so thankful for the past two months that he'd spent with the King family. He treasured the talks he shared with Hannah, and he hoped their friendship would continue to grow and blossom just as the orchard trees had.

"Hi!" Hannah's voice rang out as she approached with a large basket. "If you take all of my apples, how am I going to make a pie?"

"Did you say pie?" Stephen climbed down from the

ladder. "You can take them all if you make me an apple pie."

"Who said the pie was for you?" She grinned, and his heart warmed with the possibility that she could like him as more than a friend.

Stephen grabbed an apple from the basket and held it out to her. "If I give you an apple from my pile, would you make the pie for me?"

She took the apple and stared at it while raising an eyebrow. "Shouldn't I be the one giving *you* the apple?"

Stephen laughed. "I guess so... After all, this is Paradise. But I don't fancy myself as an Adam."

Hannah dropped the apple into her basket. "So you like apple pie?"

"There are very few pies I've met that I don't like." He leaned against the ladder. "I bet you have an *appeditlich* recipe."

Hannah frowned. "I want to get my *mammi's* recipe, but I can't convince my *mamm* to give it to me."

"Why won't she share it?"

"My *mamm* likes to be in control of things, especially my *daed*. I'm certain you've noticed that."

Stephen nodded. "I have." He glanced beyond her and spotted Jason heading toward them. His lips formed a taut line.

"Hannah!" Jason walked over to them. "I've been looking for you." He acknowledged Stephen with a slight nod.

"Hi, Jason." Hannah's smile didn't meet her eyes.

Jason looked between Stephen and Hannah and then smiled at Hannah. "I was wondering if you wanted to go for a walk with me."

"*Ach*." Hannah frowned. "No, I don't think so. Now isn't a *gut* time."

Stephen bit the inside of his mouth to stop his grin.

"Why not?" Jason's eyebrows pinched up between his eyes. "It's a *schee* day, and I came all the way out here to see you."

"I'm sorry, but I'm busy." Hannah's smile was forced. "I'll see you at church next week."

Jason's mouth gaped at her obvious dismissal. "All right, at church, then. Good-bye." He stomped off toward his buggy.

Stephen felt a surge of confidence. "Would you like to go for a walk with me?"

"Let me think about it." She tapped her finger on her chin and then smiled up at him. "I would like that."

Despite the bishop's warning, Stephen walked beside Hannah through the apple orchard. The blue sky above them was dotted with white, fluffy clouds and the sun was warm against Stephen's face, a stark contrast to the cool fall breeze.

"I'm hoping that the apple pie tastes like my *mammi's*. I've gotten my pie to come out close to hers, but I can't quite get the texture of the filling."

"I'm certain you'll figure it out." He smiled at her. "You're a *wunderbaar* baker, and you're quite sweet too."

She laughed and swatted his arm. "You're just saying that."

"How come you're walking with me, but you wouldn't walk with Jason?"

Her smile faded. "Because I'd rather walk with you." She grabbed his hand and pulled him toward the back of the orchard. "Let me show you my favorite tree that Andrew and I used to climb when we were kids."

Stephen and Hannah walked back to the tree and reminisced about their childhoods. He couldn't stop his smile as he shared stories about playing with his brother on his grandfather's farm. His heart yearned for his family, and he decided he needed to write them and share news about his new home in Paradise.

They walked around the orchard and continued to talk and laugh until they reached their basket and buckets.

"Let me give you the apples I had picked. I was going to bring them to you anyway." Stephen filled her basket with the apples from his bucket. "I'll carry it."

"*Danki.*"

Stephen fell in step with Hannah as they made their way to the house; it felt as though they were meant to walk together.

Hannah pushed the ties from her prayer covering behind her shoulders. "Fall is my favorite time of year."

"Mine too." He followed her into the kitchen and placed the basket on the table.

"*Danki* for the lovely walk. I'm going to start making the pie now." Hannah stepped over to the sink and began washing her hands.

Stephen gestured toward the stairs. "And I'm going to go upstairs for a little bit. I think it's time I wrote to my family and told them how I'm doing."

She smiled. "That's a *gut* idea."

"I'll check on my pie later." He winked at her and then took the stairs two at a time to his bedroom. He pulled out a notepad and pen from a drawer and then sat at the desk and began to write.

Dear Jacob,
Please forgive me for delaying this letter. I've
wanted to write you for a long time, but I was too
prideful to apologize to you. I'm sorry for hurting you and *Mamm*, but I believed it was the only
way for me to escape the pain of Lillian's death.
I never meant to cause you pain, and I hope you
can find it in your heart to forgive me.
    I'm living in Paradise, Pennsylvania, now. I
have so much to tell you about my life.

Stephen finished the letter by sharing the details of
his days and promising to visit Sugarcreek soon. He
wrote a similar letter to his parents before sealing the
envelopes. He wrote out the addresses and felt some of
the burden leave his heart.

Hannah frowned down at the hot apple pie. Yet again,
the recipe didn't turn out the way it was supposed to.
Not only had she left it in the oven too long, but the
crust didn't taste right. She folded her arms over her
chest and blew out a heavy sigh. One of these days she
would get it right, recipe or not.

The screen door slammed shut, and her mother entered the kitchen. "What are you doing?"

"I tried to make an apple pie, but it's not like *Mammi's*." She pointed toward the pie sitting on the cooling
rack. "I thought I had it right this time."

"It's burned." Her mother studied the pie. "And
something's wrong with the crust."

"I know." Hannah wondered if her mother enjoyed
holding back the recipe and letting her guess at her

mammi's secret. "But I tried my best. Someday I'll get it right."

"I know why it came out wrong."

"Why?" Hannah raised her eyebrows, hoping her mother would finally give her the recipe.

"Because you're still sinning, even though you were warned."

"What?"

"I saw you in the apple orchard." Her mother pointed toward the window. "I saw you walking with Stephen. You were told to avoid situations where you're together without a chaperone, but you both have continued to sin." She wagged a finger at her. "That's why your pie didn't come out right. If you were pure of heart, then your pie would be just as *appeditlich* as *Mammi's*."

Hannah stared at her mother in shock. "No, *Mamm*. That's not how God works."

"Yes, it is, and you know it."

"No." Hannah took a deep breath to calm her temper. "We have the cross to cover our sins. We don't have problems or burnt pies because of sin. We have problems because we're human, and we need God to help us. But He doesn't punish us for sinning. He forgives us because He sent us Jesus." She pointed toward the pie. "The recipe is going to turn out right eventually, when I figure it out. But walking with my friend Stephen isn't sinful, and it has nothing to do with my botched pie."

"Watch your tone with me, Hannah Mary." Her *mamm's* lower lip trembled slightly, and she turned toward the door. "I'm going to go sit with your *daed*."

Hannah rubbed her temple where a headache brewed.

Although she felt relief for standing up to her mother, she hoped that her mother would believe her words and stop punishing her for spending time with Stephen.

Chapter 14

Hannah stepped into her parents' house a week later, expecting to find her father sitting in his favorite chair reading. Her mother was visiting a friend at the farm next door. She found the family room empty, and an eerie feeling tingled down her spine.

"Daed?" She stood in the doorway to their bedroom and saw her father lying in bed. *"Daed,* are you okay?"

His answer was more garbled than usual, as if he had a mouthful of marbles.

Hannah gasped and rushed to his bedside. *"Daed? Was iss letz?"*

Her father stared at her with his bushy eyebrows pinched together as if she were speaking a foreign language.

"Do you understand me?" She spoke slowly, enunciating each word.

He continued to stare at her with a blank expression, and her heart thudded in her chest.

"*Ach*, no." She bit her lower lip to fight off her threatening tears. "I'll be right back, *Daed*. I'm going to get help."

She rushed outside and found Stephen wiping his hands on a rag as he stepped out of the barn. "Stephen! I need help!"

He dropped the rag and ran to her. "What's wrong?"

"My *daed*!" She pointed toward the door. "I think he's had another stroke. He's in bed and can't talk."

"You go sit with him. I'll call an ambulance and also call Andrew."

"Okay." She wrung her hands and looked up at the gray clouds threatening to drench them at any moment. "My *mamm* should be home soon. She's been gone over an hour."

"Go." He nudged her toward the house. "I'll take care of the calls."

"*Danki*." Hannah hurried back to the bedroom and pulled a chair up to her father's side. "It's going to be okay." She wondered if her father could understand her words. The tears she'd been holding back now spilled over, down her cheeks and onto her dress.

Hannah prayed for God to heal him. She looked out the window at the dark clouds that seemed to mirror her emotions. Why couldn't she save her father? And then the answer hit her—she wasn't in control of her earthly father; her heavenly Father was in control of everything. She needed to give her worries and her fears over to God and let Him guide her life and the lives of her family members.

"I understand, Lord." She whispered the prayer.

"Help me learn to let You take the reins and guide our lives."

She heard the back door slam downstairs and her mother's heavy footfalls. "Hannah!" Her mother rushed into the bedroom. "Stephen said your *daed* had another stroke?"

"I think he did." Hannah moved away from the bed, and her mother dropped into the chair and leaned over her father.

"*Ach*, Saul." Tears streaked her mother's full cheeks. "I thought you were sleeping when I left this morning. I didn't know."

"It's okay, *Mamm*." Hannah touched her shoulder. "God is in control."

A siren blasted outside the window.

"The ambulance is here. I'll go meet them." Hannah hurried out to the kitchen just as Stephen led the EMTs into the house. "He's in the bedroom." She pointed toward the room.

Stephen touched her shoulder. "Stay here with me. They'll need to look him over before they take him to the hospital."

"Okay." She wiped her cheeks. "My *mamm* is really upset."

"I know. She started crying when I told her. Your *bruder* is going to meet us at the hospital."

"*Gut*." She lowered herself onto a kitchen chair and silently prayed for her father while the heavy moments passed between them.

Soon the EMTs wheeled her father out on a gurney. His skin was the shade of snow, and his normally bright brown eyes were dull like mud. She gnawed her lower lip and prayed anew for his health. She also begged for strength for her mother, who trailed along behind the gurney with tears trickling down her cheeks.

Hannah and Stephen followed the EMTs and her mother out to the driveway and stood in silence while her father was loaded into the back of the ambulance. Hannah started to walk toward the ambulance, but her mother took her arm.

"I'll ride with him." Her mother hoisted a bag up onto her shoulder.

"Oh." Hannah nodded, knowing she needed to yield to her mother. "Of course. I'll call Curt for a ride."

"Andrew called Curt to drive him and Anna Ruth to the hospital. I'll take you to the hospital in the buggy." Stephen motioned toward the barn. "I'll hitch up the horse right now."

Hannah looked up at him. "You will?"

"Your *daed* is important to me, just like my *daadi* was. I want to take you." He looked at her mother. "You go in the ambulance. We'll be there as soon as we can."

Stephen hurried off to the barn while Hannah watched her mother climb into the back of the ambulance. Heavy raindrops splattered onto her face and caused her to shiver.

Stephen guided the horse and buggy over to her. "Let's go."

She settled into the seat beside him, and they rode in silence. Hannah wrung her hands and fiddled with her apron as raindrops peppered the windshield. Soon the rain pounded on the roof, and the scenery out the window became a blur.

Hannah turned to Stephen and found him white-knuckled while holding the reins.

"We should turn around and call Curt for a ride."

Stephen's voice was soft and unsure through the rain beating on the buggy.

"No." Hannah shook her head. "We have to get to the hospital. My parents need me."

Stephen sniffed, and Hannah spotted a tear trickling down his cheek.

"Stephen? Are you okay?" She realized what was wrong. "You're thinking of the accident."

He nodded, keeping his eyes trained on the road ahead. "We need to go back. I can't get you there safely."

"Yes, you can." She placed her hand on his arm. "This is the moment that you have to know that your past is covered by the cross. You can do this, Stephen. We will get there safely because God is in control."

He met her gaze and nodded slowly. "You're right, Hannah. All things are possible with God."

"Always." Hannah settled in the seat, and Stephen wiped his tears before loosening his hands on the reins.

"*Danki* for reminding me." His voice was calm and controlled as he squeezed her hand. "Everything is going to be fine."

Later that evening Hannah stepped out into the hallway outside her father's hospital room and watched the doctor speak to her mother. They'd met Andrew at the hospital and then waited hours for her father to undergo tests and be admitted. She was thankful for Stephen, who had sat by her side and held her hand.

Now he touched her gently. "Your *daed* is going to be fine."

"I know." She smiled up at him. "I'm glad you're here."

"I am too."

They stood in silence until her mother walked over to them.

"What did the doctor say?" Hannah clasped her hands together.

"It was a stroke." Her *mamm* frowned. "He's going to have to spend a few days in the hospital, and then he'll need physical therapy. The doctor said it could've been much worse, and it's a good thing we brought him right to the hospital."

Hannah felt the muscles in her shoulders relax. "*Gut.*"

"You and Stephen should go home. It's late, and Andrew is about to leave. Everyone is tired." Her *mamm* motioned toward the room. "I packed a few things, so I can stay the night with him. You can come back in the morning."

"Okay." Hannah went to her father's bedside and watched him sleep for a moment. She then kissed his forehead. "You take care, *Daed. Ich liebe dich.*" She felt a hand on her arm and turned to find her mother waiting for her.

"I want to talk to you alone before you leave." Her mother took her hand and led her out to the hallway.

Hannah watched her mother pull a piece of paper from her apron pocket. "What's that?"

"I was planning on giving this to you tonight, but then everything happened with your *daed.*"

Hannah took the paper and gasped when she spotted her *mammi's* handwriting. "The apple pie recipe!" She smiled up at her mother. "*Danki.*"

"I'm sorry, Hannah." Her mother wiped away a tear. "I should've given it to you a long time ago. And I'm sorry for what I said about the apple pie. Your heart is pure, and Stephen is a *gut* young man."

Hannah hugged her. "I forgive you. *Ich liebe dich, Mamm.*"

"I love you too." Her mother smiled. "And I want you to make this pie as soon as your *daed* gets home. I'm certain yours will be just as *gut* as *Mammi's.*" She sniffed. "And the books were fine. They were off because of a mistake I'd made. You've always been competent."

"Thank you for believing in me, *Mamm.*"

Her mother cupped her hand to Hannah's cheek. "I always have. I'm sorry I never told you."

Hannah smiled and felt hot tears welling up again. She knew God was guiding the hearts of her family members, and she was more than thankful.

The sky was clear when Hannah settled into the buggy seat during the ride home. When they reached the house, she climbed out and looked upward. Her mouth gaped as she took in the beautiful golden and orange hues of the sunset. "Look, Stephen. Isn't it beautiful?"

Stephen nodded. "God paints with the most *schee* paintbrushes."

She smiled. "*Danki* for all you've done for my family. Not only today, but since you arrived. You're a blessing to us."

He took her hands in his. "And *danki* for all you've done for me. You reminded me about the power of our faith."

He leaned down, and Hannah's heart raced. His lips brushed hers, and the sensation sent her stomach into a wild swirl. Heat rushed up her neck to her cheeks, and her heart thudded in her chest. She felt light-headed when he broke the kiss.

He ran his fingers down her cheek. "It's late. I better put the horse up."

"Okay." Hannah started toward the house and sighed deeply.

Stephen climbed the stairs, all the while thinking of Hannah. She truly was a blessing to him. Although the decision to make the trip to Paradise had seemed hasty, he knew now that it had been God's path for him in order to guide his healing.

He stepped into his room and sat on the edge of his bed, which creaked under his weight. He knew that God had forgiven him for his past, but he still needed to release his guilt. That meant he also had to release his memories. And those were memories of Lillian. He knew now that Hannah's resemblance to Lillian had only been a coincidence. He wasn't supposed to live with her memory ever present in his life. He had to let Lillian go and live for the present, which was Hannah.

Stephen scanned his room looking for something that connected him to Lillian. He spotted his duffel bag in the corner and remembered the special birthday letter that Lillian had written him. He fished it out of a pocket in the duffel, then found a pack of matches on the desk.

He made his way outside and hurried behind the barn, away from the two houses. He knelt on the ground, and the cool moisture from the grass seeped through his trousers to his knees.

Stephen closed his eyes and sent a prayer up to God.

Lord, please relieve me of my burdens and cleanse me of the guilt. I know I'm not worthy of Your love, and I'm only forgiven by Your grace. Please lay Your pre-

cious hand on my heart, and help me forgive myself for all of my sins.

He then lit a match and set Lillian's letter on fire. He watched the letter burn and breathed in the smoky scent as if it were incense, an offering to the Lord. A heavy weight lifted from his shoulders as the paper was reduced to ashes.

Be still and know that I am God.

Stephen looked up at the stars blinking in a clear sky. "Lord, is that You?"

Calmness settled in his heart, and for the first time since the accident, he didn't feel the heartache or guilt coiling through him.

"*Danki*, Lord, for sending me to Paradise. I've found peace."

When Hannah heard the back door bang, she pulled on her shoes and a cloak and went to investigate the smoke that was billowing up from near the barn.

"Stephen? What are you doing?" She stepped toward him. "What are you burning?"

"Hannah." He stood and brushed off his hands. "I was burning a letter from Lillian that I had saved."

"Why?"

"Because I needed to let go." He took her hands in his. "Lillian was my past, but you are my present." He put his arms around her shoulders and pulled her close.

* * * * *

ACKNOWLEDGMENTS

As always, I'm thankful for my loving family members. I'm more grateful than words can express to my patient friends who critique for me—Stacey Barbalace, Janet Pecorella, and Lauran Rodriguez. Special thanks to Stacey, who helped with the recipes and research.

I'm thankful for my Amish friends who patiently answer my endless stream of questions. To my agent, Mary Sue Seymour—thank you for all you do! I'm grateful to my wonderful editor, Natalie Hanemann, for her guidance. Special thanks to Beth Wiseman and Kelly Long for their friendship and assistance with this novella.

Thanks most of all to God for giving me the inspiration and the words to glorify You. I'm so grateful and humbled You've chosen this path for me.

The author and publisher gratefully acknowledge the following resource that was used to research information for this book: C. Richard Beam, *Revised Pennsylvania German Dictionary* (Lancaster: Brookshire Publications, Inc., 1991).

ABOUT THE AUTHOR

Amy Clipston is the best-selling author of the Kauffman Amish Bakery series. Her novels have hit multiple best-seller lists including CBD, CBA, and ECPA. She and her family live in North Carolina. Learn more about Amy at amyclipston.com.

Amish Recipes

RECIPES FROM
A RECIPE FOR HOPE

PROVIDED AND TESTED BY
BETH WISEMAN

RACHEL'S BOILED COOKIES

½ cup butter
½ cup milk
2 cups sugar
3 tablespoons unsweetened cocoa
½ cup chunky peanut butter
1 teaspoon vanilla
¼ teaspoon salt
3 cups quick oats (not instant)

1. In small saucepan, combine butter, milk, sugar, and cocoa; cook on medium-high heat and bring to a boil for 1 minute.

2. Remove from heat and stir in peanut butter, vanilla, and salt. Mix in oats.

3. Drop by teaspoon on wax paper and allow to stand unrefrigerated for 1 hour.

AMISH HAYSTACKS

4 cans Campbell's cheese soup
Milk
1 lb saltine crackers, crushed
3–4 cups cooked rice
1 large head lettuce, shredded
4 tomatoes, diced
1 onion, diced
1 large bag tortilla chips, crushed
3 lbs hamburger, browned and seasoned
1 cup chopped boiled eggs

1. Heat cheese soup; add milk to make a cheese sauce of desired consistency.

2. Place remaining ingredients on individual plates in order given; top with cheese sauce. Makes 15 servings.

ROSEMARY AND EVE'S CHICKEN IN A CLOUD

3 ½ cups hot mashed potatoes prepared with cream cheese and only a little milk, no butter

FILLING:
1 ½ cups cooked cubed chicken
1 (10 ½-ounce) can cream of chicken soup
¼ cup milk
½ teaspoon dry mustard
¼ teaspoon garlic powder
¼ teaspoon pepper

TOPPING:
1 ½ cups shredded cheddar or Monterey Jack cheese

1. Grease shallow 2-quart baking dish.

2. Spread mashed potatoes on bottom and sides of baking dish. Top with chicken filling.

3. Top with 1 ½ cups shredded cheddar or Monterey Jack cheese.

4. Bake uncovered at 375°F for 40 minutes.

SOUR CREAM PANCAKES

2 cups flour
4 teaspoons baking powder
½ teaspoon salt
¼ cup sugar
2 eggs, beaten
1 cup (8 ounces) sour cream
1 ½ cups milk
1 teaspoon vanilla
⅓ cup butter, melted

1. Combine dry ingredients in bowl and stir to mix.

2. In second bowl, beat eggs, then mix in remaining wet ingredients.

3. Slowly pour wet ingredients into dry mixture, stirring just until combined.

4. Pour ½ cup batter on hot griddle or skillet and cook. Turn when light brown to brown both sides.

CRUNCHY POTATO BALLS

2 cups very stiff mashed potatoes
2 cups chopped cooked ham
1 cup shredded cheddar or Swiss cheese
⅓ cup mayonnaise or sour cream
1 egg, beaten
1 teaspoon prepared mustard
½ teaspoon pepper
2–4 tablespoons flour
1 ¾ cups crushed cornflakes

1. In bowl combine potatoes, ham, cheese, mayonnaise, egg, mustard, and pepper. Mix well. Add enough flour to make a stiff mixture.

2. Chill, covered, for 1 hour.

3. Shape into 1-inch balls. Roll in cornflakes.

4. Place on greased baking sheet and bake at 350°F for 25 to 30 minutes. Serve hot.

ZUCCHINI CASSEROLE

2 cups hamburger
4 cups zucchini, sliced into ¼-inch slices
½ cup diced onion
4 eggs, beaten
½ cup milk
2 cups toasted bread crumbs
1 tablespoon oleo, melted
½ cup shredded cheese (your choice)
Pepper and salt to taste

1. Combine first 5 ingredients. Top with toasted bread crumb mixed with melted oleo.

2. Bake at 350°F for 1 hour. Add cheese of your choice and put back in oven until cheese melts.

QUILTERS SALAD

1 cup slivered almonds
2 teaspoons vegetable oil
1 pkg. shredded coleslaw mix or equivalent shredded
cabbage
½ cup diced scallions (optional)
1 package Ramen chicken noodle soup mix (discard
seasoning packet)

DRESSING:
½ cup oil
3 tablespoons sugar
2 tablespoons white vinegar

1. Toast almonds in 2 teaspoons oil in skillet.

2. Pat dry on paper towel and cool.

3. Combine almonds, cabbage mixture, scallions (if using), and noodles.

4. Mix dressing ingredients and toss with salad mixture. Serve immediately.

ROSEMARY'S APPLE CRUMB PIE

6 cups peeled and sliced (or chopped) apples
1 ⅓ cups sugar
3 tablespoons flour
¾ teaspoon salt
⅓ cup half-and-half
½ teaspoon cinnamon
Refrigerated pie shell

CRUMBS:
½ cup butter, cold.
½ cup brown sugar
1 cup flour

1. Combine all pie ingredients and place in unbaked pie shell.

2. Combine crumb mixture and sprinkle on top.

3. Bake at 325°F for 55 minutes or until apples are tender.

ROSEMARY'S TOMATO PIE

6 medium tomatoes
2 cups baking mix (such as Bisquick)
⅔ cup milk
1 teaspoon garlic salt
½ teaspoon dried or fresh basil leaves
1 teaspoon dried or fresh oregano leaves
1 teaspoon salt or to taste
¼ teaspoon pepper
1 cup grated Parmesan cheese
1 cup shredded mozzarella cheese
1 ½ cups mayonnaise or sour cream

1. Preheat oven to 400°F.

2. Drop tomatoes into boiling water for 10 seconds to loosen skins, then peel and slice into a colander to drain.

3. Mix baking mix and milk in bowl. Spread mixture evenly in greased 10-inch pie plate.

4. Mix spices in small bowl.

5. Mix ½ cup Parmesan cheese and ½ cup mozzarella cheese with mayonnaise or sour cream.

6. Place a layer of tomatoes over baking mix in pie plate; sprinkle with half of spices and half of remaining cheeses.

7. Repeat with another layer of tomatoes, spices, and cheeses.

8. Spread mayonnaise/cheese or sour cream/cheese mixture on top.

9. Bake at 400°F for 35 to 40 minutes. Can be covered loosely with foil for final 10 minutes.

AMISH WINTER SOUP RECIPE

1 ½ cups water
1 cup cubed red potatoes
½ cup thinly sliced carrots
½ cup celery, sliced ½-inch thick
½ teaspoon white pepper
1 cup cubed cooked ham
¾ lb Velveeta cheese

1. Bring water, potatoes, carrots, and celery to a boil.

2. Reduce heat and simmer for 10 minutes or until vegetables are tender.

3. Add remaining ingredients.

4. Cook, stirring occasionally until cheese is melted. Don't add any salt!

Rosemary's Kaffi Cake

2 cups brown sugar
2 cups all-purpose flour
¾ cup shortening
1 teaspoon baking soda
1 cup strong coffee, hot
1 egg, lightly beaten
2 teaspoons vanilla
1 teaspoon cinnamon

1. Mix brown sugar, flour, and shortening until crumbly. Do not mix until creamy.

2. Reserve 1 cup to use as topping.

3. Dissolve baking soda in hot coffee and add to flour mixture.

4. Add egg, vanilla, and cinnamon.

5. Spread in 9x12x2-inch pan; batter will be thin.

6. Sprinkle with reserved topping.

7. Bake at 325°F for approximately 30 minutes.

GERMAN BREAKFAST SKILLET

1 lb ground pork sausage
2 tablespoons butter
6 medium potatoes
½ cup chopped onion
½ cup chopped green or red bell pepper
1 ½ teaspoons salt
½ teaspoon pepper
3 eggs, lightly beaten
⅓ cup milk
2 cups shredded mozzarella cheese

1. Brown pork sausage in butter in large skillet.

2. Shred potatoes and place on top of meat; add chopped onion and pepper, then salt and pepper.

3. Combine eggs and milk; pour over all.

4. Cover and simmer for 30 minutes or until potatoes are tender.

5. Sprinkle evenly with cheese and cover until melted.

Sour Cream Fruit Dip

1 cup sour cream
2 tablespoons brown sugar
½ teaspoon vanilla
5–6 drops red food coloring

1. Mix sour cream, brown sugar, and vanilla.

2. Add drops of red food coloring one at a time, mixing between each drop, until dip appears a pale pink.

3. Let stand in refrigerator for flavors to combine (at least 1 hour, even better overnight).

4. Cut fruit such as apples, bananas, pears, and strawberries into pieces, chunks, and wedges as desired. Serve fruit with dip.

HAM AND CHEESE STRATA

12 slices thin sandwich bread with crusts removed
1 lb sliced ham
2 (10-ounce) packages chopped frozen broccoli
¾ lb shredded sharp cheese

SAUCE:
3 eggs, beaten
3 cups milk
½ teaspoon dry mustard
½ teaspoon salt
1 tablespoon Worcestershire sauce

TOPPING:
1 cup crushed cornflakes
1 tablespoon butter, melted

1. Butter 9x13-inch baking dish.

2. Place 6 slices of bread on bottom of dish.

3. Cover with ham, then broccoli.

4. Sprinkle with cheese, then cover with 6 slices of bread.

5. Mix sauce and pour over casserole.

6. Cover and refrigerate overnight.

7. Mix topping and sprinkle on top of casserole. Bake at 300°F for 1 ½ hours.

Peach Sweet Potatoes

6 medium sweet potatoes
½ cup brown sugar
⅓ cup coarsely chopped pecans
½ teaspoon salt
¼ teaspoon ground ginger
1 (15-ounce) can sliced peaches, drained
Butter

1. Place potatoes in large pot. Cover with water and bring to a boil.

2. Reduce heat, cover, and cook 30 minutes or until potatoes are tender. Drain, allow to cool, and then peel and cut potatoes into 1-inch cubes.

3. In small bowl, combine brown sugar, pecans, salt, and ginger.

4. Put half of potatoes in baking dish sprayed with nonstick spray. Top with half of peaches and half of brown sugar mixture.

5. Repeat layers, then dot with butter.

6. Cover and bake at 350°F for 30 minutes. Uncover and bake 10 additional minutes.

Recipes from
A Spoonful of Love

Provided and Tested by
Amy Clipston

GRANOLA

¾ cup butter (or 1 ½ sticks)
1 teaspoon vanilla
2 tablespoons peanut butter (optional)
5 cups oatmeal
1 ¼ cups brown sugar
1 cup wheat germ or oat bran
1 cup coconut (optional)
1 teaspoon salt

7. Melt butter in saucepan and remove from heat.

8. Add vanilla and peanut butter. Mix well. Pour over dry ingredients.

9. Mix well and place in 2 shallow baking pans.

10. Bake at 350°F for 30 to 35 minutes or until brown. Stir once or twice while baking.

BREAD

1. Combine the following and let sit for 10 minutes.

   1 tablespoon yeast
   ½ cup warm water

2. After 10 minutes, mix in:

   2 tablespoons sugar
   2 tablespoons oil
   2 teaspoons salt
   2 cups warm water
   5 cups bread flour

3. Form into a ball and let rise for 15 minutes in a warm place.

4. Punch down and let rise 15 more minutes. Repeat this step three more times.

5. After the fourth punch, shape into loaves and place in greased bread pans. Let rise to the top of the pan.

6. Bake at 400°F until golden brown. Makes 2 or 3 loaves.

Soft Pretzels

1 ⅛ teaspoons active dry yeast
1 ½ cups warm water
2 tablespoons brown sugar
1 ¼ teaspoons salt
1 cup bread flour
3 cups regular flour

1. Sprinkle yeast over warm water in mixing bowl. Stir to dissolve.

2. Add brown sugar and salt. Stir to dissolve.

3. Add flours and knead dough until smooth. Let rise for 30 minutes.

2 cups warm water
2 tablespoons baking soda

4. While dough is rising, mix 2 cups warm water with 2 tablespoons baking soda. Stir often.

5. After dough has risen, roll pieces of dough into long ropes (no more than ½ inch thick).

6. Shape into pretzels or keep in strips. Dip in baking soda solution and place on greased baking sheet. Let dough rise again.

7. Bake at 450°F for 10 minutes or until golden brown.

2–4 tablespoons melted butter
Coarse salt

8. Brush with melted butter and sprinkle with coarse salt. You can also sprinkle with cinnamon and sugar.

MOIST BANANA BREAD

2 eggs
½ cup butter
2 tablespoons milk
½ teaspoon lemon juice
1 cup sugar
3 medium bananas, mashed
2 cups flour
1 ½ teaspoons baking powder
½ teaspoon salt
½ teaspoon baking soda
¼ teaspoon nutmeg

1. Beat together eggs, butter, milk, lemon juice, and sugar.

2. Add mashed bananas and mix.

3. Add dry ingredients and mix just until flour is moist.

4. Pour batter into greased loaf pan.

5. Bake at 350°F for 45 to 50 minutes.

Shoofly Cupcakes

2 ½ cups flour
½ cup shortening
1 ½ cups light brown sugar
1 ⅛ teaspoons baking powder
1 ⅛ teaspoons baking soda
1 ½ cups boiling water
Cinnamon

1. Mix together flour, shortening, and light brown sugar.

2. Set aside 1 cup of this mixture for top of cupcakes.

3. Add remaining ingredients to above mixture. Mix well.

4. Spoon into paper cupcake cups and top with reserved mixture. Sprinkle with cinnamon.

5. Bake at 350°F for 20 minutes. Makes 18–24 cupcakes.

PUMPKIN WHOOPIE PIES

2 egg yolks
2 cups brown sugar
1 cup oil
1 teaspoon vanilla
2 cups cooked pumpkin
3 cups flour
1 teaspoon salt
1 teaspoon baking soda
1 teaspoon baking powder
1 teaspoon cloves
1 teaspoon cinnamon
1 teaspoon ginger
Pinch of nutmeg

1. Beat eggs yolks, brown sugar, and oil until smooth.

2. Stir in remaining ingredients and drop onto greased cookie sheet in 2-to 3-inch circles.

3. Bake at 350°F for 12 minutes. Cool and fill with filling.

FILLING:
2 teaspoons vanilla
2 tablespoons milk
2 egg whites, unbeaten
4 tablespoons flour
1 lb powdered sugar

1 ½ cups shortening

1. Combine all ingredients and mix well. Spread between cookies.

APPLE ROLL-UPS

2 cups flour
4 teaspoons baking powder
1 ¼ teaspoons salt
2 tablespoons sugar
4 tablespoons lard
¾ cup milk
4 medium apples, sliced
Nutmeg
Cinnamon
1 pint water
1 ½ cups brown sugar

1. Combine first 6 ingredients to make dough.

2. Roll out as for pie dough (¼ inch thick). Spread apples on top and sprinkle with nutmeg and cinnamon.

3. Roll up as for jelly roll and cut in round slices. Place slices in greased cake pan with open side up.

4. Boil together 1 pint water and 1 ½ cups brown sugar. Pour over apples slices.

5. Bake at 350°F until brown.

SCHNITZEL BEANS

4 slices bacon
3 medium onions
1 quart fresh string beans
2 cups chopped tomatoes
1 teaspoon salt
½ teaspoon pepper
1 cup boiling water

1. Fry bacon and then crumble.

2. Slice onions and fry until soft.

3. Cut beans into 1-inch pieces and brown slightly with onions.

4. Add bacon, tomatoes, seasonings, and boiling water.

5. Cover and cook slowly until beans are tender. Add water if necessary to make a little sauce to serve with beans.

APPLE PUDDING

6 large apples
¾ cup sugar
1 teaspoon cinnamon
2 eggs
¼ cup shortening
¾ teaspoon salt
1 cup flour
1 teaspoon baking powder
½ cup water

1. Pare and slice apples and place in greased baking dish.

2. Combine sugar and cinnamon and mix into apples.

3. In separate dish, place well-beaten eggs, shortening, and salt and mix thoroughly. Add flour, baking powder, and water. Pour over apples.

4. Bake at 350°F for 30 minutes.

GERMAN POTATO PANCAKES

2 large potatoes, grated
2 medium onions, grated
2 eggs
½ teaspoon salt
⅛ teaspoon pepper
1 ½ tablespoons flour
1 tablespoon chopped parsley
1 teaspoon baking powder
Butter for frying

1. Combine potatoes and onions. Add eggs.

2. Add salt, pepper, flour, parsley, and baking powder. Mix well.

3. Form into thin cakes and fry slowly in butter until browned. Makes about 8 cakes.

CHILLY DAY SOUP

1 large carrot
2 cups water
1 large onion, chopped
1 quart diced potatoes
⅓ cup macaroni
1 teaspoon salt
¼ teaspoon pepper
2 cups milk
2 tablespoons butter
1 cup cooked meat (optional)

1. Chop carrot and cook in 2 cups water.

2. When carrot is partially cooked, add onion, potatoes, macaroni, salt, and pepper.

3. Add enough water to cover and cook until tender.

4. Add milk and butter and heat well. Add meat if desired.

DUTCH COUNTRY MEAT LOAF

2 cups bread crumbs
2 cups milk
2 lbs ground beef
1 lb ground pork
3 eggs
1 medium onion, chopped
Salt and pepper

1. Soak bread crumbs in milk for 2 minutes.

2. Combine meats, bread crumbs, eggs, onion, and seasonings. Mix thoroughly and shape into a loaf.

3. Place in roasting pan, add ½ inch water, and bake at 375°F for 1 ½ to 2 hours.

PEACH STRUDEL

Fresh peaches
Cinnamon and sugar
Butter
1 cup sugar
1 cup flour
1 teaspoon baking powder
¾ teaspoon salt
1 egg

1. Put a thick layer of peaches in bottom of buttered baking dish.

2. Sprinkle with cinnamon and sugar. Dot with lumps of butter.

3. Sift dry ingredients and then add egg. Spoon over peaches.

4. Bake at 350°F until brown.

Amish Chicken and Corn Soup

12 cups water
2 pounds boneless skinless chicken breasts, cubed
1 cup chopped onion
1 cup chopped celery
1 cup shredded carrots
3 chicken bouillon cubes
2 cans (14 ¾ ounces each) cream-style corn
2 cups uncooked egg noodles
¼ cup butter
1 teaspoon salt
½ teaspoon pepper

1. In large pot, combine water, chicken, onion, celery, carrots, and bouillon. Bring to a boil.

2. Reduce heat; simmer uncovered for 30 minutes or until chicken is no longer pink and vegetables are tender.

3. Stir in corn, noodles, and butter; cook 10 minutes longer or until noodles are tender.

4. Season with salt and pepper.

CREAMED CELERY

3 cups diced celery
3 tablespoons butter
3 tablespoons flour
1 teaspoon salt
¼ teaspoon pepper
1 cup milk
½ cup water in which celery was cooked

1. Cook celery in boiling salted water until tender and then drain, saving ½ cup of the liquid.

2. When celery has cooked, make a white sauce with the other ingredients.

3. Pour sauce over cooked celery, heat, and serve.